AN AGREEABLE ALLIANCE

ALSO BY KASEY STOCKTON

Ladies of Devon Series

The Jewels of Halstead Manor

The Lady of Larkspur Vale

The Widow of Falbrooke Court

The Recluse of Wolfeton House

Women of Worth Series

Love in the Bargain

Love for the Spinster

Love at the House Party

Love in the Wager

Love in the Ballroom

Stand-alone Historical Romance

His Amiable Bride

A Duke for Lady Eve

A Forgiving Heart

All is Mary and Bright

Scottish Historical Romance

Journey to Bongary Spring

AN AGREEABLE ALLIANCE

KASEY STOCKTON

For Rebecca and Alyssa— your friendship means the world to me, and I love you both! And to save our friendship: these characters are not my interpretation of your personalities.

Also for Kellie— just clean your glasses already. (And I love you too!)

CHAPTER ONE

May 1816
Somerset, England

W as there anything quite as dull as spectating an eternally long cricket match? The ball getting whacked repeatedly, men crossing each other to reach wickets, the other team standing idly in the fields. Nothing about it was particularly engaging, except for the remarkable plum cake and the refreshing lemonade provided by the hosts. Rebecca Turner shifted on her uncomfortable seat beneath the shaded canopy, pushing her spectacles higher on her nose. Her gaze swept over the expanse of lush, green lawn up to the imposing country estate, Briarwood Manor.

This entire outing was an exercise of extreme patience, for Rebecca had such little time for frivolities. But she came here with a purpose, and she would not leave without seeing her task complete.

"Which team shall we cheer for?" Alicia asked, smoothing a hand down her stiff, black skirt. "I'm partial to the gentlemen, of course, but the other team is quite handsome." Alicia brought her cup of lemonade to her smirking lips. Her blonde hair was a stark contrast to her black bonnet, but her rosy cheeks softened her pale complexion, making her look every bit the grieving daughter.

Aunt Langley scoffed. "Surely you jest."

"Why?" Alicia faced her mother, raising her chin. "You cannot mean to imply that I should look no lower than a gentleman in my pursuit of a husband. Is Margaret's Lord Buxton not enough for you? Must we have *two* lords in the family?"

Rebecca suppressed the temptation to sigh. This same tired argument had been volleying between her aunt and cousin since they'd set out from Bath that very morning. The cricket match—pitting a group of gentlemen against a group of men who worked for their living—was being held at the home of Aunt Langley's friend, and that had given them a reason to attend despite their state of mourning.

"It hardly matters now," Aunt Langley muttered. "But regardless, darling, that is precisely what I mean, and you well know it." She shot Rebecca a commiserating look before tipping back her cup and emptying her glass in a harsh, frantic manner. It was rather a miracle the woman hadn't splashed liquid down her chin.

Rebecca's heart reached out to her aunt. She had lost her husband five months prior on the tail of her eldest daughter, Margaret, becoming engaged to a viscount. It had been a boon and a blow in quick succession, leaving the three Langley women, Rebecca's aunt and two cousins, quite alone and, even worse, forcing Margaret to postpone her wedding.

"Until I put off these wretched black gowns, I shall look at whomever I please," Alicia said. "Regardless of their station."

"Be grateful I allowed you to attend at all."

Alicia made a soft, irritated sound. "Of course, Mother. May I fetch some cake? I do promise not to engage myself to a stablehand along the way."

Aunt Langley narrowed her eyes. "Only if Rebecca accompanies you."

Rebecca startled, pulling her gaze from the men gathering on the lawn. The gentlemen's team was moving into field positions so the working-class men could bat. She had analyzed each of them but had thus far failed to find any indicators that any of them possessed the skills she needed.

How she would determine that any of these men were doctors without directly inquiring of them was beyond her, but she searched for clues anyway. A leather satchel containing his tools, or perhaps just the sort of intelligent gaze a man full of healing remedies would wear.

It had been a whim of hers to attend the cricket match with her aunt and cousin. When she'd learned that the team set to go against the gentlemen were a group of working men, it had seemed like an opportunity for her to meet a new doctor. A younger, fitter man who could be persuaded to help.

And she needed help.

Alicia stood. "Come, Rebecca, let us drown our loneliness in cake."

"Loneliness?" Aunt Langley scoffed. "That's rich. You spend nearly all your time together."

Rebecca rose beside her cousin before leaning over to give her crotchety aunt a kiss on her rosy cheek. "Shall I bring you another lemonade?"

"Only if it is accompanied by a heaping plate of pastries."

"Of course," Rebecca said, accepting Aunt Langley's empty, rose-painted cup.

Aunt Langley settled in her chair more comfortably, muttering softly to herself. "Loneliness. Bah. I think I know a thing or two about it."

Rebecca slipped her hand around Alicia's arm and walked the length of the spectators, tugging her along each time she slowed to admire a handsome man. The grounds of Briarwood were absolutely teeming with them, and it was all Rebecca could do to keep her cousin on a straight path to the refreshment table.

It wasn't Alicia's fault she was so beautiful, but it was her design to bring that beauty to the maximum attention of anyone she happened to be nearby. God had blessed her with a perfect complexion, a dainty nose, and pure, nearly white blonde hair over laughing blue eyes. Alicia walked as though she knew her worth and expected everyone else to appreciate it as well.

Rebecca would heartily dislike her cousin if she did not love her so dearly.

"You must allow my maid to do your hair for our next outing," Alicia said, tugging at a loose lock of Rebecca's auburn hair. "It has so much potential."

"I like my hair precisely the way it is." And she did. Rebecca had never felt the need to primp herself, but she owned that some of her indifference was likely due to her cousin. What was the point of attempting to look pretty when her pointy chin and spectacles could never compete with Alicia?

"You would like it *more* if you let me do something with it." Alicia paused, scrunching her nose. "Well, not me. My maid. I would be hopeless with a handful of hair pins."

Rebecca chuckled politely, hoping Alicia would let the

4

matter drop. They were not alone, people milled around them filling plates and chatting amiably, and Alicia's voice tended to carry. For all of her ignorance, Alicia did have a generous, caring disposition.

A table sat before them overladen with pastries, cakes, and turnovers, and Alicia hovered near the bowl of lemonade while Rebecca took up a rose-painted plate to fill for her aunt. She shouldn't have left Alicia alone by the drinks, but it would only take a moment to fill her plate—

Drat. A man had already approached Alicia, and judging by his motions, was offering to pour her drink. Rebecca filled Aunt Langley's plate swiftly and passed a couple admiring the blancmanges. Side-stepping a man stuffing a napkin-wrapped bundle into his bag, she reached her cousin.

"I assure you, it is a compliment," the man said to Alicia. "Do you live nearby?"

"We live in Bath," Alicia said. "I am eager to resume my attendance at the assemblies, but for now I must satisfy myself with frequent, brief visits to the Pump Room."

The man looked down at Alicia with rapt attention, nodding as he held her glass. "I only returned to Bath a few weeks ago, but I have found the company to be particularly engaging."

Rebecca was completely certain that neither of them had even noticed her approach. If her cousin had, she was plainly ignoring it.

Alicia smiled radiantly. "I do hope you intend to remain in Bath for some time."

"That was my intention, yes," he said, his voice squeaking just slightly. He cleared his throat and offered her the glass, quite clearly becoming lost in her gaze. He was tall, possessed of sandy-brown hair that peeked out beneath his hat, and a well-made, worn coat. It was impossible to tell whether the man was here in support of the gentlemen's team or the working men.

Rebecca was tempted to ask him, if for no other reason than to startle him out of his lovelorn gaze.

Alicia brought her cup to her lips and took a minuscule sip. Her tongue darted out to lick her lip, and she made a noise that resembled a cat more than a woman. "This is quite delicious."

The man swallowed noticeably. Good heavens, Alicia may have taken this too far. Rebecca opened her mouth to steal her cousin's attention when the man turned abruptly toward her and dipped his head. The weight of his gaze shocked her, though he seemed flustered. His cheeks were rosy, and she doubted it was from the heat.

"May I pour you a glass as well, miss?"

Rebecca was quite at a loss. She was not typically given attention when standing beside Alicia, especially from unfamiliar gentlemen. Judging by the slight pulling of Alicia's blonde eyebrows together, she was just as surprised.

"Yes, I thank you." Rebecca offered him Aunt Langley's empty glass and watched him smoothly fill it before returning it to her. The man glanced down at her plate, heaping with cakes and pastries, and his lips twitched, giving her the strongest desire to explain that the whole of the contents on her plate were not intended for her alone. Though she did plan to indulge in another slice of plum cake.

"May I help you carry your things back to your seat?"

"No, that is quite all right," Alicia said, drawing his attention once more. She took Rebecca firmly by the arm and spun her away, but not before catching disappointment flash over the man's pale blue eyes.

"You shouldn't flirt so obviously," Alicia hissed, dragging her away from the refreshment tent. "You need to be more subtle if you wish for a man to take interest in you."

Rebecca choked on air, coughing once before she righted herself. Alicia could not be serious, surely. But one look proved her wrong, for Alicia's pinched mouth was a sign of irritation.

"He quoted a poem to me," Alicia admitted, lowering her voice. "I thought he was being rude, but he promised his intention was to offer me a compliment."

"Which poem?"

Alicia screwed up her nose. "I haven't the faintest. Something about a lion or bear, I believe."

That was odd. Men did the strangest things when they found themselves faced with Alicia's beauty and this creature was no different, it seemed.

They seated themselves beside Aunt Langley, quiet settling over the women as they watched the match and picked at the pastries. A tall, dark-haired man picked up the cricket bat, and Rebecca watched him prepare for his turn. All the while, her mind turned over the image of the man at the refreshments, and the way he had looked at her.

She was not foolish enough to believe he found anything desirable in her countenance, but he was possessed of kind eyes, and his desire to be inclusive had been obvious. Rebecca could not, if it was within her power, allow *this* man to pursue Alicia once they returned to Bath. Alicia would merely play with him as though she were the cat and he the ignorant mouse.

Alicia was but nineteen. While Rebecca was only two years her senior, she sometimes felt she possessed the maturity of a middle-aged woman. Life and its circumstances had required it of her, and she would not trade her social or economic awareness with her cousin's beauty for anything. Alicia was far more beautiful, but Rebecca would never be taken in and swindled by a shallow gentleman.

She feared that one day Alicia's games would catch up to her, and she would be the victim of just that sort of thing.

She returned to her perusal of the men dotting the pitch when a large crack rent the air, screams shortly following it.

Alicia gasped, clutching both of her hands to her breast. "Lord Ryecombe!" she breathed.

"What is it?" Rebecca asked, craning her neck to see over the crowd rushing toward the earl.

"He was hit with the ball," Aunt Langley supplied, rising from her seat.

Voices in the distance echoed the alarm pulsing through Rebecca.

"Is he injured?"

"Who hurt him?"

"Come," Alicia said, taking Rebecca by the arm, "let us go closer."

Both teams of cricket players rushed toward Lord Ryecombe's seat, not too far from where they were situated, and Rebecca caught a glimpse of the man from the lemonade table jogging that direction, as well.

"Is there a physician?" someone shouted.

"Make way, please!" The man from the refreshments tried to push his way through the crowd which surrounded Lord Ryecombe. "I'm a doctor."

Rebecca's heart stuttered. He was a doctor? Of all the men in attendance, she'd found a physician and hadn't even known it.

Alicia pulled Rebecca through the throng, giving them a good view of the injury. Lord Ryecombe clutched his mouth, his wild eyes blazing. "I'm more than well, Cooper," he grumbled, his voice sounding gurgly. "Continue with the match!"

Cooper. His name was Dr. Cooper.

"Forgive me, my lord, but I must insist that you allow me to see to the wound, if only to ensure nothing worse comes of it."

"You are thimply trying to throw the game," Lord

Ryecombe shouted, a clear lisp coloring his speech. "Upon my honor, he'll pay for thith!"

"Did you see who hit him with the ball?" Alicia asked. "I was not paying attention."

Rebecca had, but she was not about to search the crowd for the man responsible. No, her sights were set on the doctor tending to the irascible earl's wound. His patience and directness were commendable, and his persistence estimable. And aside from that, he had something about his manner that led Rebecca to believe she might actually have a shot of convincing him to help her.

He was absolutely perfect. Now, she just needed to obtain a legitimate introduction.

CHAPTER TWO

J ared Cooper had treated his share of obnoxious, entitled
men during the course of his career, but Lord Ryecombe
ranked among the most vexing of them all. He checked the
man's mouth, ensured there were no broken teeth, and forced
the earl to prove that his jaw hadn't sustained significant
damage. He cleaned the earl's blood away, obtained a glass of
something far too strong for a daytime cricket match to calm
Lord Ryecombe's well-disguised nerves, and promptly returned
his attention to the match.

The earl's mouth would undoubtedly swell if the size of his
lip was any clue, and he would suffer from a speech impedi-
ment for a few days, but the damage was not nearly as bad as it
could have been. Jared had tried to say as much to Lord
Ryecombe, but sometimes there was no getting through to
block-headed old men.

Thomas Hawkins raised his copper eyebrows as Jared took
his place on the lush, green pitch. "Got everything sorted,
then?"

"Yes, though it took twice as long as it ought to have done. Which is typically a result of treating a small child."

"Well . . ." Thomas shrugged, a smile pulling at his lips. He indicated the opposing team. "The pompous fools just pulled ahead, but I think we still have a real shot at taking the game."

Jared nodded, his gaze drawing back to the spectators' canopy and the young woman seated beneath it. He'd scarcely allowed himself to look at another woman since the rejection over two years ago that had shredded his heart, but something about the blonde woman he'd spoken with at the refreshments table had grabbed his attention and refused to let go.

He hadn't meant to quote *The Tyger* to her, but she was stunning, and the words of William Blake that he had read just the day before had filtered through his mind and escaped his mouth without his approval. She'd been offended, but when he explained the poem, she'd looked at him as though she'd truly found him interesting; it had been so long since anyone had found worth in what Jared had to offer. It was intoxicating.

"Did you find anything of interest at the refreshments tent?" Thomas asked, his rumbling stomach a clue of where his mind was at—far from the cricket match.

Wide blue eyes swam before his mind's eye, but Jared squashed the image. He wished he'd asked the woman her name, but it was no matter. She had made her interest quite clear when she had mentioned how she liked to frequent the Pump Room. Jared knew exactly where he was going to begin spending his mornings.

"Nothing good?" Thomas asked, tilting his head to the side. A copper curl flopped over his forehead, his fisted hand resting casually at his waist. He'd been a good friend to Jared since he'd stumbled into Thomas's stables a few years ago in search of a new mount, and they had bonded immediately over their shared appreciation for equines.

It was Thomas's connections that had gotten Jared an invitation to play cricket. Most everyone in Bath knew of Hawkins's superior stock. His stables flourished—right alongside his social calendar.

"No, quite the opposite in fact." Jared *had* found something amazing beneath the refreshment tent. Or so he hoped. And the food hadn't been too bad, either.

The remainder of the match passed in a flurry, broken up by Jared sneaking glances at the woman who so captivated him. He was pleased when it finally ended—his team had won, which was immensely gratifying—and he found himself gravitating toward the blonde angel's general vicinity.

For the last hour, Jared had weighed the likelihood of seeing the woman at the Pump Room and obtaining a proper introduction there. She'd been dressed in black from head to toe, and he had to assume the person for whom she mourned was a close relation, given the extent of her clothing and that of the older woman seated beside her.

The spectacled woman who had accompanied them, however, was conspicuously in pale colors, and he briefly wondered why, and what her relationship was to them.

Thomas clapped Jared on the back, his grin stretching widely over his freckled face. "I need a slice of cake and a glass of ale."

"You're bound to be disappointed in the drink selection, I feel."

Thomas scowled. "Do not say Ryecombe has offered nothing stronger than lemonade."

"Not for his guests, no. At least, not that I could find." Jared would keep to himself how quickly the servant had produced brandy when he'd required it to calm Lord Ryecombe's nerves.

"Let's skip the social and head directly for the pub then."

Jared looked to his friend, gauging the sincerity of that

comment, and found a deep groove between Thomas's eyebrows. Blast. The man meant it. "Of course. Do you not wish to sample the plum cake first?"

"I suppose," he said with a sulk.

Thank heavens. Jared meandered toward the refreshments, searching the crowd for the black-clad woman with pale blonde hair. The longer he looked, however, the more panicked he became, for she was nowhere to be seen. He paused on the lawn, a soft breeze tickling his perspiring neck, and surveyed the guests but came up empty.

She was gone.

Thomas retrieved his cake and was pulled into a conversation with a man from their team with whom Jared was unfamiliar. Jared perused the crowds while he waited for his friend, side-stepping a couple deep in conversation and narrowly missing trampling the woman's blue pelisse under his shoe.

Jared circled the tent, doing his best to swallow his disappointment. He'd been taken in by a pair of beautiful eyes, and he was likely fooling himself that the woman felt any returned interest. Though she *had* told him where to find her once they returned to Bath. He must hold on to that hope.

A soft, warm breeze lifted the scent of baked goods and damp earth. People milled around the tables, congratulating their friends or offering brave support, depending on the team they'd cheered for.

Jared turned the corner of the long pole holding up the shade canopy and pulled up short to avoid running directly into a young woman. His breath caught as he took in the heart-shaped face and round, wire-rimmed spectacles. He'd found the angel's friend.

"Good day," he said, realizing that he was grinning like a fool and doing his best to level it. He dipped his head in a soft bow, and she returned the courtesy with a curtsy.

"Congratulations on your triumph," she said meekly.

"Yes, well, I do not think I had much to do with winning the match—"

"I was referring to your successful treatment of a particular patient at the start of the match."

Was Jared wrong, or did he detect a degree of mirth coloring the woman's words? Her eyes sparkled with mischief behind the glass that helped her see, and he chuckled softly. "I thank you most heartily. It was an accomplishment, indeed."

She seemed to pause and gather her thoughts before speaking. "Tell me, do you practice medicine in Bath?"

"I have not done so yet, no."

Her face fell, and he had the oddest desire to put the smile back on her lips. Besides, if he pleased this woman, perhaps she would help him find her friend once again. "I plan to eventually, but I have only just moved to the city, and I must gain patients first."

She sucked in a breath and held his gaze. "Perhaps I can be of some assistance."

What did she mean by that? Her hands fidgeted slightly where she'd clasped them before herself, almost as if she was nervous.

"Do you know of someone in need of medical care?"

"I do." She delicately cleared her throat, her eyes darting behind him before resting upon him once more. "If you would give me your direction, I'd be glad to send round a note with the appropriate information."

"Certainly. You can direct your note to Mr. Jared Cooper," he said. Surprise flashed over her face, and he swallowed back his irritation.

"Mister? You are not a physician?"

"No, I'm a surgeon. But I assure you I am perfectly capable—"

15

"Do not mistake me," she said, lifting her hands to stave off his irritation. "I am pleased with the discovery. The last physician I contacted . . ." She failed to complete her sentence, her cheeks infused with a delicate shade of pink. "It will be well."

Jared gave her his direction, suppressing the thread of apprehension that was working its way down his spine. Was the woman's mother the patient in need of help? Why would Jared's position as a surgeon be a good thing in that case? He wanted to ask exactly what the patient suffered from when Thomas approached, a bit of his plum cake clinging to his clean-shaven chin.

Jared indicated his chin, and Thomas brushed the offending crumbs away. "Good day . . ." He turned to look expectantly at Jared, but he could only shrug lightly. He didn't know the woman's name.

"We've yet to be introduced," Jared explained. "Though we hope to remedy that at the Pump Room shortly."

"Can no one here do the honor?" Thomas asked, looking about as though someone who knew both parties would simply appear. His thumb hung from his waistcoat pocket.

"No, I'm sorry," the woman said. "I know no one outside of my own party, and they are awaiting me in the carriage now. If you'll excuse me." She dipped in a quick curtsy and hurried away.

Jared remained, unable to move, his jaw slightly slack. He wasn't entirely certain what had just occurred between himself and the woman, but he had a feeling it was a sign of good things to come. He'd nursed his wounded heart for so long, and all the while Evelyn Trainor, the woman who had hurt him, remained happily married, unaware of the extent of the pain she'd caused. But now things were going to be different.

"I haven't seen you speak to a woman in the entire three weeks you've been in Bath." Thomas grinned, snapping Jared back to the present and shoving away his errant thoughts of past heartbreaks. "How about we celebrate that with some ale?"

Shaking his head, Jared chuckled. "Any excuse to go to the pub will do, eh?"

"Of course not." Thomas mocked offense. "I wouldn't need to go to a pub if we had a perfectly acceptable drink available right here."

"Ah, I see. Important distinction."

"Isn't it, though?"

They made their way toward the carriages when a slim figure dressed in pale green caught Jared's attention, and he watched the woman with the heart-shaped face climb into a burgundy carriage with black trim. A servant closed the door behind her, and they were shortly on their way. His heart buoyed with the hope of seeing her again, and he didn't bother fighting the smile that came naturally to his lips.

━━━━━━ ⌾ ━━━━━━

Jared had sipped slowly at his tankard of ale. He'd never been one to heavily imbibe; one never knew when one's medical skills would be called upon, and he preferred to always have his wits about him. Thomas was satiated after two glasses and had been persuaded to return to Bath before it grew too late and they would be forced to travel in the dark.

"Are you glad I convinced you to attend the match with me today?" Thomas asked, his shoulders swaying with the motion of the carriage.

Jared was glad, but he didn't want to admit it so easily. He held his tongue.

"Oh come now, you might as well thank me. If nothing else, you were able to treat the earl, and you appear to have collected your first client in Bath."

17

Jared watched hills roll by through the window, pretending not to hear his friend. Thomas was correct, but he wasn't sure it was a good thing. Jared wasn't certain he even wanted to build a practice in Bath. He'd been unceremoniously booted from Derham, and that was an assault on his pride he never wanted to experience again. He returned his attention to the window and hoped his scowl wasn't obvious. The landscape of green, rolling hills was marred by the road, and something in the distance on the side of the lane caught his eye.

"You are quite hilarious. Did you know this?" Thomas asked drily. He crossed his arms over his chest and leaned back on the tufted bench.

"I did, in fact," Jared agreed absently. The waning light made it difficult to see, to say nothing of the wavy glass pane in the carriage, but he was nearly certain the carriage they were approaching looked exactly like one he'd seen at Briarwood Manor earlier that afternoon.

Their coachman slowed a little, pulling as much to the side of the narrow road as he was able. When they passed the familiar burgundy carriage with black trim, Jared caught sight of a matronly woman in a black dress speaking to a man at the horse's heads and immediately stomped his foot on the floor three times to garner his coachman's attention.

"What the devil was that for?" Thomas asked, his hands splayed over the bench seat on either side of him.

Jared smiled sheepishly. "Forgive me, chap. I should have warned you."

"Indeed."

"There's a carriage on the side of the road over there, and I believe its only inhabitants were women from Briarwood."

Women that Jared had met at the refreshment table and again after the match, that he had taken a liking to and hoped to see again.

He hadn't imagined it would be *this* soon that they would meet, but fate had delivered him an opportunity, and Jared was not about to pass it by. To say nothing of the fact that these women appeared stranded, and it was his duty to ensure that all was well, of course.

"We must help them, I suppose," Thomas said, running a hand through his curly, copper hair.

"Yes. We must."

Thomas threw the door open once they'd rolled to a complete stop and hopped onto the packed dirt before the servant could come around and let down the step. He might grumble, but he wasn't against helping in these sorts of situations. It was part of why Jared liked him so well.

The sun was on its way to setting, and the late afternoon was much cooler, helped along by a soft breeze. Two men stood at the head of the horses, appearing to be deep in conversation. The woman in black had likely retreated into the carriage for safety.

"Good evening," Jared called when they approached. "Are you in need of any assistance?"

The older gentleman turned and appraised Jared and Thomas. "The axel's broken, gov."

"Have you dispatched a man for another carriage?"

"Not yet." He flicked his head toward the younger man beside him. "About to send him, though."

"Do you carry passengers who were recently at Briarwood?" Thomas asked.

The coachman nodded, his eyes narrowing.

Jared stepped forward. "Will you ask them if they would like us to transport them home in our carriage? We came from Briarwood Manor as well. Jared Cooper and Thomas Hawkins."

The coachman waited a moment, running his hand over his

chin before saying something quietly to the groom and nodding.

Thomas leaned over and spoke softly in his ear. "Do you know these women?"

"I believe this carriage belongs to the party of the woman I spoke to just before we left."

If Thomas was surprised, he hid it well. "The woman with the spectacles."

Jared nodded. He hoped he was correct. How many burgundy carriages with this same black trim would be on the road to Bath at this time containing women dressed in black? Chances were high his blonde angel was inside.

The coachman spoke to the passengers in the carriage before helping an older woman step out onto the pocked road. She looked at Jared, her mouth pinched and eyes wary.

"Good evening, ma'am." He bowed. "We've just come from the cricket match as well."

Her eyes were wrinkled, difficult to see in the waning light, and her gray hair was arranged neatly under her wide-brimmed bonnet, which further shadowed her face. "Yes, you look familiar, but I do not recognize your names."

"I treated Lord Rycombe's injury at the beginning of the game." Jared was tempted to explain that he'd spoken to the other women in her party, but he had a feeling that would not help his case at present. It certainly wasn't gentlemanly of him to carry on a conversation with a woman to whom he had not been properly introduced, and he'd done so with the spectacle-clad woman twice. He gestured to Thomas's carriage up the road. "We have plenty of room and are returning to Bath now. May we convey you home?"

The woman looked to be struggling with indecision. She glanced from Jared and Thomas to her own carriage, worry etched on her wrinkled brow. The sun moved closer to the horizon, the sky taking on a hazy hue as it prepared to shift into full darkness. Time was not on this woman's side, and she appeared to know it well.

"Yes, I thank you," she said at length, and Jared did not miss her uncomfortable, pinched lips. "We would appreciate your assistance, Doctor."

"Mr. Cooper, ma'am." He smiled kindly at her.

She seemed to understand his meaning and nodded at him before turning to retrieve the other women in the carriage.

"I did wonder if she was going to ask which side we played for at the match today," Thomas whispered, mirth in his tone. "The gentlemen or the winners."

"I'm certain she knows now," Jared said, ignoring the joke. A few years ago, he'd been given the opportunity to go to university and be trained at Guy's Hospital in London as a physician, but the career had never interested him much. It was not in Jared's nature to stand aside and allow other men to heal his patients. He much preferred the hands-on approach of being a surgeon, and if that forced others not to see him as a gentleman, then so be it. Jared was a man of the people—the people he cared for and healed. He needed no more accolades than that.

Continuing his education was important to him, but he did so in other ways.

The women were helped from the carriage and ushered toward Jared and Thomas. The blonde angel dipped her chin and looked up at him, her eyes round and warm and sending a flurry of something much like a wave of tiny flying insects through his stomach.

He cleared his throat. "Allow me to introduce myself. Mr. Jared Cooper," he said, bowing, "and my friend Mr. Thomas Hawkins."

"Mrs. Langley," the older woman said, before gesturing to

the women beside her. "This is my daughter, Miss Alicia Langley, and my niece, Miss Turner."

Alicia. What a beautiful name for such a lovely creature.

"We are pleased to make your acquaintance, but it is mightily unfortunate to do so under such circumstances." He proceeded to guide them toward Thomas's carriage and help them inside—one of the advantages of Thomas owning a livery and breeding horses, the man was always good for a horse or a carriage when Jared had need of one—then asked for their direction and gave it to the coachman. Once they were all settled snugly inside the carriage and on their way, Jared had difficulty keeping his gaze in one place. It flicked around from face to face, jumping to the sunset painted on the window and down to his hands in his lap.

Thomas pressed his shoulder lightly against Jared's, and he stilled. Was his fidgeting so obvious? He glanced up and caught Miss Turner's eye and paused. She gave him a kind smile that seemed to melt away his anxious fettering, and he smiled in return.

His spirits settled, he directed his attention to Miss Langley. "So, do tell me, how long have you resided in Bath?"

CHAPTER THREE

Rebecca could not believe her good fortune. She sat at the far end of the bench pressed against the lacquered wall, her knees knocking against Aunt Langley's leg in motion with the swaying vehicle. She could not determine whether it was due to the number of bodies packed into the small space, or proof of the quality of the carriage that she was so warm. The cool wind that had descended on them as they'd left their broken vehicle and climbed into the gentlemens' was cut off at the door, and as Rebecca had the terrible habit of most often feeling cold, this was something for which she was prodigiously grateful.

"Carriage trouble always occurs at the most inconvenient times," Mr. Hawkins said, shaking his head sadly.

"Indeed," Aunt Langley replied with feeling. "It would have been much more agreeable had we already arrived in Bath, at the very least."

"But that would have prevented us from making the acquaintance of these fine gentlemen," Alicia purred.

"Very true, darling," Aunt Langley stoutly agreed. She'd

been hesitant when she'd fetched them from the broken carriage, but Rebecca could see that the men had swiftly changed her opinion of them. "It is always best to look for the good, even in unfortunate situations."

Mr. Hawkins nodded sagely, a copper curl falling over his forehead. "A very noble way to approach one's view on life."

Rebecca peered at him, unable to ascertain whether the man was entirely genuine or having a bit of fun at Aunt's expense.

Mr. Cooper shifted on his seat. "I am somewhat new to the area. Is there anything in town you think I ought not to miss?"

"Have you walked the length of the Circus?" Alicia asked. "It is a magnificent thing to behold."

"I have, yes," he answered, nodding. "I've yet to partake of the waters, though—"

"Do not bother," Alicia said, pulling a face. "Horrid stuff."

"Though they have been proven helpful for many," Aunt Langley said. She had the tone of someone who wanted to ensure that others were not offended. Perhaps she believed Mr. Cooper would take offense from Alicia's opinion since he was a medical man.

Rebecca had tried the waters as well, but she hadn't felt any different afterward. Of course, she did not possess any need for healing within her body. Unless one counted eyesight, but she was certain the waters wouldn't make her vision less blurry. Shame, though. She would drink tubs of the *horrid stuff* if it meant she could discard her spectacles for good. It was dratted difficult to find a husband under her current circumstances, and the spectacles certainly didn't help her case.

Alicia laughed, the sound bouncing about the small carriage. "I hardly think a doctor would find value in the waters."

"I know of one who did a few years ago," Mr. Cooper said

kindly. "Though he has since decided that it is not effective as a sole treatment, but better in conjunction with other remedies."

Silence fell over the occupants, and Rebecca hurried to fill it. "He sounds like a wise man."

Mr. Cooper looked at her then, his eyes warm and grateful. "Indeed. The wisest of men."

Alicia laughed. "I for one do not care how sick I become, I shall never again drink the waters unless they are forced upon me."

Mr. Cooper's gaze shifted to Alicia, the warmth he carried magnifying when he settled his attention on her. He was besotted with her, that was plain to see. Rebecca wondered if that would help or hinder the proposition she planned to put forth to him.

Though she hated to admit it even to herself, envy formed in the pit of her stomach, swirling like an unpleasant storm cloud. She squashed the feeling as she'd done so many times in her cousin's presence before and pasted a smile on her face. "We shall endeavor to keep that from happening, Alicia."

They rolled to a stop, and a servant came around to open the door and let down the step. The men exited first, then turned to assist the women. Mr. Cooper helped Alicia down, and Mr. Hawkins helped Aunt Langley. Rebecca scooted over on the seat and curled her gloved fingers around Mr. Cooper's offered hand. He squeezed her fingers, and a blast of low heat started at her hand and swept through her body, stunning her into soft silence.

Rebecca stepped awkwardly on the uneven paving stones, her ankle turning and jerking her sideways. She shot out her free hand and gripped Mr. Cooper's coat sleeve, managing to keep herself upright. His hand went around her waist to support her, and her heart jumped.

Oh, dear. This was not good. She enjoyed being touched by the man far too much.

Bending his neck, Mr. Cooper surveyed her face, his eyes so close to her that she could easily discern the varying shades of blue, even with nothing but the warm light from the street lamp to see.

"Are you hurt?"

"No," she said, quickly disentangling herself from his grip and stepping back.

He glanced down at her feet.

She was quick to dissuade any notion that she'd been injured. "I believe I caught myself before any damage could be done to my ankle."

"Shall we ask the good doctor to look at it, Rebecca?" Aunt Langley asked.

Alicia nodded. "It would be wise, I think."

Embarrassment enveloped Rebecca, bleeding heat up her cheeks. "No, that is quite all right. I assure you, I am entirely well, and so is my ankle."

The very last thing Rebecca felt she could stomach at that moment was more of Mr. Cooper's fingers on her. She had felt such a strong jolt of reaction from the contact, she was certain one small touch from him would send her into a fit. Which was alarming, for Rebecca was not the sort of woman who swooned.

Mr. Cooper appraised her. "I do not wish to cause Miss Turner further distress. But please, if it comes to bother you, do send a note."

"May we have your direction, Doctor?" Aunt Langley asked, as if it were just occurring to her that she did not know where the man lived. "You must promise to dine with us this week, both of you."

The gentlemen began to politely decline when Aunt Langley raised a sturdy hand, silencing them both. "You will allow me to thank you for the service you've provided. Wednesday next?"

The men appeared to find no fault with this scheme and graciously accepted before bidding farewell and leaving in the carriage.

Aunt Langley sighed merrily once the front door was closed behind them. "Such nice young men."

"Regardless of their status?" Alicia countered.

"Mr. Cooper is a doctor," she said crisply.

"Ah, yes. But a *surgeon*, Mother, not a physician."

"Little does that matter. He is still a doctor." She huffed, clearly forgetting her prejudices from earlier in the day. "He claims a noble profession and with proper guidance could build his esteem, I should think." She seemed to consider her own words, then gave a slight shake of her head. "Though I do not think that even with our help he would be accepted among your father's family. Such a pompous set, the lot of them. You're best setting your sights elsewhere, darling."

Was it not lost on anyone but Rebecca that Aunt mirrored her in-laws' prejudice by advising against Mr. Cooper?

"Mr. Hawkins was a kind man," Rebecca said.

"Very handsome, too," Alicia agreed. "Is he also a doctor? He was on Mr. Cooper's team at cricket today."

Rebecca paused, searching the conversation, but the subject of Mr. Hawkins's employment had not come up. "I'm not sure."

"He possessed a very nice carriage," Alicia mused. "And his coat was well-made. Did you notice that?"

Aunt Langley peered strangely at her daughter. "One can be wealthy and still in trade, dear. It is quite common."

"I know that, but does that not change things even a little?"

"That would depend entirely on what Mr. Hawkins does to earn his wages, of course."

Rebecca was tired, the evening was growing late, and she had heard enough of this conversation today. Had it not occurred to her aunt even once that Rebecca's own father was engaged in trade at present? Or was his business of selling wine out of France acceptable because he was family? "I must go home," she said sadly, though the opposite was true. She looked forward to the quiet solitude awaiting her and to delivering her report to her mother. She was always a little anxious leaving Mama, but her endeavors had been worth it today.

A frown marred Alicia's flawless brow. "Will we see you tomorrow, Rebecca?"

Aunt Langley answered. "Of course we shall. The Assemblies in the Upper Rooms, you'll recall? We will come for you at half-past six."

Alicia turned sharply. "Why so early?"

Aunt's lips twisted wryly. "Tomorrow we must walk."

Rebecca lifted a hand. "I'm not sure I can attend. I must go home and see to Mama first."

"Of course, dear," Aunt said, her face scrunching. "Will you come for a visit tomorrow, at least?"

"I will send round a note to inform you whether Mama is feeling up for it or not in the morning."

Aunt Langley squeezed Rebecca's hand before pulling her in for a light embrace. "Take Rupert with you when you walk home."

"Yes, Aunt."

Rupert, the footman, was sent for, and they were soon outside and on their way to the rooms Rebecca and her mother were renting. She was situated in a far less fashionable part of town, but it had never bothered Rebecca. Aunt Langley had offered for them to stay at the Royal Crescent with her, but Mama had her pride, and she was determined to support herself until Father returned from France.

28

Letting herself into the townhouse, she thanked Rupert for seeing her home safely and climbed the narrow staircase to her rooms. It was a comfortable arrangement they shared with the woman who owned the house. Rebecca and her mother promised to be quiet tenants—not a particular struggle since Rebecca did not have access to a pianoforte and the only souls they had to speak to were each other and their maid, Mullens —and the landlady provided delicious hot meals. Two servants kept the building clean, three cats kept it rodent-free, and Rebecca was certain she would be happy there for as long as it took her father to finish his business and return home to them.

She missed him heartily, but she understood that they needed the money and was grateful he was doing his best to provide for them. She did not have the same prejudices against men in trade that her aunt held. But she would feel much more at ease if Father would only send word.

Rebecca let herself into the small sitting room she shared with Mama to the sound of the squeaky door hinges. Fire burned in the hearth and a thin blanket was thrown over the back of the sofa, opposite a delicate rocking chair containing an even more delicate looking woman. Mama's chin was tucked down against her chest, bent at a seemingly uncomfortable angle as a soft snore floated through the room.

Rebecca couldn't help but chuckle. She set her reticule on the end of the sofa and approached her mother, kneeling before her on the soft blue rug. "Mama," she said, gently shaking her knees. "Mama."

Her mother stirred, blinking lazily at Rebecca, and straightened in her seat, a sweet smile crossing over her face. "You've returned."

"Where is Mullens?" she asked, surprised their maid was not sitting awake by the fire with Mama as she usually was.

"I sent her to bed. She was tired, and you are much later than we anticipated."

"Aunt Langley's carriage had trouble. But never mind that. She will retrieve it tomorrow."

"Oh, dear. I am glad you've returned home safely. Was your day enjoyable?"

"It was lovely," Rebecca said. "The team of working men won the match, which you know put Aunt Langley into something of a mood and only made Alicia crave attention from a stable boy or a clerk."

Mama's smile widened. She covered a yawn with her cupped hand. "My sister never did like to bet on the losing side. But I would imagine Alicia giving attention to a clerk would vex her dearly. You must know she only wants security for her daughters. You know how difficult it was for my sister and me, living in such a debt-ridden household as children."

Indeed, Rebecca knew of their troubles all too well. Their father's inability to stay out of debt had them losing houses to the bank and their father to the debtors' prison. Mama had been raised on charity, and while she was grateful for it, she wouldn't allow the same for her family. Aunt Langley's fears were rooted in the same need for financial security.

"Will they not have security once Margaret marries the viscount?"

"A title does not guarantee wealth, and wealth does not guarantee security. Especially if he is a man with poor habits or weakness in character."

"Does Lord Buxton possess a gambling addiction?" Rebecca asked, trying to hide her amusement. She rocked back on her heels, watching her mother's face for a reaction to her boldness.

Mama simply pressed her lips together and shot a

reproving look at Rebecca, showing *exactly* what she thought of her boldness. "You know I refuse to gossip."

"Yes, Mama." Rebecca sighed. "You are a righteous bore."

Mama chuckled as Rebecca picked herself up from the floor and sat at the end of the sofa, curling her legs beneath her.

"I'd much rather be righteous and a bore than speak ill of others."

"Gossip is not always speaking ill," Rebecca defended.

"But it *is* speaking of others without their knowledge."

Rebecca said no more. She understood Mama's point and conceded that it was the better way to be. It was a worthy and commendable trait to be able to keep all secrets. Rebecca was no gossip, but neither was she perfect. She did find the little things her aunt shared about their friends interesting. But part of that could be because Rebecca did not know of whom her aunt spoke, more often than not.

"Were there any handsome young men present?" Mama asked.

"Yes, and I've asked one to call on us shortly. You will like him, Mama. He has none of the pomp or arrogance we've so often seen with other physicians."

Mama's eyebrows rose. "He is a doctor?"

"Yes, but he is different. I promise you will like him."

"So you've said." She peered at her daughter with a funny, appraising expression. "When will the handsome doctor come?"

"Handsome . . ." She realized her mistake, and her cheeks flushed. "I only have interest in his ability to see to your illness, Mama. And I have not invited him yet, for I wanted to speak to you first. I need your blessing."

Mama swept her arm out like she was the queen on her throne instead of a sickly woman on a rickety rocking chair. "If we can afford it, you have my blessing."

Wonderful. That was the first step out of the way. Rebecca breathed a sigh of relief. She had fought and fought to convince her mother to move to Bath in search of proper medical care, to leave the home they both loved dearly tucked in the south-western corner of Somerset for this bustling, aged metropolis. Their town had no redeemable doctor, and Mama needed help.

Now, with Father's promised funds missing and no response to any of her pleas for assistance, Rebecca only needed to come up with a way to pay for it.

Mama pulled her blanket tightly about her shoulders and leaned forward. She pushed herself up to a stand and wobbled on her feet, and Rebecca jumped up, ignoring the slight twinge in her ankle, and slid her hand around Mama's waist to help her into the adjoining bedroom. They were confined to small quarters, but the rooms were well-designed and well-outfitted, making a comfortable, cozy atmosphere for the Turner women. It was nothing compared to the opulence of Aunt Langley's apartment in the Royal Crescent, but Rebecca and her mother were perfectly comfortable.

After helping Mama into her bed, Rebecca pulled the warming pan from the fire and slid it under the blankets near her feet. It was summer, but Mama was always cold, like Rebecca.

"Mama," she asked quietly, "did we receive any post today?"

"No," she answered sleepily.

Rebecca leaned over and kissed her mother's temple before retreating to the dressing table to remove her pins. She pulled the emerald brooch from the small, pearl-encrusted jewelry box and turned it over in her hands. It had been passed down to each woman in her family on their eighteenth birthday over four generations and was the only thing of value that Rebecca owned. Mama had forbidden her to sell it, and selfishly,

Rebecca had been relieved. But it still belonged to her, and she would sell it if she had no other choice. Mama's health was more important than an heirloom.

Mr. Cooper had seemed like a kind man, and furthermore, he was absolutely taken with Alicia. Rebecca wasn't certain entirely how she was going to accomplish it yet, but she was determined to convince him to help. What other choice did she have?

CHAPTER FOUR

Rebecca had never seen her aunt so livid in her entire life. Aunt Langley stood before her own drawing room windows, red-faced and pinched-lipped, clutching a letter from her brother-in-law, the Langley patriarch, in her fist.

"Surely he could not mean it the way you are understanding," Mama said, looking warily at the abused missive from her position on the sofa. "Your brother-in-law understands how dearly you loved your husband."

"Does he?" Aunt Langley snapped. "He would not mention the precise number of weeks since the man's demise had he not intended to bring attention to my *lurid behavior* and *unscrupulous socializing*." Her round chin wobbled, tears pooling in the rim of her eyes before she crumpled onto the end of the sofa nearest the window, burying her head in the bend of her elbow.

Rebecca looked to Alicia, but she did not move from her place at the pianoforte, hands paused above the quiet keys. Mama moved closer to her sister's side and rubbed a soothing palm over her bent shoulders.

"All will be well," Mama crooned.

Aunt Langley sat up, her mottled cheeks streaked with tears, and frowned. "Will it? My own family cannot understand that I grieve quietly while allowing my daughters to attend carefully chosen social events. I have not resumed at-home hours, despite my poor sweet Alicia's need for company, I have not allowed her to dance at the assemblies, despite passing the requisite three months of mourning. She is *still* in black at nearly four months. Does that not prove our loyalty?"

"It does," Mama said. "Your Mr. Langley has certainly been grieved in this home, and the careless words his brother wrote were not likely meant to be interpreted in such a way."

"You are too kind to see the malice in others, Sister," Aunt Langley said. "I cannot interpret Arthur's words in any way other than that which they were given. He has called me careless, and the worst of it is that I do not wish to give him the satisfaction of having him believe that I agree with his accusation. I do not want to keep Alicia from Society in an effort to prove his opinion of me wrong." She took a shuddering breath. "But my pride will not allow for any other course of action. I fear we must extend our mourning another two months."

"Two months?" Alicia all but shouted, rising so quickly from her bench that she knocked it over, sending a crash through the room.

"We've no other choice," Aunt Langley said.

"Uncle's opinions matter little to me," Alicia wailed. "He cares for nothing but utilizing his control over us. He has always used his influence over Papa, and now that Papa is gone, he will continue to force us to heed his ludicrous schemes."

"He is not so bad as that," Aunt Langley said, though her voice lacked the power of conviction.

Silence sat heavily in the room as Alicia's eyes flared and Aunt Langley sobbed quietly into her handkerchief. Mr.

Arthur Langley was a frustrating man, and even Rebecca would despise being under his thumb. He never seemed to have any sound reasoning to his madness, but the Langleys did what he asked of them regardless. Rebecca was exceedingly grateful that the man was no relation to her.

"I cannot wait two more months to dance, Mother. Margaret should not have to wait to marry her Lord Buxton, either, not with the wedding already planned. Why must we suffer because of the opinions of an old, stuffy ogre?"

"Watch your tongue, Alicia."

Alicia glared at the wall.

Aunt Langley looked from her daughter to the letter again, her voice soft and defeated. "We have no choice. We are at the mercy of your uncle's generosity."

Alicia sucked in an outraged gasp.

Mama pulled back, surprised. "Did Mr. Langley not provide—"

"He provided well enough," Aunt said. "As well as he was able. The girls' dowries remain untouched, and my settlement is mostly intact. Though you well know, Sister, how little that was."

Rebecca struggled to understand the magnitude of what her aunt was saying. If Aunt Langley was reduced to a similar income as Rebecca and her mother, then how was she able to afford her carriage, horses, and fashionable home? She drew in a worried breath. Certainly they were not living *entirely* on credit. How could Aunt Langley do so after watching her own father spend his life in and out of a debtor's prison? "What does this mean for you, Aunt?"

Aunt Langley closed her eyes, the tiredness seeping through her limbs and drawing her down into a slouch. "We must retrench and economize until Margaret can marry Lord Buxton. Or we can swallow our pride and do our best to please

Arthur in hopes that he will not cease footing the bill for this house."

Alicia continued to seethe, but it was apparent that even she could see the importance and magnitude of their situation. They could have freedom of choice or fine things.

"This is wildly unfair," Alicia said before storming from the room.

Rebecca rose to follow her when Aunt Langley lifted her hand. "Allow her to suffer in peace, Rebecca. You may go to her in a half-hour when her sorrows have properly drained, and she is receptive to your support."

Nodding, Rebecca sat again, folding her hands demurely in her lap. The blow from learning that her aunt and cousins had not been left as well-provided for as they'd allowed Rebecca and her mother to believe was acute, and she reeled from its effects. Her hurt was only a small portion of what Alicia must be feeling, but it was unwelcome, the way she felt that she'd been lied to. Did Aunt Langley believe Rebecca or her mother would think less of them for the change in their circumstances?

"How long does Arthur expect you to remain in mourning?"

Aunt Langley lifted the fisted, wrinkled letter. "He expects a year from me, which I am more than happy to oblige. I should never think of wearing a happy color while my sweet Mr. Langley is gone from this world." She sniffed.

Rebecca had trouble thinking of her portly uncle as sweet. The man had been quiet, indolent, with mottled red jowls and a bored countenance. He slept, ate, or otherwise relaxed, but he hardly embodied the concept of *sweet.*

It was strange sometimes how death could change a person in the eyes of those they left behind. It could erase the negative parts of them, leaving a singular, positive representation. Rebecca hoped her loved ones would not paint her in a saintly light after her death. She was imperfect—everyone was—and it was those flaws which made up her character, which, coupled with her strengths, made her unique.

"You wear black so well," Mama said, and Aunt Langley nodded in agreement.

Then her face crumpled. "Alicia does not wear black well. I believed once that she would be radiant in anything, but black makes her skin pale and drawn. She deserves to wear colors, and the world deserves to see her in them."

Good gracious, they were only considering two months more of mourning for the girl, not the rest of her life. "She will not be in mourning forever, Aunt," Rebecca said softly.

Delivering a shuddering breath, Aunt Langley nodded in agreement. "That is a small comfort." She seemed to collect herself. "Will you go to her now, Rebecca? I think sufficient time has passed, and I must write to the Gastrells to inform them that we will not be able to join them in the Upper Rooms this evening. And we must cancel the dinner with the Johns. Oh, dear. So much to do."

Mama rose and crossed to the writing table. "I will pen the notes, dear. You simply tell me what you'd like them to say."

Rebecca left them to it but paused at the door and peered back at her mother. Her hands clasped the edge of the writing desk, her breaths even and deep as if she were focusing her efforts on maintaining a steady rhythm. Sunlight bled through the windows and fell over her face, and Rebecca squinted, trying to determine if the greenish tint to Mama's skin was a trick of the light. Unease rippled through her abdomen, and she forced herself to turn away.

Alicia's distraught wailing carried down the corridor, and Rebecca steeled herself before opening her cousin's bedroom door. But Alicia wasn't alone. Margaret sat beside her on the edge of the bed, stroking Alicia's hair as she cried in her sister's lap.

"I hadn't realized you were home," Rebecca said, closing the door behind herself.

Margaret wrinkled her dainty nose. "Lord Buxton was called to London on some important matter and doesn't intend to return for a fortnight at least. I only went to bid him farewell and came directly home."

"I am sorry for it," Alicia said. "But at least you have a Lord Buxton." Her face fell again, and she buried it in the folds of Margaret's skirt. "I don't have any lord at all," she wailed.

She could have one if she wanted, the moment she ceased playing games with men's hearts and gave them her authentic attention. Rebecca swallowed her admonition and sat on the other side of Alicia, rubbing her back. "Two more months is not so very long. Surely it will pass, and you will be back in the Upper Rooms before you know it."

Alicia sat up slowly, her eyes sparkling and red-rimmed. Her crying had only made her lovelier. Unfair, in Rebecca's opinion. Crying had only ever made her face puff like a feather pillow.

"It feels difficult now," Margaret said. "But Rebecca is correct. It won't last forever."

Sniffling, Alicia pulled herself from her sister's lap and sat up straight, using a damp handkerchief to wipe her tears. "I suppose I ought to be grateful for all we still have, but I only feel angry."

"You will not feel this way forever. Do your best to suffer elegantly, Alicia. It will be good practice for when you are married." Margaret grinned.

Alicia scoffed. "You can only say that because you love your Lord Buxton, but there are plenty of people unhappy in marriage. I vow I shan't be one of them."

"Neither shall I," Rebecca said, the words slipping free before she could trap them inside. She hadn't meant to say so aloud, and both of her cousins looked at her in varying measures of surprise.

Margaret filled the silence. "If you choose to find love, then I'm certain you shall."

"It will be awfully difficult to find anything when you are confined at home more often than not."

Alicia was correct, and the reality of her statement hit Rebecca with the force of a charging stallion. If Aunt Langley and Alicia were choosing to remain home and avoid social functions for another two months, that meant Rebecca would not be leaving home either. The only time she could attend assemblies, dinners, or routs was when her aunt took her. Mama was much too weak and tired for any sort of frivolous socializing, and Rebecca did not hold it against her. The only place Mama went when she left her home was Aunt Langley's house.

They'd moved to Bath to find Mama a cure shortly after the death of her uncle, and Rebecca had immediately dived into finding a physician who could help with Mama's illness. The trouble was, they were all much too expensive, these fancy Bath doctors, and she'd yet to find one she could afford. Her only hope now was to find one in possession of a heart and willing to make a trade for treatment like her country doctor was willing to do.

Her experience approaching the physician recommended to her by her aunt's friend was fresh in her mind. Warmth crept up her neck, heating her ears. The man had laughed at her request to offer services in lieu of money. He'd *laughed*. Mama had overheard and vowed to return to Welton immediately. Rebecca had taken great pains to convince her to remain. Surely not every doctor in Bath was as pompous and rude as he'd been.

Rebecca had begun to lose hope. Until Mr. Cooper, of course. She'd never been so glad she'd attended a wretched cricket match. Luck had shone down on her that blessed day in placing Mr. Cooper in her path. But the deal hadn't closed yet, and Rebecca needed to see him again, to ask him the question she'd been dreading asking since she met him.

How could she pay him to see to her mother's health? What could she offer him?

She'd only attempted that question one more time after the first doctor had laughed her to shame; the second doctor's response was so disturbing, Rebecca had felt the need to go home and bathe. But Mr. Cooper was different. He wouldn't be vile and require things of her that she could not give.

She also suspected Mr. Cooper would be willing to give Mama medical care without a fee, but neither did Rebecca want that. She simply didn't know what else to offer the man.

Truly, how difficult could it be to diagnose whatever it was that ailed Mama and give Rebecca a list of treatments? She didn't want extended care. She only wanted a little help.

She'd made a promise, after all. Father hadn't sent word in weeks, but the last time Rebecca had seen him before he set sail for France, he'd looked her in the eye and asked her to take care of her mother. Mama had no one else to depend upon. Rebecca could not let her father down now.

CHAPTER FIVE

Jared was growing restless. He'd been in Bath nearly four weeks and hadn't treated a single patient beyond the grouchy earl at the cricket match. If he hadn't relied on his parents' charity, he would not have been able to remain in the city. One could not pay for boarding or meals when one was not receiving patients. He was grateful his father had come into a little money from Jared's great aunt a few years prior, and that it paved the way for his father to retire when he needed to, but Jared could not rely on his parents' generosity forever.

And besides that, he missed the thrill and the gratification that accompanied the act of healing.

He'd attempted to speak to his father a few times regarding his gout, but the man had been a doctor longer than Jared had been alive and didn't subscribe to what he considered gimmicky, modern treatments. Jared had learned nearly everything he knew from his father, but he liked to read the *London Medical and Physical Journal* of his colleagues and continue to learn. He'd recently heard of the pure water trend and thought it could be on to something, but Father was having none of that so-called nonsense.

Father read the journal too, but only for argument fodder.

Jared stepped through the front door of his parents' home and tossed his hat on the table, pulling at his gloves one finger at a time to remove them as well. He'd considered taking his own rooms when he came to town, but until he had the funds and decided where he wanted to settle—and he was not convinced it would be Bath yet—he felt it best to avoid anything of a permanent nature.

Slapping his gloves on the table beside his hat, Jared suppressed a sigh. He'd had another unsuccessful day at the Pump Room, and the injury of feeling rejected was beginning to smart. Three mornings in a row he'd gone to the fashionable watering hole and promenaded far too long before he was forced to leave without laying eyes on Miss Langley. Or her cousin, or her mother. He'd yet to see anyone from their party, and he was growing increasingly frustrated.

Thankfully, he had the dinner invitation to supply him with hope, but that was not to occur for another six days, which seemed an awfully long time to wait.

Climbing the stairs, Jared let himself into the sitting room. Mother looked up from her embroidery, smiling beneath her knit cap and halo of gray curls. "Did you enjoy yourself?"

"I did hold an interesting conversation with Dr. Fielding about the new concept of pure water, but apart from him, there was no one present who I knew."

Mother frowned. "I really ought to have gone with you and performed more introductions."

He waved the concept away with a flick of his wrist and lowered himself on the wingback chair across from her. Reaching forward, he pilfered a small chunk of muffin and popped it in his mouth.

"The only introductions you've provided thus far have been to stodgy old doctors or their wives."

"I would hardly call your father's friends stodgy."

Jared lifted an eyebrow but said no more on the subject. He pinched another large chunk of muffin.

"I received a letter from Julia," Mother said, setting her embroidery on the cushion beside her and sliding the needle through the edge of the fabric. Jared stilled, the muffin in his mouth turning to sand.

The last he'd seen of his sister was when he'd angrily packed his belongings and vowed never to return to Derham. He remembered the moment clearly. The pain in her eyes reflecting his hurt, and the way he'd made her promise not to tell their parents of his indiscretion.

But though he'd tried to leave behind what had happened in Derham, he'd brought the feelings with him, and he had a hard time letting them go. As his horse had pulled away from the town he'd been raised in, he'd wondered if he would ever doctor again. Alas, it was quite literally in his blood. He couldn't put that part of himself away, as evidenced by the way he'd run to Lord Ryecombe when the ball had hit him in the face. Jared had found his feet moving toward the injured man before he'd consciously chosen to act.

He could not see a person in pain or in need and turn them away. That was something he and his father had in common. And, ironically, why *both* of them had fled to Bath. Father had retreated to Bath in his retirement to heal his gout and remove himself from an environment where he knew everyone and thus could not stop working even though he'd tried. Jared had far less altruistic motives. He'd simply run away.

"Julia mentioned that she is feeling the babe kick more and more, and she is prepared for the sleepless nights ahead of her, for she is already lacking in that department." Mother lowered the letter, a gleam in her brown eyes. "It was just the same way for me before you and your sister were born."

Jared gave her a soft smile. "When do you plan to go to her?"

"Not for another four weeks."

Jared nodded, his nerves rising. He had a month to tell his parents of what happened before they went to Derham and learned of it themselves. He swallowed hard, searching for the words to introduce his mother to the idea that he'd done something wrong.

"Oh, speaking of letters," Mother said as if she'd just recalled something. "You received a few this morning."

As the topic of conversation shifted away from a potential confession, relief poured through Jared, and the tension in his shoulders eased, no longer bending in accordance with the weight of the necessary conversation.

Another day, Jared thought to himself. There was still time.

Mother took two folded notes from the stack of correspondence on the table nestled into the side of her sofa, and Jared rose to retrieve them from her hand.

He did not recognize the handwriting on either letter, but hope bloomed in his chest that one, at least, would be from Miss Langley or Miss Turner. Breaking the wafer, Jared unfolded the first missive and scanned the document, his stomach tightening.

Mr. Jared Cooper—

I regret to inform you that we must postpone the dinner party planned for Wednesday. We have been premature in the disbanding of our mourning restrictions and must beg your forgiveness and hope you will be willing to receive our gratitude at a later date.

Yours, etc.
Mrs. Ellen Langley

Jared swallowed a curse. He'd been rejected, and Mrs. Langley had failed to even cite a decent reason for it. To postpone was acceptable, but she hadn't even named a future date. Something was off, and it didn't sit well with him.

He glanced up to find his mother watching him and formed a smile to ease her worried brow.

Taking the next letter, he ripped it open and read it quickly.

Mr. Cooper—

In regard to the patient we spoke of briefly, I would like to meet and discuss our options prior to introducing you to her. There is a little bench at the edge of Sydney Gardens on the end of Great Pulteney Street. You will find me there at half past noon today. If it is agreeable to you, I look forward to discussing this patient.

Gratefully yours,
R.T.

R.T. could be no other than Miss Turner, and the note she'd sent, while cryptic, reinstated a fraction of his hope. Surely she would be able to provide Jared with insight as to why the Langleys had canceled their dinner. Or had they merely removed him, alone, from their party?

He rose. It was nearly noon, and he needed to get out the door if he were to make it to the park in time.

"Have you received bad news?" Mother asked.

"No," he said at once, pausing halfway to the door and making an effort to smooth his brow. He'd forgotten she was there, so caught up in the letters as he'd been. He gave her a reassuring smile. "One of the letters contained a request for medical advice."

"Ah," Mother said, nodding and sitting back in her seat. His preoccupation with healing was something she knew well. "Someone we know?"

"No, it is a woman I met at the cricket match." He moved to his mother's side and bent to kiss her on the cheek. "I will return in an hour or so, and then I would love to hear about the rest of Julia's letter."

"I hate to disappoint you, but I have already shared everything she wrote." Her expression shifted into the adoring smile of a woman who was about to be made a grandmother. "She is uncomfortable and longs for the day when she is less round. Quite typical behavior for a woman in her situation, I assure you."

"I am glad to hear it," Jared replied. He'd helped a fair number of women with births and was as knowledgeable as any doctor on the subject of pregnancy normalities. But he bit his tongue. Mother only wanted to share.

"You may want to take an umbrella," she said, looking to the window behind him. "It looks like rain. Such odd weather for summer."

He followed her gaze to the gray sky beyond the glass panes. Blast. It had been raining off and on for weeks now, but during the cricket match, they'd had something of a break from dreary weather. He hoped the rain wasn't back to stay.

Jared retrieved his black umbrella, gloves, and hat and slid on his greatcoat before venturing outside. The chilly air nipped at his nose and wrists as he picked his way down the road and turned onto Great Pulteney Street. He didn't live too far from

Sydney Gardens, and he picked up his pace when the rain began to drizzle.

Once the park was in view, Jared found the bench unsurprisingly empty. The rain was falling in earnest now and the bench was wet, water pooling along the wooden slats. He searched the mostly empty area until his eyes fell upon a slim figure in a forest green cloak, the hood brought up and covering her hair. A glint from the mostly hidden sun bounced from the glass of her spectacles, and a smile fell unbidden to his lips.

It was her.

Rebecca had stood under the cover of the tree for ten minutes, anxiously appraising each gentleman who strode by and finding herself increasingly disappointed that none of them were Mr. Cooper. Minutes stretched on until the appointed time came and passed, and she forced herself not to give up hope.

She'd been foolish, perhaps, to choose such a public meeting area, but anywhere more private than an open park would have been inappropriate. She was prepared to offer whatever Mr. Cooper thought fair in exchange for his services, so long as her reputation remained intact and the brooch stayed in the pearl-encrusted box.

"Miss Turner?"

Rebecca glanced toward the voice, startled that Mr. Cooper had come upon her without her awareness. A smile stretched over his lips, revealing a soft dimple to the side of his mouth, and her stomach flipped. He wore a large, black coat underneath a black hat and umbrella, and looked mostly dry. The opposite of herself, she couldn't help but notice.

"Good day, Mr. Cooper. Thank you for meeting with me."

"How is your ankle faring?"

"It is well, I thank you," she said, surprised that he recalled her small injury.

He looked behind her, sweeping his gaze over the park, and she suppressed her blush as best she could. She hoped he would attribute her pinking cheeks to the cold and not her nerves. Clearing her throat, she gestured to the bench she'd previously mentioned in the letter. "It is too wet to sit, I fear."

"Do you not have an umbrella?" he asked, concern flashing in his eyes and in the furrow of his brow. "You are quite wet."

"I did not think it would be necessary," she said, feeling her blush deepen. She could hardly use her umbrella in Mr. Cooper's company anyhow, not when one side absolutely refused to fold up all the way and was obviously broken. She'd rather be wet than carry a broken umbrella before him. She did have *some* pride.

He straightened his arm toward her. "Here, take mine."

"I couldn't." Rebecca backed up until her shoulder blades bumped into the tree behind her. "I thank you, sir, but it is unnecessary. My cloak and hood cover me well enough."

He didn't look convinced, but he did not press the issue. The tree was doing a marvelous job blocking the majority of the rain anyway.

"Can you tell me about the patient?" he asked. He did not mince words, did he?

"First, we must discuss payment."

She'd surprised him, she could see that.

She held her sopping, muddy ground. "I do not feel comfortable moving forward, and neither would my mother, until we've discussed fees."

"Very well," he said. He'd taken on a congenial, businesslike mien, and Rebecca wondered if this was his doctoring face. It fell somewhere between pleasant and serious, and she liked it. It was sophisticated and suited him well, though his dimple was absent. "I assure you, I am very reasonable. For a typical daylight visit, I charge no more than a shilling—"

"I will stop you right there, sir. I cannot afford to pay in the typical fashion."

Mr. Cooper's eyebrows rose. Had he been wondering exactly why she'd brought him to the park to discuss payment and then promptly refused to pay? She must appear mad, she knew that. She hurried to continue. "But I will pay somehow. My father is away, and should soon be sending us money, but until I have it, I hoped to offer something of a trade. I am skilled in many ways; I can bake, embroider, play the pianoforte, and sing. I am not above taking in washing, scribing, or—"

"You propose, Miss Turner, to make a trade for the service of seeing to your mother's health?"

"Indeed." She nodded to punctuate her word, shame climbing up her spine and coloring her neck. She didn't mean to beg, but he needed to know the lengths she was willing to go. Rebecca would do anything wholesome in order to avoid debt.

Mr. Cooper screwed up his face in indecision, and she instantly knew a moment of fear. Not once in all of her planning since meeting the doctor at the cricket match had Rebecca thought that he would deny her. He'd seemed so affable, so generous and kind. It had felt, to Rebecca, a matter of *how* she would pay him and not *if* he would accept a trade.

Now the quiet stretched between them, and she questioned herself. Had she seen good in a man who did not actually possess it?

"I'm not certain I need any of the services you mentioned, but I am more than happy to come meet your mother and see what I can do to help."

Charity. The man appeared to be offering her charity. That rankled, somehow, more than an outright refusal. She was willing to beg and work, but she was not willing to accept a hand-out. Mist from the rain fogged up her spectacles, and Rebecca did her best to wipe them with the interior of her cloak so she could see clearly, all the while fighting the most ridiculous urge to cry.

Releasing a frustrated huff, she squared her shoulders and forced herself to hold Mr. Cooper's handsome blue gaze. Evidently, she would need to keep looking for a doctor. "I thank you for your time, Mr. Cooper, and I shan't take up any more of it today."

Before he could say anything else, she slipped around him and into the rain, lifting her hood further in front of her face to guard her glasses from becoming wet and blurring her vision. A shadow passed above her head, and she looked up to find Mr. Cooper holding his umbrella over her.

She stopped on the paving stones immediately, and he continued on, halting when he noticed that she was gone. The streets were all but empty and she had to speak up to be heard over the rain.

"I do not require an escort, sir."

He faced her. "You must allow me to walk you home, Miss Turner. The rain is only increasing."

No. Because then he would know where she lived. If he was not going to accept payment, he would not be learning where to find her mother. She lifted her stubborn chin. "I cannot accept your generosity, but please understand that I do know it was kindly meant."

He dropped his hand which held the umbrella and studied her as rain fell over him, pooling on the brim of his hat and running onto his shoulders. "Do you refer to the umbrella or the offer to see your mother?"

"Both."

"Then you must understand that I cannot, in good

conscience, allow you to walk into the rain when I have a perfectly fine umbrella. My umbrella is not being utilized, which is really silly when one considers that refusing its help will in no way stop this rain."

Rebecca didn't know if Mr. Cooper intended the umbrella scenario to be a metaphor for her mother's health, but she could see the parallels quite clearly. What he failed to know, however, was that Rebecca inherited her stubborn pride from her mother. Neither of the Turner women would admit him into their home without an agreement to pay in some way.

If Mr. Cooper was not the doctor for them, all that meant was that Rebecca's search would start from the beginning. Again.

"Please, allow me to help," he pleaded. It was sweet, the rain dripping down his face, gathering on his lashes and falling from his chin as his umbrella lay idly in his hand, collecting water in its upturned base. "I promise to allow you to pay in some way, and we can worry about the details later."

Rebecca's stomach swirled with indecision, but Mr. Cooper's wet eyelashes blinking away rainwater decided for her. He was right. Turning away a perfectly good and willing doctor was senseless when he was available, and Mama's poor health wasn't going to change on its own. "You promise to allow me to pay in some way?"

"I do," he said firmly.

"And we will determine a method of payment soon? I cannot abide debt."

He nodded. "Very soon. I promise."

She let out a small sigh and reached for his umbrella handle, tipping it to the side to empty the water and then lifting it until it covered his head. Water dripped from the rounded edge and onto her hood, and Mr. Cooper stepped forward until the umbrella covered both of them, his proximity heating her body from the inside. His hair looked darker from the water and the shadow of his umbrella, and his eyes were a deep, dark ocean, the glint of light like white-crested waves on their surface. If she wasn't careful, she would drown in their depths.

"Shall we go now?" he asked, his gaze locked on hers.

But Rebecca's throat was dry. This doctor was doing things to her stomach that she'd never before felt, and it simultaneously delighted and terrified her. She dropped her hand, burying it in the folds of her cloak.

"Yes. Follow me."

CHAPTER SIX

Jared followed Miss Turner into the narrow townhouse and hesitated near the door in the entryway. She removed her sodden cloak and untied her bonnet, avoiding his gaze through her rain-speckled glasses.

"Would you mind waiting a moment so I can warn my mother of your presence?"

"Of course not." Jared smiled reassuringly at her before he watched her retreat up the stairs. He could see her pride in the way she carried herself, her back straight and shoulders stiff, though to call the woman prideful could very well be an understatement. Her mother was in need of medical assistance, and when she'd believed Jared to be offering charity—which in all fairness, he *had* been—she had been willing to walk away. He wasn't entirely sure how he was going to accept payment from her when there was nothing she could offer which he had a need of.

He supposed, if it came down to it, he could request that she teach him a song on the pianoforte. She'd mentioned that she could play, and he had always been interested to learn.

Though it would be odd, of course. And he wouldn't want others to have the wrong impression of his feelings for her.

He'd stayed away from women so resolutely for the last two years—nursing a broken heart had required it of him—that he was certain to elicit no small amount of speculation the first time his parents or friends found him seeking the attention of a woman. He would need to be careful, whatever he chose.

Miss Turner appeared at the top of the stairs and quietly beckoned him upward. Jared left his wet overcoat, gloves, and umbrella near the front door before ascending. There were no servants to take his things, so he hoped he'd left them in an appropriate place. In his line of work, he had visited every type of household, and he'd grown comfortable blending in with varying classes of people.

Miss Turner waited before a partially open door, light spilling from the room into the dimly lit corridor. The storm had descended upon them in earnest, darkening the sky and drawing a blanket of thick clouds over the sun. Though it was the middle of the day, it looked as though it was nearing night-fall indoors.

Miss Turner opened the door to reveal a small sitting room and an older woman perched on a spindly rocking chair near the large fire. A white, lacy cap covered her dark hair much like the one his mother often wore, and fine lines fanned out from her eyes and the corners of her mouth. She smiled softly at Jared, and he lowered his hat in his hands, immediately assessing the unnatural hue of her skin. He wished he would have retrieved more information from Miss Turner ahead of time, but he'd been so focused on convincing her to allow him to treat her mother that he'd thought of little else.

The young woman was unpredictable, but he liked her.

"Mama, this is the man I spoke to you about, Mr. Cooper." She gestured to the woman, her worried gaze latching on to him. He could feel the desperation lacing her words as though it was a physical force. "Mr. Cooper, this is my mother, Mrs. Turner."

He sketched a bow. "It is good to meet you, Mrs. Turner."

She nodded but didn't rise, and he was happy to sit at the end of the sofa when she invited him to. A short, slight woman bustled into the room with a tray of tea and startled when her gaze fell upon Jared. She set the tea on the small table before them and retreated from the room, likely to fetch another cup.

Mrs. Turner offered him tea, which he graciously declined, and he watched Miss Turner flit about the room like a busy honeybee, closing the door to the corridor, straightening the shawl about her mother's shoulder before fetching a small blanket for her lap, then lifting the poker to stoke the well-burning fire.

"Rebecca, really," Mrs. Turner said, looking at her daughter with exasperation. "Mullens just stoked the fire minutes before you arrived. Now be seated. Your anxious fretting is going to soon become contagious if you do not force it into submission."

Rebecca stared at her mother, fire poker dangling from her hand and her eyes wide with surprise. Her auburn eyebrows were raised high above the thin wire of her spectacles, and Jared studied her briefly. Her character was every bit as strong and steadfast as her name, and he thought it suited her well.

Rebecca placed the poker against the hearth and folded her hands together before crossing the room and seating herself at the other end of the sofa.

Jared cleared his throat and pulled a small notebook and pencil from his coat pocket. "Mrs. Turner, are you able to tell me what ails you?"

He'd noticed the unhealthy pallor of her skin when he stepped into the room, and further observation confirmed that it was not due to the lighting but was most likely owed to the woman's health. The window shades were pulled open, and the fire burned bright. But aside from the greenish tint to her skin, there was nothing visibly wrong with the woman. She merely appeared frail.

"We aren't certain, exactly," she said, a reedy quality to her voice.

"She has lost her energy," Rebecca explained.

"What little I had."

"And her appetite has fled. She's fainted on occasion this last year—"

"Only twice," Mrs. Turner cut in. She smiled wryly, but her chair had ceased rocking. "Rebecca would like to make me sound worse than I am, Doctor."

Rebecca huffed softly. "I would like to ensure that Mr. Cooper has the entire truth of the matter so he might be able to help you, Mama. I am not fabricating your symptoms or exaggerating them by any means."

"You made it sound as though I fall over every time I try to stand up," Mrs. Turner argued.

Rebecca seemed to gather her strength from an invisible source and then spoke, her voice calm and collected. "I do not believe one can equate fainting *on occasion* to *daily*, Mama. If I exaggerate, then you just as easily deemphasize your trouble."

At what point was it appropriate for Jared to step into the conversation and bring it to a stop? He glanced between the stubborn women and held his tongue. His answer was never. He should never step between a mother and daughter in the midst of a disagreement on health and wellness. Or anything else, for that matter.

"We are getting away with ourselves," Rebecca said. "I believe the only other issue of note is that Mama doesn't sleep well."

Jared nodded, noting the final symptom in his book. He

gave his patient his full attention. "When did all of these things begin to occur?"

"I have struggled with many of them for most of my life to one degree or another, but the culmination and the severity have increased significantly in the last two years."

Jared nodded, noting that as well. "Can you describe a typical day's diet to me?"

"Currently or before we moved to Bath?"

"How long have you lived in Bath?"

"Three months."

"Then both, please."

Mrs. Turner proceeded to break down her daily diet and how it had altered since moving to Bath. She explained her habits from before, and Jared took copious notes, as he always did, because it helped him to process the information and think thoroughly. But he'd known her illness from the moment he saw the woman's skin, and her explanations had done nothing but consistently confirm what he believed to be the case.

He would hate to explain it to these women and give them a false idea of the ease with which she could be healed. Understanding the ailment was only half of the problem. *Fixing* it would be an entirely different beast to tackle. No two people were cured in the same way. Some people were never cured.

Mrs. Turner and Rebecca both blinked at him, and Jared realized that he had allowed his mind to run away.

"Are your feet often cold, Mrs. Turner?"

Her eyes widened, almost imperceptibly, but she nodded.

"And do you mind if I listen to your pulse?"

"Of course not, young man."

Jared swallowed his mirth. He liked this woman excessively. Setting his hat on the cushion beside him, he crossed the small sitting room rug and knelt beside her, where he took her proffered wrist and pressed his fingers lightly to the underside.

He detected her pulse, and it beat quickly, but not as strongly as he'd hoped.

Regardless, it confirmed his suspicion. Releasing her wrist back to her lap, Jared rose and retook his seat on the sofa. "I believe you have what is called green sickness, Mrs. Turner."

"What is it?" Rebecca asked, fear bubbling into her voice.

Jared did his best to reassure her. "It is not fatal by any means, and it can be managed. It most often presents as a lack of energy, appetite, and ability to sleep, among other things." He directed his attention back to his patient. "Until you have an understanding of what helps you to feel better, however, your situation will not change."

"What do we do?"

He glanced at the window. "I would typically prescribe fresh, warm air—at least two hours daily—but that might be impossible at present. If you can manage it, take a walk outside whenever the sun is out. As soon as this storm passes, you will want two hours minimum. Twice daily would be ideal."

He could see that Rebecca was surprised. "Is that all?"

"No, but I've seen it do a world of good. This will be a slow process, but it can be righted. Do you have access to horses?"

Rebecca's shoulders slumped, a furrow appearing on her brow. "Not at present, no."

He should have known. Horses in a town such as Bath were an exorbitant cost that many could not afford. And yet, he'd read recently about the importance of implementing riding into one's regimen to heal green sickness, that it did wonders for the circulation. Perhaps if he was able to obtain a few horses, Mrs. Turner could utilize one of them for a time.

"The sunlight and fresh air really are quite important," he said. "I will write you a recipe for tablets, and you'll need to take two each day, one pill in the morning and one at night."

He turned to a fresh page in his notebook and wrote out the

ingredients she would need for her medicine. Iron, ipecacuan powder, aromatic powder, extract of gentian . . . He quickly added the amounts of each and how many pills to divide it into before tearing the paper away. "When this order is complete, I will write a new one. We must change the dosage a little at a time until you are feeling yourself again, Mrs. Turner."

"Thank you, Doctor," Mrs. Turner said. "We will adhere to your advice exactly."

"I will go to the apothecary directly," Rebecca said, rising and taking the recipe from him. She folded the paper and tucked it into her wet, discarded reticule.

Jared stood as well. "I will see myself out. Please strive for sunlight and maintain the medicine regimen for a fortnight, and I will come see you again to assess your progress and determine what should next be done."

"Thank you, Mr. Cooper," Mrs. Turner said, and her genuine tone made Jared pause. She appeared slightly skeptical of his prescription for sunlight, but she was clearly grateful, and he appreciated her gratitude.

After what Jared had endured in Derham, Mrs. Turner's quiet acceptance and thankfulness was a balm over what still felt a gaping wound.

Rebecca pulled the creaky door open, sending a squeak through the room.

Mrs. Turner huffed. "Ask Mrs. Brown about the door as well while you're down there, Rebecca."

"I'm not certain a third request will do us much good. Not if the first and second didn't see it done." She looked at her mother and swiftly added, "But I can ask."

Jared bowed farewell and stepped into the corridor, pausing to allow Rebecca to precede him down the stairs. Rain pattered the windows, and the house was quiet, making the falls of his boots echo loudly down the stairwell.

They reached the entryway and Rebecca paused. She pushed her glasses up on her nose and held his gaze. The glass seemed to make her eyes bigger, and the green irises were just the shade of the lush green lawn they'd played cricket on. Had he noticed the color before? It was striking, even in the dimness of the dark entryway. He found himself wondering exactly what shade they would be with the sun's light filtering through them.

"Now," she said, her tone sturdy and clipped. "As for a matter of payment—"

He cut her off. "First, I wondered if you could clarify something for me."

She waited expectantly, and he knew a moment of unease. Swallowing, he pressed forward. "I have received a note from your aunt postponing my dinner invitation."

Rebecca nodded. "She felt awful, but she didn't have a choice."

"Because of her mourning?"

"Indeed. Did she mention as much in her letter?"

She spoke with such ease, lacking any contrivance, that Jared had no trouble taking her for her word. "Yes. But it was very brief, and I admit I was taken quite by surprise."

Rebecca crossed to his umbrella and picked up his gloves from the table beside the door. She looked down at them, running the black leather through her fingers as though she was too lost in thought to deliver them to his waiting grasp. Jared lowered his outstretched hand.

"I can see why you might be confused, but my aunt attended the cricket match for Alicia's sake and has since felt it necessary to extend their mourning for another two months. She will not be attending social functions, and she felt uncomfortable hosting a dinner, given the circumstances." Rebecca looked up and held his gaze. "If she implied that the dinner would be postponed, then I am certain she intends to deliver another invitation at a later date. She will be true to her word."

Disappointment filled Jared's stomach like a heavy, water-laden basin. It was just his luck that the first woman he found of interest had immediately become unavailable for a time. Was it conceit that he felt she'd returned his interest? No, it was not. Not when the woman herself had given him reason to feel that way by her marked attention and mention of the Pump Room. Surely two months would pass quickly, and in that time he would be patient.

He'd waited two years to find a woman who sparked his interest after having his heart broken. What were two additional months?

"You will see your aunt and cousin in the interim though, I presume?"

"I will."

Jared considered her and nodded. He wanted to inquire further, to ask if Miss Langley had said anything about him, but the impulse felt childish, and he bit his tongue.

She chewed on her lower lip, bringing to mind Miss Langley doing something very similar at the cricket match. Though it had been evident that Miss Langley knew of the power she wielded with such a trick, and Rebecca appeared to be using no such artifice. She raised her gaze to meet his. "I wonder if you will settle a curiosity for me."

"Of course, if it is within my power," he said.

"Alicia mentioned that you quoted a poem to her, but she could not recall the name."

His neck warmed. The words had slipped from his tongue, and recalling the moment was embarrassing when faced with the steadfast Rebecca. He nodded. "Ah yes, *The Tyger*."

"By William Blake."

"Indeed, the very one." Jared was impressed she had recognized the author so speedily. And yet, it had been named for the animal it was centered upon, and Alicia could not recall its name?

Rebecca squared her shoulders. "Now for the matter of payment—"

"We can discuss it another time." Jared pulled his watch from his pocket and checked the time before tucking it away again. "I must be off. But do not fear, I will not conveniently forget this. I will allow you to pay when I have need of a service you can provide."

She looked uneasy, and he didn't blame her. It could not be comfortable to feel as though she was in his debt. "Thank you, Mr. Cooper. You cannot know what this means to us. My mother has sought help, and no one has been able to do anything for her. Although, no one else prescribed sunlight and horses. Perhaps we were going to the wrong men all along."

He bowed to her. "I do sincerely hope she will quickly feel a difference. May I escort you to the apothecary? I can wait if you need to fetch a servant." He wondered about her traveling alone that morning without a maid to follow her. It couldn't be safe, especially in such a large town.

"Heavens, no. I assure you I am perfectly capable of completing this task."

Capable, yes. But it wasn't what was typically done. He waited for her to continue, to explain herself, but she turned away and slipped her dripping cloak over her shoulders.

Jared pulled on his gloves and opened the door. The rain had slowed some, but it was still falling in earnest. Raising his umbrella, he waited until Rebecca looked at him to speak. "You will take my umbrella, at least."

"Nonsense," she said, flashing an impatient smile. "I have my own."

"Oh, lovely." He stood by the door, waiting for her to

retrieve it, but she did not move. Her foot began to tap out a restless pattern on the smooth, wood floor, the rain quietly falling behind them. "I do not mind waiting."

"Please, Mr. Cooper. Do not allow me to keep you. Did you not just say that you must be on your way?"

He wanted to wait longer, but she had him there. Blast the woman. He was determined to be chivalrous, and she seemed determined not to let him. He sketched a low bow, holding her gaze as he rose. "Until next time, Miss Turner."

Placing his hat upon his head, Jared stepped into the rain, the pattering of drops on his umbrella muting the sound of the passing carriage. He strolled down the block and paused when he realized that he had not asked Rebecca if she planned to attend the assemblies the next evening.

He liked her. She had an easy way about her that made him comfortable, and in a town where he hardly knew anyone, her soothing presence would make the assemblies much more enjoyable. He glanced over his shoulder and caught sight of her leaving her townhouse, her head bent and umbrella raised to keep off the rain. Jared opened his mouth to call to her when she turned slightly, and her umbrella pivoted as well. It was round on one side and flat on the other. If Rebecca didn't hold it in the correct position, it was sure to scrape her shoulder.

Jared hesitated drawing attention to himself and instead watched her hurried pace down the path and around the corner until she was gone.

CHAPTER SEVEN

Rebecca sat at the pianoforte in her aunt's drawing room and picked out the notes of the Mozart piece leaning against the music stand. Her heart wasn't in it, for she was far too distracted listening to her mother describe the drapes featured in the most recent installment of *Ackermann's Repository of Arts*.

Nearly a week had passed since their appointment with Mr. Cooper, marking a full six weeks since they'd heard from Father. It was not the first instance Father had gone a length of time without writing. He tended to be forgetful in some ways, so it was not a long enough stretch to cause alarm to Rebecca or her mother. But since the money had ceased as well, she had an uneasy feeling all the same.

"You look pale, Sister," Aunt Langley said, narrowing her gaze. "Perhaps I ought to send for some lemonade."

"I feel better today than I did yesterday." Mama smoothed her skirt down her legs. "But I will never refuse a cold glass of lemonade."

Aunt Langley called for a servant and requested refreshments. She leaned back in her plush seat, sighing. "It is such a shame Alicia's gowns are lying in waste. By the time she is able to don yellow or pink again, all of her new dresses will surely be out of fashion."

"You always choose such elegant styles. I am certain they will not be out of fashion entirely," Mama said.

Rebecca did her best not to shake her head in mirth at the ridiculous nature of Aunt Langley's concerns. She loved her aunt, even though the woman was sometimes denser than an overcooked scone.

"How does Margaret fare?"

"She left this morning to stay with her Langley cousins in Brighton for the next few weeks."

Alicia scowled down at her lap.

Mama nodded. "She is fortunate to get away."

"You mentioned that you sought the advice of a doctor," Aunt Langley said. "Was he helpful?"

"I liked him immensely. We will see if he was helpful over time, I suppose." Mama's forehead wrinkled in thought. "I do believe he will be, though. I had a good feeling about him."

"That is wonderful news, Aunt," Alicia said. She smiled, absently fingering the fringe of the pillow beside her.

"I believe you know the young man," Mama said. "Rebecca mentioned that she'd met him at the cricket match."

Alicia's head shot up, her gaze piercing Rebecca across the room so strongly, she could feel the weight of it even from a distance.

"Oh, is that so?" Aunt Langley asked, tilting her head to the side. "Was it Mr. Cooper?"

"Indeed. Such a nice young man, and so very knowl-edgeable."

"Rebecca," Alicia whined. "You did not mention this to me. What a clever idea to ask for Mr. Cooper's assistance."

"He has such a pleasant countenance," Aunt Langley said. "It is too bad, really, that he is only a surgeon. He would sound much better as Dr. Cooper, do you not think?"

"He is still a doctor, regardless of how he trained," Mama said.

Alicia stood abruptly. "I need to fetch something from my room. Rebecca, will you accompany me?"

Rebecca's hands stilled on the keys, the silence reverberating through the room as loudly as the song had before it.

Alicia crossed to her and took Rebecca by the hand. She dragged her out of the drawing room, a look of mischief in her eye that dumped a rock into the pit of Rebecca's stomach.

"Come, I have something to ask of you."

Rebecca swallowed, following her cousin up the stairs and toward her bedroom. Neither of them said another word until they were safely ensconced within the chamber, the bright yellow walls and cream *fleur-de-lis* drapes a sunny backdrop to Alicia's growing grin.

Sitting on the edge of the bed, Alicia waited for Rebecca to settle beside her. "You do plan to go to the assemblies at the Lower Rooms this evening, correct?"

"I hadn't planned on it, no."

Alicia scowled. "Whyever not?"

"I have no interest in going." Rebecca had not come to Bath to socialize. She'd come to find her mother the help she needed. In the days since Mr. Cooper's visit, Mama had yet to see any significant changes, though she felt marginally better. But they had hope, and that was a powerful cure in itself. It had been so impressive how easily Mr. Cooper had been able to diagnose and treat Mama, that Rebecca couldn't help but be awed by his skill.

Alicia implored her, taking her hand in both of hers. "I need you to go tonight."

"Who will accompany me?" Rebecca asked, lifting an eyebrow. She removed one of her hands from her cousin's grip to slide her glasses back up her nose. "My mother surely will wish to remain home and rest, and Aunt Langley has chosen to forgo all entertainment for the next eight weeks."

Pouting, Alicia's blonde eyebrows pulled together, and she stared hard at the opposite wall. "Can you not convince your mother to attend the assemblies just for a set or two?"

"Why is this so important?"

Alicia paused, then released a long breath and lowered her voice. "I need you to deliver a letter to someone for me."

Unease slipped into Rebecca's stomach and curled into a tight ball. "To whom?"

"Just . . . a gentleman. I want to thank him, and I need you to do it for me. I cannot send the note to his address, for what would I do if it was discovered?"

Alicia had been reckless in the past, but this was too much. "You cannot ask me to participate in this clandestine activity. What if *I* am caught, and it is discovered that you are passing letters to a man to whom you are not engaged? You could put yourself in a position to *never* be engaged following that."

"Please, Rebecca." She laughed lightly. "You know that is unlikely to happen. You can be discreet."

That did not make it less of a danger to either of their reputations. "No, I cannot do it. I will not be party to your indiscretions."

Alicia huffed in frustration. "It is nothing vile, I assure you. I merely want to tell Mr. Cooper that I found the poem which he referred to and learned for myself what a compliment his reference was. It is completely innocent."

"Can I not simply tell him that information myself?" she asked, biting back the odd jealousy that flitted through her empty stomach.

"Of course not." Alicia tucked her chin. "It would not be from me if you were the one to say it."

She had a point, but still, it sat uneasily on Rebecca's chest. Alicia had not yet courted a man in earnest, but she had received her share of admirers, her court large and constantly fluctuating. Men adored Alicia. Her sweet, dimpling personality coupled with her beauty was a consistent draw that kept the number of suitors on a constant rotation. But surely Alicia did not intend to draw Mr. Cooper into her nest of admirers, not when he was a lowly doctor with little to recommend him in the eyes of Aunt Langley or even the *ton*. Alicia cared far too much for the opinions of Society to consider such a match. Didn't she?

Rebecca avoided elite society when she was able, but Alicia and her mother were very much involved and wished to be more so. No, Alicia couldn't intend to add Mr. Cooper to her line of suitors. She would never have him for a husband, and even she was not so callous as to string a man along.

Surely her note was innocent. Perhaps Rebecca could take it to put her cousin at ease, but she certainly wouldn't deliver it unless the right opportunity presented itself. Alicia wouldn't have to know that Rebecca didn't *truly* intend to deliver it.

"I might be persuaded to give him the note, but I cannot go to the assemblies. We must find another venue. Mama needs her rest, not an evening in a stuffy room with little to do but watch young people dance about the floor and old people gossip."

Alicia stood, a smile playing at her lips. She crossed to her writing table and retrieved a small sheet of paper, penning a quick note before sanding and folding it. Returning to Rebecca's side, she placed the folded paper in her hand. "You take this, and I will manage Aunt Turner. We've already purchased your subscriptions, so it would be a waste not to use them, anyway." She nearly shook, her knees bouncing in her excitement. Clearly remaining at home was boring poor Alicia, and she needed to find some way to entertain herself.

But she had a good plan. If anything could persuade Mama to go to the Lower Rooms, it would be the idea of avoiding waste. "I will agree to this mad scheme of yours, but you must understand that if my mother is unwell, I will put her needs above any promise to deliver a note."

Alicia almost looked wounded. "Of course you will. I would never expect otherwise."

Rebecca rose, following her cousin from the room. She had the oddest feeling that she had just been swindled, though she could not tell exactly how. Never mind that. She was confident that Mama would never feel up to attending a function that evening anyway.

CHAPTER EIGHT

Rebecca had been wrong. Not only had Alicia managed to convince Mama of the merits of putting their tickets to the Lower Rooms to use, she had also managed to persuade Rebecca to borrow one of her gowns. It had never been worn, and it was going to waste in her wardrobe—a fact that plagued poor Aunt Langley.

Fingering the soft, butter-yellow silk, Rebecca watched the fabric cascade down her leg in ripples much like waves, pooling around her slippered feet. A string stuck out from the toe of her slipper where she had repaired it earlier that evening and had forgotten to snip the thread, and she tucked her foot further under the skirt, grateful Alicia was just tall enough to make the skirt skim the floor and hide her ratty, old dancing shoes.

"The room is so bright and cheerful," Mama said, a satisfied smile on her lips. "I do think the color on the wall would be lovely in our sitting room. What do you think?"

"Yes, it's very nice," Rebecca said, sending the sea-green walls a cursory glance. "Let us find you a seat."

Rebecca took her mother's arm and led her around the edge

of the dancing couples toward an open space on the bench that lined the long wall. She felt the edges of Alicia's letter poke into her ribs where she'd tucked it into the wide ribbon around her bodice, the small rectangle burning into her side with the heat of guilt. Passing a letter to a gentleman in a crowded ballroom was reckless, and she wasn't going to do it unless she could be absolutely certain they would not be caught.

She would be happy if the opportunity did not present itself at all.

The master of ceremonies announced a cotillion and couples formed into sets for the dance as Rebecca settled beside her mother on the hard bench seat. She swept her gaze among the occupants of the room, looking for a tall man with sandy-brown hair and laughing blue eyes.

It was difficult to see the other side of the room from where they were seated, despite the raised bench they sat upon, but Mr. Cooper was nowhere in the immediate vicinity.

"What a crush," Mama said, surprise lacing her tone. "It has been so long since I attended a dance in Bath, but it is just as lively as I recall."

The general trend toward older patrons in the room was obvious, as more heads contained gray or white hair than any other color. If Mama considered this lively, she certainly needed to leave their sitting room much more often. Rebecca had only attended a few private balls since coming to Bath with her aunt and cousin, but they were much younger and livelier than this.

It turned out that Mama hadn't been very difficult to convince at all. Rebecca wanted to believe the medicine and daily walks were helping, but her mother had still suffered from restless sleep and her appetite had thus far failed to revive. "Are you glad you came? Remember, we can leave at any time."

Rebecca only needed to deliver Alicia's dratted note—or

discern that it was unsafe to do so—and they would be free to go.

"I am glad we came, and you really needn't fuss so. I needed to see more than Mrs. Brown's lovely furnishings and the gray sky from my window."

"You see much more than that each day when we go to Aunt Langley's house."

"Ah, but that does not count. It is not quite a relaxing endeavor when one must spend their time consoling." Mama smiled sheepishly. "Not that I mind being a support, of course. You know I love my sister. But her home does not exactly foster relaxation. Not like this."

Rebecca was flummoxed. She looked to the dancers in the middle of the room, the spectators gathering in groups and chatting loudly, the matrons analyzing each other through raised eyeglasses. None of this was very relaxing to her.

"You should have worn Grandmother's brooch," Mama said, a wistful smile on her lips. "It would have shone against Alicia's gown."

"I did not think of it," Rebecca said. In fact, she had avoided that piece of jewelry when she dressed for the assemblies. She could have sold it and paid for her mother's care ten times over, but she knew Mama did not wish for her to part with it. It made her feel awful, however, knowing it was there while she asked to trade for doctoring services instead of paying outright.

"Rebecca," Mama said quickly, lowering her voice. "Mrs. Gastrell comes this way. Do remember to ask after her sickly dog. It will make her like you straight away."

Her sickly *what*? Mrs. Gastrell was upon them before Rebecca could ask for further clarification. She knew the woman from their previous visits to Bath—Mrs. Gastrell was a particular friend of Aunt Langley—but Rebecca was unaware of any canine troubles.

"Good evening, Francis," Mama said kindly.

"How is your dog, ma'am?" Rebecca asked, hoping her mother had steered her in the right direction.

Mrs. Gastrell appraised Rebecca in approval. "She is much better, I thank you. She seems quite restored."

Mama's hand pressed to her heart. "I am glad to hear it. I was so worried on your behalf."

Mrs. Gastrell's countenance relaxed in appreciation.

"Have your children joined you this evening?" Mama asked.

"They have, but they are dancing." Mrs. Gastrell shot Rebecca a look before turning her smile on Mama. "I am certain Henry will wish to greet Rebecca, though. He asked me just the other day if we were planning to see you again before you left."

"We have no intention of leaving soon, I assure you," Mama said. "And we will give notice to our friends before we quit the city. I find there is much to do in Bath, and we are quite enjoying ourselves."

"Oh, is that so? I was under the impression that you haven't been able to see much of the city yet."

"Not as much as I'd like to, but we are not in a hurry to leave Bath at present."

Mrs. Gastrell smiled, the twinkle in her eye seemingly genuine. "I am glad to hear it. Perhaps we can devise a list of the places you ought to see before you leave. I do recommend the Pump Room, but only if you wish to see and be seen. It is quite the social gathering place, as I'm sure Rebecca can confirm."

Mama seemed to warm to the idea of planning, and Mrs. Gastrell settled in beside her on the bench. They bent their heads together and began planning a list of the fashionable haunts of Bath, discussing what Mama had previously seen and what she hadn't visited in ages. Since the Langleys had always lived in Bath, Rebecca had visited often over the years, but they hardly left the company of her aunt, uncle, and cousins during those visits. Now they had time to explore. Though, Rebecca was surprised Mama felt she had the energy for such an endeavor.

"Henry and Georgiana would be happy for such an outing on the next sunny day we have." Mrs. Gastrell sighed heavily, and Rebecca wondered which outing they were speaking of now. "Though I'm beginning to wonder if we shall ever see the sun again."

"It doesn't feel that way yet," Mama agreed. Her face brightened as she looked beyond Rebecca's shoulder. "Good evening, Mr. Cooper. What a pleasant surprise this is. Do you know Mrs. Gastrell?"

"I'm afraid I haven't had the pleasure," he said from just behind Rebecca. His warm voice washed over her skin, prickling her neck with awareness, and she avoided turning to meet his gaze in the event that it might incite a blush. The letter she had from Alicia was like a hot coal in her side, and it made her feel daring and nervous. The last thing Rebecca wanted was for her mother to misinterpret her sense of danger and believe that she was developing any sort of fondness for the doctor.

Mama performed the proper introductions, and Mrs. Gastrell proceeded to question Mr. Cooper on his situation.

"I am staying with my mother and father for the time being. They have been very happy in Bath for the last few years," he explained.

"Where did they live before coming here?"

"A little village in Wiltshire called Derham." He delivered an amused smile. "My father was also a doctor, and when he retired, he found it difficult to stop himself from seeing patients when there was a need, despite my presence in town. So my mother brought him to Bath so he could fully retire. They hoped the break would ease his own ailments."

"Wiltshire is a lovely part of the country," Mrs. Gastrell said.

"Indeed. It is a little oasis. But I find Somerset to be beautiful, too."

Rebecca shifted on the seat to see him better and was immediately taken aback. He wore a sharp, white cravat over a bronze waistcoat, and his black coat was sleek and fitted. He cut a very dashing figure that seemed to grip her in the stomach and tighten it. Had she ever before seen a man so handsome? She likely had, but none came to mind.

None of his clothing looked expensive, but somehow Mr. Cooper still looked every bit as dapper as the men of affluence around her. Even more so, in her opinion.

He regarded her thoughtfully, and she fought the desire to shake herself. Good gracious, it was just a man in a well-fitted coat and cravat. *Most* men were dashing when they took such care with their appearance. An image of Mr. Cooper standing in the rain flashed in her mind, his hat dripping a steady stream of water as droplets clung to his eyelashes. He'd been just as attractive in a drenched, worn morning coat as he was dry.

"Miss Turner, can I interest you in a dance?"

"Yes, Mr. Cooper," she heard herself say. "I would like that very much."

It was the perfect opportunity to give him the letter from Alicia. Or rather, to tell him of her errand and devise a plan to sneak him the letter later. If she handed him a folded missive in the center of the assembly hall, they would certainly be discovered.

They were forced to wait the better part of a half-hour for

the current set to end, all the while chatting about their favorite Bath entertainments. Mr. Cooper mentioned a concert at the Upper Halls in a fortnight that he'd been considering attending, and Mrs. Gastrell contributed the abbey to the list of places for Mama to visit.

The master of ceremonies announced the quadrille, and Mr. Cooper stepped forward, offering his hand to her. Rebecca placed her gloved fingers within his and allowed him to pull her away from her mother to take their place for the dance. Her fingers were warm where they connected with him, and her pulse sped, thrumming steadily in her throat. When Mr. Cooper released her hands and stood at her side, she drew in a steadying breath.

She needed to tell him of the letter, but the words lodged in her throat. What if *he* disapproved of accepting a letter from Alicia? Until this moment, Rebecca had not considered the possibility. But facing this man in the flesh made her insecure in a way she wasn't used to feeling. It was true that Rebecca often took a step back in social situations, Alicia and her consistent throng of suitors required it of her, but this felt different. Mr. Cooper was different.

Only, she could not place exactly what it was about him that gave her pause. Yes, he was handsome. Quite a few men were, and they still did not incite these feelings of insecurity within her.

"Has your mother been keeping up with her regimen?" he asked, pulling her away from her spiraling concerns.

"The rain has made it difficult."

His brow lowered. "Yes. Horseback riding is out of the question in this weather."

"It already was out of the question," she reminded him.

The instruments began to play, their soft music floating through the massive hall and covering some of the din. Mr.

Cooper stood sentinel beside her as the couples to either side of them began their part in the dance. "If I can procure horses, and the heavens would oblige us with some sunlight, would you be willing to ride out of Bath with me for a time?"

The phrasing of Mr. Cooper's request very much sounded like he was asking Rebecca alone to spend time with him, and her chest constricted. His blue eyes flicked toward her, and she straightened immediately, facing the dancers completing their steps before her. Her body felt warm and cool simultaneously, and it was growing uneasy to draw a breath.

Whatever was happening to her? Rebecca's body tensed, her stomach turning over as though she were growing ill, but that was madness. This man had merely asked her to ride with him, and she'd lost control of her senses. Goodness, maybe she had contracted her mother's green sickness.

"Do you enjoy riding, Miss Turner?" he asked, a slight tilt to his head.

She spoke quickly, fumbling over her words. So silly, really, when she knew the words well. They were words she had been saying her entire life. "Oh, yes. I do enjoy it very much."

"Then is there another reason for your hesitation?" He paused as though considering something and turned more fully toward her. He needed to maintain his position though, for it would soon be their turn to move to the center of the couples and dance. "It will not cost me anything if that is your concern. I read recently about the importance of riding when taking one's daily exercise for green sickness, and I truly believe your mother could benefit from it."

The truth of the situation crashed upon Rebecca like an enormous wave, roaring past her ears and rushing through her body. Mr. Cooper had not been inviting her on an outing. He'd been doctoring her mother.

She should be thrilled the man cared so much for healing

that he would spend time considering the matter on his own, but it stung her pride, and she faced away from him immediately, her cheeks flaming with heat from the embarrassment of where her thoughts had quickly jumped.

"I think convincing my mother would take some time, but I could probably manage it." Particularly since Mr. Cooper had explained that it would not cast them into further debt. That she owed the man at all was uncomfortable, skittering over her skin like small bugs and leaving her uneasy. She would find a way to pay him back soon, or she would need to cease accepting his help. After what Mama had endured under the canopy of a debt-ridden childhood, she would never abide the debts Rebecca had placed on their shoulders now.

It was a blessing Mama left the finances mostly to Rebecca, or she'd have been found out already.

"That is excellent to hear," Mr. Cooper said, a smile spreading over his lips. The couples beside them moved back to their original places, and it was time for them to begin their portion of the dance.

Rebecca moved through the motions, unable to hold Mr. Cooper's gaze when they came together, or when he took her arm and circled her about. She was mortified over the brief moment that she'd believed him to hold interest for her, especially when a note from her cousin was currently burning a hole in the side of her bodice.

She needed to execute the remainder of the dance, complete her errand if the opportunity presented itself, and be done with it. Mr. Cooper was doing odd things to the rhythm of her pulse and inciting a warmth in her stomach that was difficult to remove.

And she would be better off without him taking residence in her mind.

CHAPTER NINE

J ared had no idea what he'd said to put Rebecca in a mood, but she had acted strangely since the moment he came upon her and her mother and now was acting stranger still. He watched her move through the motions of their dance, studiously turning her face at just the right angle to avoid his gaze. He admitted it was difficult to converse during a dance, but surely she was not purposefully avoiding him. He didn't believe he'd done anything in particular to lose her esteem.

They completed their portion of the dance and stepped back into their original positions, waiting as two other couples stepped forward for their parts.

"There is an Italian opera singer promised to perform at the concert in the Upper Rooms in a fortnight," he said, his gaze pasted to the dancers as he spoke softly to his partner. "Have you any interest in opera?"

"When it is sung by a trained musician, yes. I enjoy it immensely."

"Have you heard opera sung by someone who was not a trained musician?"

Rebecca was quiet for so long that he turned to look at her and found an amused smile playing on her lips.

Her gaze flicked up and caught his, and her smile broke out in earnest. "We had a neighbor near our cottage who believed she would have been a proficient singer had she been given the proper guidance."

"I see," he said, though he didn't. Not really.

Rebecca pushed her spectacles up the bridge of her nose. "She did not allow her lack of training to stop her from practicing her craft, of course. Often loudly and with her windows open."

Jared laughed. "I now understand your caveat."

Rebecca grinned and placed her hand on his proffered arm as they moved forward to perform their portion once more.

The remainder of the set passed in a similar fashion, sparse conversations sprinkled among the dancing, and Jared could not recall the last time he had enjoyed a dance more. He offered his arm when it was time to escort Miss Turner back to her mother, and she tugged softly at his elbow, slowing his steps.

"I must speak to you with some urgency," she said quietly, her gaze darting about them.

"What is it?"

She stepped forward just a little. "My cousin—"

Alarm gripped him. "Is she hurt?"

"No, nothing of the sort. She asked me to give you a note. Will you accept it?"

He stood in the midst of Bath's Society and tried not to gawk at the woman. She did understand how inappropriate such a thing was, did she not? Judging by the hesitancy in her manner and the fidgeting in her hands, she knew it well.

Mrs. Turner caught his eye from across the room, her eyebrows knit together in question, and he felt the urgency of the situation. Smiling cordially down at Rebecca, he nodded. "Yes, I will accept it."

Relief swept over her features, and she followed him across the room, allowing him to lead her toward her mother. When he bid her goodbye, he took her hand, and in it felt the rough rectangle she pressed into his palm. He swiftly closed his fist around the letter and tucked it into his pocket, holding Rebecca's smile.

Accepting a note that Miss Langley had penned specifically for him sent a thrill coursing through his body, and he did his best to temper his eagerness.

"I will send a note when I am able to procure the horses," he said.

"Thank you, Mr. Cooper. We look forward to it."

Was her gratitude directed at him for accepting Miss Langley's letter, or for offering to obtain the horses? He turned away from the women and left the assemblies entirely. Neither Thomas nor Jared's parents had chosen to accompany him that evening, and now that he'd seen Rebecca and her mother, he felt no further enticement to remain.

The letter weighed down his pocket as though it was made of lead, and he walked briskly toward home, eager for privacy to see what Miss Langley warranted worth risking her reputation in this way. It was uncharacteristically cold for an evening in May, and the rain continued to drizzle around him, the soft mist giving everything a water-colored illusion.

Jared reached his parents' home and let himself inside, leaving his umbrella, hat, and gloves with his father's servant before sloughing off his greatcoat. The door to the sitting room at the top of the stairs had been left open and light from the roaring fire poured into the corridor.

Mother sat beside father on the sofa, reading from her book

in the waning light. She set the book on her lap and smiled at Jared when he came into the room.

Father sat up as best he could, his wrapped, ailing foot propped up on a stool before him. "You've returned early."

"Did you enjoy yourself?" Mother asked.

Jared lowered himself on the chair opposite his parents. "I managed to make some new acquaintances, so the night was not a total waste."

"Would they be anyone we might know?"

He slid his hand into his pocket and played with the folded missive, distracted by the need to see what it contained. "Well, are you familiar with Mrs. Gastrell?"

Mother's forehead wrinkled in thought. "I don't believe I've heard the name."

"She is a friend of Mrs. Turner."

"The woman you treated for green sickness?" Father asked, perking up, his neck raising like a dog who knew its dinner was on the way.

"Indeed, the very one."

"How long ago did you prescribe her medication?"

"Just a few days ago."

"Did she appear better this evening?" Father asked, pushing himself straighter in his seat. He winced and lowered again, regaining a comfortable position with his injured foot on the tufted stool.

"Not noticeably, no. But a few days are hardly enough time for iron to make a noticeable difference."

"That is true." Father bobbed his head, his distracted gaze narrowing. "Did you explain the benefits of horseback riding—"

"I did, but in this weather, that is hardly a reasonable option. She intends to take daily walks."

Father's face contorted into one of careful thought, his white, trimmed beard quivering as he chewed on his cheek. "Would it not be more advisable to urge her to remain indoors while the rain persists? Is the wetness in the air not perhaps worse for her lungs?"

Jared considered the point but disagreed. "I think the benefit of fresh air and the circulation of her blood as a result of her exercise will outweigh any negative effects from the moisture in the air."

"Ah," Father said, lifting a solitary finger in the air, his eyes shining with pride, "quite a good point, Son. You have no need of my expertise, I see."

"I will always find value in your opinions, Father. The moment we believe we know everything is the moment we know nothing. It is dangerous to close one's mind to other possibilities, for it halts learning and growth and narrows the potential to become better."

Mother nodded. "Well said, Jared."

His curiosity had grown too large for him to postpone reading his letter any longer. Rising, he leaned down and kissed his mother on the cheek. "That is enough philosophizing for one night. I shall see you both in the morning."

"It is not yet ten o'clock," Mother said.

"Indeed." Jared didn't defend his early night but left the room and made his way up to his bedchamber. The fire had been lit and was already warming his room, and he took the seat beside the hearth, the cushion warmed from its proximity to the fireplace. Removing the letter from his pocket, he broke the wafer and unfolded the thick paper.

Mr. Cooper,

Regarding the poem you referenced at Briarwood Manor. It has been on my mind since that meeting, and I located it to read

*in its entirety. I understand your meaning now, and I wanted to
thank you for the compliment you paid me.*

Yours, etc.,

Alicia Langley

Jared leaned back in his chair and let the letter fall onto his lap.
He hadn't known what to expect, but he was certain this wasn't
it. If anything was clear to him, though, it was that Rebecca had
nothing to do with the letter and was clearly unaware of its
contents. Could she not have merely relayed the fact that Alicia
was grateful?

She certainly could have. Which proved that Alicia was
reaching out to Jared because she wanted to show her interest
in him. For what other purpose would this serve? He sat back,
smiling, the glow of excitement and possibilities warming his
chest.

He'd been in this position before, on the precipice of poten-
tially finding happiness, when the lady had decided to reject
his marriage proposal and had wrecked his heart. He'd begged
her to accept him, and she had refused. In her words, she cared
about him too much to marry him when she knew that he loved
her, and she could never be certain she would fall in love with
him in return. He now understood that she had just been
madly in love with someone else, but it was difficult to move
beyond a rejection of that magnitude. Allowing himself to
entertain the idea of courting Miss Langley, even if he must
wait two months from now, was opening his mind and heart to
the potential to love again. It was likewise opening him up to
the potential of hurt, but in this case, he felt it a risk worth
taking.

He lit a candle and placed it on his writing table, then
prepared his writing implements and straightened the sheet of

clean, white paper. If he wrote to Alicia, he was committing himself to seeing this through, for corresponding was not only dangerous to their reputations, it was a declaration. He dipped the quill in the inkpot and tapped away the excess, pausing. He was on the precipice of something great, but would it bring love or pain?

Drawing in a breath, Jared pushed away his worries and fears and began to write.

The next morning, the Pump Room was full of familiar faces from the assemblies the evening before. Jared joined the promenade, searching the room for a shorter woman with wire-rimmed spectacles. He'd been careful to keep the letter he'd penned to Alicia at the very surface of his thoughts, allowing her to set the standard to which they divulged their feelings and interests.

Mother had chosen to join him that morning, and she clung to his arm, forcing him to maintain a sedate pace when he really would have preferred to search quickly. He was eager, and the moment his gaze rested upon the reddish-brown hair and heart-shaped face which belonged to Rebecca, his heart leaped in his chest.

"Mother," he said, hoping his tone remained steady and did not betray his excitement. "Would you like me to introduce you to Mrs. Turner?"

"The woman with the green sickness?" she asked quietly.

He nodded, and she squeezed his arm. "I would like that."

Jared steered her in the direction of the Turner women and concentrated on maintaining a leisurely pace. Why was it so blasted difficult to walk slowly when one's body was humming with excitement?

"Good day," he said when he approached them, bowing.

They exchanged pleasantries, and Jared introduced the Turner women to his mother.

"You must enjoy having your son visit," Mrs. Turner said, her kind eyes wrinkling alongside her smile.

Mother agreed. "It is most welcome having him nearby. My husband does not practice medicine any longer, but he adores discussing it, and Jared graciously provides him with an outlet in that regard."

"It is my pleasure," Jared said with a dip of his head, eliciting chuckles from the women.

Mother inclined her head. "Mrs. Turner, would you like to take a turn about the room with me?"

"I would love that."

The mothers linked arms and walked sedately along with the rest of Bath's elite. Jared and Rebecca fell into step behind them, keeping their hands to themselves.

He wished he had the audacity to be forward and request her help with the letter directly, but it was not in his nature to be so bold. Searching for a neutral topic, he asked, "Did you enjoy the assemblies last night?"

"I did," she said, though she sounded somewhat surprised by this fact. "It was good for my mama to see some of her old friends. She has not gotten out much since coming to Bath, not until you prescribed fresh air and exercise for her."

"I hope that has not been a burden for you."

"No, on the contrary, actually. The most I could convince her to venture forth before was for daily visits to her sister's house. Now we are planning to see much more of Bath—albeit, a rainy Bath."

"Then I am glad."

"So am I. More than you can imagine. We had used a doctor before, back home, but he was snobbish and far from helpful. It has been a blessing to make your acquaintance, Mr. Cooper. I will forever be grateful to you." She lifted a gloved finger to push her spectacles back up her nose and looked at him. "I do think I will be even more relieved when I have contrived a way to pay you. I wish it could be done properly, but until my father sends word—"

"I have thought of something, actually."

"Oh?" Her auburn eyebrows lifted. "What is it?"

"The letters."

Rebecca's brow furrowed. "What letters?"

He felt a fissure of apprehension. "To Miss Langley."

Rebecca was not skilled at covering her surprise, and he hoped he hadn't shocked her too much. Rebecca had been willing to deliver a letter already, hadn't she?

He cleared his throat and lowered his voice to avoid being overheard. "If you would be so kind as to take the letter I've written to Miss Langley, I will consider your debt paid in full."

CHAPTER TEN

P*aid in full.* The words were so beautiful to Rebecca's ears that she forgot to breathe for a moment. She glanced up at Mr. Cooper's hopeful blue eyes and swallowed her hesitation. What was the harm in passing one last letter? Surely she could do so discreetly and then wash her hands of it. "Yes, I can agree to that."

He smiled broadly, revealing a set of even, white teeth. Rebecca knew a moment of jealousy that the reason for this man's smile wasn't because of her directly, even if it was her agreement that led to it. Someday, she hoped a man would smile like that at her, and that it would have nothing to do with her cousin.

She loved Alicia, but she wanted to be loved as well. To be admired and cared for. She wanted to be the whole world to someone—aside from her parents—and it hurt to find herself drawn to a man who seemed to only have eyes for Alicia.

Trampling those ridiculous, disloyal thoughts, Rebecca pasted a smile on her face. And then she recalled that her mother would need another appointment and a different prescription in just another week and a half, and her smile slipped. "What will we do when you come and visit again? If my father was to return before that time—"

"I cannot speak for Miss Langley, but I have reason to believe I will have future need of your services in this regard."

Recognition swept through her, and Rebecca forced her gaze to remain on her mother's back ahead of her, tracing the straight lines of the blue striped muslin. Mr. Cooper was asking her to pass their letters for the foreseeable future. It was a risky endeavor, though Rebecca herself carried very little risk. As long as she was not caught, it would never be discovered that she was a liaison in this improper alliance.

She shook away her reservations. "So long as I continue to help you, you will consider it payment for seeing to my mother's illness?"

"I believe it is more than enough," he said. "I realize I am asking quite a lot of you. I need to know that it is a suitable arrangement for you, Miss Turner. I would never wish to put you in a position which compromised your comfort or morals."

He was so kind and thoughtful, and his considerate gaze was like a tiny dagger twisting in her heart. He presented an opportunity for Mama to receive help without throwing them into debt or forcing them to accept charity. She saw her cousin nearly every day, so it was not a hardship, either. Rebecca would be a fool *not* to accept this arrangement, but that didn't make the idea of passing letters between Alicia and Mr. Cooper any less painful.

This was the best thing for everyone. Squaring her shoulders, she nodded. "Yes, it is a suitable arrangement for me."

Mr. Cooper smiled at her. "I rather think you are a good person to have on my side, Miss Turner. You make for an agreeable partner."

She laughed to cover her surprise. "Perhaps you ought to

keep that to yourself. If word spreads that I am willing to participate in orchestrating clandestine arrangements, surely I will be bombarded with requests from bereft lovers across the city."

"The post will then beg your assistance, and you will become so busy helping others that I will be out of luck. No, we must endeavor to keep this between us."

"Us and Alicia," Rebecca amended. "Now, am I correct in assuming that you've brought a letter with you today?"

"Yes, though I think we should find a discreet way to pass it. There are a lot of eyes in this room that are particularly attuned to ladies and gentlemen who choose to walk side by side for any prolonged periods of time."

"Oh, dear. That is true." She looked about the room and noticed the beady gazes that watched couples promenade. It was surely busier than average due to the relentless rain. "Perhaps I can drop my reticule and you can retrieve it for me?"

"That could certainly work," he agreed.

"I will widen the opening beforehand to make it easy for you to slip the letter inside."

His lips ticked up into a smile, the soft dimple appearing to the side of his mouth. "How considerate of you."

Rebecca fought a smile. She should not be enjoying this discourse so much, but it was the most amusing thing she had experienced in quite some time. After months of mourning her uncle, worrying over her mother's health, and doing her best not to feel too anxious over the lack of letters from her father, the light-hearted banter was a soothing balm on her overwrought mind.

He leaned closer, lowering his voice. "Perhaps you can prepare now and drop the offending item once we've turned the corner up there."

"Excellent plan." Rebecca removed the corded handle from her wrist and widened the drawstring opening, pretending to look inside for something. Her nerves skittered and danced, fear of being discovered clashing with her enjoyment. As they neared the wall, she tossed the bag a little where it fell conveniently beside a pillar that jutted out partially from the wall. "Oh, goodness," she said, careful not to raise her voice too much.

"Allow me, madam." Mr. Cooper bent to retrieve it. If he slipped the letter within as he rose, Rebecca missed it. But when she accepted the reticule back she pulled the drawstrings tight and caught sight of a white rectangle tossed on top of her things.

"That was rather smooth, was it not?" she asked as they fell into step behind their mothers once again, though much further back.

"Careful," Mr. Cooper admonished. "It is unwise to grow too confident in one's ability."

"Unless you are treating a patient, of course."

"Actually, I believe the opposite to be true. I think humility is even more important when treating a patient. I was just discussing this with my father last night, in fact. I think . . ." He looked at her quickly and chuckled. "Never mind. I wouldn't wish to bore you."

"On the contrary, Mr. Cooper. I am quite interested in hearing what you have to say."

He peered at her, and she held his gaze. "Well, while I do believe one must be confident in one's abilities in order to accurately treat the ill and afflicted, it is my belief that it can be harmful to grow *too* confident. If I believed myself to have a perfect understanding, what would be the enticement to continue to learn new scientific developments or treatments? How would I know of discoveries doctors make in Edinburgh or even in the colonies if I ceased seeking to learn? Growth is such an important part of doing my work and accomplishing it well."

Mr. Cooper's desire to heal and help people was evident in the way he spoke, and Rebecca admired and respected that about him.

"I did tell you it wasn't very interesting," he said, smiling down at her.

"You're mistaken, Mr. Cooper. I believe that makes quite a lot of sense. I am certain it makes you a better doctor."

"I am not the only doctor to feel this way. Many people agree with me. It is the reason medical journals and the like exist, and I am grateful for them."

He reached for her hand and squeezed her fingers, sending a jolt of heat from her hand to her heart and robbing her of breath. Surely this was not a feeling typical between friends, for it was much stronger than anything she'd ever felt before. Swallowing against a dry throat, Rebecca could only nod in agreement. Her head was swimming with the realization that she had liked that contact far better than she ought, all the while carrying a letter from this man to her exceptionally beautiful cousin on her person.

It was a horrible twist of fate that the day Rebecca would finally feel something of a romantic nature toward a man, it was a man she was helping to make a liaison with someone else.

Well, drat.

"Shall we join our mothers?" he asked, drawing her mind back to the room. He still held her hand, and she forced herself not to tug it from his grip, lest she make things uneasy between them or draw attention to her discomfort.

"Yes."

Mr. Cooper placed her hand on the crook of his elbow, his other hand resting over it as he led her toward where their mothers had found a seat. Affection seemed to settle between them like a warm haze from the gentle way he handled her to the warm smile sitting comfortably on his lips.

"We should be going," Mama said. "Or your Aunt Langley will wonder where we are."

Mr. Cooper's fingers tightened over hers, and Rebecca forced a smile. "Yes, we should be on our way." She turned to Mrs. Cooper. "It was very nice to meet you."

The older woman moved to rise from her seat, and Mr. Cooper dropped Rebecca's hand in order to offer his mother help. Neither mother needed assistance, and they all bowed and curtsied and said the things which were proper before Rebecca and her mother left to collect their umbrella at the door.

Mama took Rebecca's arm as they left the Pump Room.

"You seemed to like Mrs. Cooper," Rebecca said.

"Oh, I like her excessively." Mama sent Rebecca a conspiratorial smile. "She was so amiable and thoughtful. It is no wonder her son is such a good man."

Rebecca looked away, the implications tightening her gut. "There is nothing between Mr. Cooper and myself, Mama."

"No, I agree. It is much too soon for that."

"It will never be appropriate, I assure you."

Mama frowned. "You cannot write him off so quickly, dear. Not when—"

"He has taken a liking to Alicia."

They waited at the edge of the street for a carriage to pass before crossing the road. When they reached the walkway on the other side, Mama sighed. "I see. And you are certain of this?"

"He has told me as much," Rebecca said. Mama paused, turning to look at her hard, and she knew a moment's temptation to reveal the letter in her reticule. If nothing else, it would prove that she knew what she was telling Mama to be true.

If Rebecca must fight these feelings emerging for Mr. Cooper, it would be much easier without Mama pressing her toward him.

"I enjoy Mr. Cooper's company, but it will go no further than friendship between myself and the doctor. If he has his way, he will end up married to my cousin."

Mama seemed to consider this. "And if my niece does not feel the same?"

"I believe she might," Rebecca answered honestly. "But it hardly matters. Do you believe I could care for a man who would prefer Alicia?"

A moment of difficult silence passed before Mama shook her head. "No. I can see how that would be impossible. It is a good thing you love your cousin so dearly, or this would be more difficult."

"It is far from difficult, I assure you. I have known Mr. Cooper for one week, Mama, which is not nearly enough time to engage my heart beyond repair."

Mama looked wary. "Well, I hope that is true. He is a handsome man."

"Comments like *that* will surely slow my progress."

Mama cringed, but she started forward again, and Rebecca kept pace beside her. She couldn't help but notice how her mother had spent the greater part of a half-hour promenading and was now walking to Aunt Langley's house with little trouble. Could Mr. Cooper's medication have taken effect that quickly?

She made a mental note to ask him when she next saw him, and hoped, despite herself, that the occasion would arrive swiftly.

They reached the Langley townhouse and went up to the drawing room where Aunt Langley and Alicia waited for them on the sofa. Alicia rose the moment they entered the room and crossed toward Rebecca, taking her by the hands and drawing her toward the pianoforte on the other side of the room. Her black dress was stark and bold, broken only by the cream fichu tucked into the bodice, but she still looked beautiful.

"I have some new music I'd like to show you," she said loudly, clearly for their mothers' benefit.

When they reached the pianoforte, Alicia pulled Rebecca down on the bench beside her and lowered her voice. "Tell me right away. Have you seen the doctor?"

"I have."

Alicia grinned, her sparkling blue eyes vivid against her creamy, perfect skin. "He was at the assemblies?"

"He was, and I gave him the letter."

Alicia watched her expectantly. "Well, did he dance with you? Did he mention a desire to see you again? Tell me everything which occurred and leave nothing out."

Rebecca relayed the events of the previous evening to Alicia's apparent delight, followed by the meeting at the Pump Room that morning.

Alicia listened, her mouth parted, her head nodding. "When do you plan to see him again?"

Rebecca pulled away, her cousin's enthusiasm tempering her own mood. "I'm not sure. I suppose I will see him at the concert in the Upper Rooms in a few weeks."

"Unless you go to the Pump Room again in the morning and he is there."

"Yes, but I do not plan on it."

Alicia looked displeased. "When does he intend to visit Aunt Turner next?"

"A fortnight from the first visit."

Alicia leaned back, her frown deepening.

Suspicion planted in Rebecca's belly. "Are you so eager to deliver another letter to the man?"

"A letter? No."

"Then why are you so anxious for me to see him again?"

Alicia's mouth opened and closed again like a fish. She wrinkled her small, rounded nose and pursed her lips in thought. "I suppose I am so lonely here, with so little in the way of entertainment. I am starved for anything to divert me."

Something was missing. Alicia had thought too hard to devise her reply, and it caused Rebecca to believe that her cousin was hiding something from her.

"What are you not telling me?" Rebecca asked.

Alicia looked to where their mothers sat on the sofa before speaking again. "Nothing. I truly am dying of boredom. I think it is vastly unfair that my uncle has control over my circumstances. But what choice do I have but to heed his decree?"

"Hardly any," Rebecca agreed. Though she was tempted to remind Alicia that she had made a choice between her freedom and having nice things. She understood that it was a difficult scenario for a woman so used to having everything.

Rebecca opened her reticule and retrieved the letter, her back facing her mother to hide it. But when she tried to give it to Alicia, her cousin shrunk back.

"It is from Mr. Cooper," Rebecca said, slightly flapping the missive.

Alicia stared at the folded sheet of white paper as though it was a foreign object. She shook her head. "I do not want it."

"Whyever not? You were eager for news about the man just minutes ago."

"News, yes. But I do not wish to actually correspond with him."

She recalled Mr. Cooper's cheerful expression just an hour before when he had explained that he had reason to believe they would write to one another. "He is expecting a reply."

Alicia shrugged. "Then you write one," she said flippantly.

Rebecca's hand tightened around the missive. If Alicia failed to write to the doctor, he would have no need for Rebecca's services as a courier, which would, in turn, leave her without a way to pay him for seeing to Mama's health. Rebecca needed this. *Mama* needed this. She drew in a fortifying breath. "Do you not at least wish to see what he has written prior to determining your course of action?"

"No, it will only make me feel obligated to reply, and I loathe corresponding." Alicia gasped quietly, turning to Rebecca with wide eyes. There was a calculation in her gaze as she appraised Rebecca that spoke of scheming. It was the same sort of look Alicia wore in their childhood before playing a trick on the stable boy or as she hid Rebecca in the closet so they wouldn't be forced apart when their holiday ended and the Turners left Bath for their home in Welton.

Alicia was all but buzzing, bouncing slightly in her seat. "I know just the thing! I said it in jest, but what if I meant it? *You* may write to Mr. Cooper, and he will be completely unaware that it is not me. You know our handwriting is nearly identical."

Rebecca's mouth fell open. "But why? I cannot do something so dishonest."

"Whyever not?" She pursed her lips thoughtfully. "I did not say I have *no* interest in the man, merely that I do not wish to correspond. If it is something he desires, then you can appease him."

Surely Alicia could not be in earnest. It was one thing to sneakily deliver letters to a man, but it was another thing entirely to write those letters pretending to be someone else. "Alicia, if you do not hold Mr. Cooper in high regard, it would be wrong to lead him to believe otherwise."

"Of course I hold him in high regard. But I do not want to write letters." She gripped Rebecca's hands. "If you write the letters for me, you would be doing me a great service."

"Good heavens, Alicia. I would feel awful misleading him so." She would simply have to find another way to pay him for seeing after her mother. "You wrote the last letter without any provocation."

Alicia laughed. "Well, it was very short, and nothing more than a declaration of my gratitude." She narrowed her eyes. "You said he wishes to continue our correspondence?"

"Yes."

She nodded. "Do you like him?"

Rebecca stilled. "Do I like him?" She did. A little too much.

"Yes," Alicia said. "Do you approve of the man?"

"Of course."

She shrugged. "Then I do not see the harm in it. Once my mourning is over, I would be more than happy to see him again. But for now, I simply cannot bear the pressure of continued correspondence."

Rebecca chewed on her lower lip. She removed her spectacles and cleaned the dried raindrops with her skirt before placing them back on her nose. Her head warred with her heart, and she moved to place the letter in her cousin's lap. "Just read it yourself—"

Alicia stopped her with a hand on her wrist. "You may read it and respond if you so desire. I have already told Mr. Cooper all that I wished to say until we meet again."

Rebecca shoved the letter back in her reticule, frowning. Something did not add up. If Alicia did not have a secret objective, then why had she schemed? And yet, in what way would Rebecca writing letters under her name help her? She leveled her voice. "What game are you playing, Alicia?"

"Nothing. I swear to you, I have no ill intent. I am merely lazy."

"You must forget that I know you much better than that."

Alicia's soft blue eyes rounded, her lips falling open in hurt.

"You doubt me? I would *never* agree to anything which might harm you, my dearest cousin and friend." She lightened her voice. "You are helping me, really."

"And these letters. How shall I write them? As though I am you? That my opinions are yours?"

"Heavens, no. How could you guess at all of my thoughts?"

Rebecca certainly was not guessing at them now, she'd concede that much.

Alicia ran her fingers along the piano keys, a groove lining her forehead. "I suppose it makes the most sense for you to answer as yourself. When I see him again, I will merely have changed my mind if our opinions do not line up. Surely Mr. Cooper is enough of a gentleman to own that a woman's mind is allowed to alter."

Rebecca perched on the edge of the piano bench as though she balanced on the precipice of a cliff. Could she walk that dangerous line, balancing on the slippery edge, or would she fall?

Alicia sighed. "Shall we play a duet?"

Rebecca faced the keys, sliding her reticule up on her arm so it would not be in the way of playing. She wasn't entirely sure what was going on, but she knew two things. The first, that Alicia had something up her sleeve. The second, that Rebecca would *not* be writing to Mr. Cooper.

CHAPTER ELEVEN

J ared knocked sharply at the Turners' door and stepped back. He hadn't seen Rebecca since the Pump Room nearly a week before when she'd taken his letter to Alicia, and he had grown restless searching for her in the crowded rooms since. Indecision plagued him, and after their easy conversation while promenading the Pump Room, he'd felt the strongest urge to speak to her again. He'd been called on by a few neighbors and a friend of Thomas's for various injuries and illnesses, and his name was beginning to spread about their social circle as a reputable surgeon, but he wasn't sure if that was something he wanted for himself.

It was all too easy to lose one's reputation, as Jared well knew, and the more his esteem grew in this town, the more important it became for him to decide if creating a life in Bath was something he even wanted. His mother and father had succeeded in making a home for themselves here, but it hadn't felt exactly right to Jared yet. He hoped it would soon, however, for he longed to find a place to build a home for himself.

The door to the narrow townhouse swung open to reveal a

short, plump woman with rounded, rosy cheeks. Mrs. Brown, he presumed. The landlady who repeatedly failed to fix the Turners' squeaky door hinge.

"Good day, ma'am. I've come to call on Mrs. Turner. Are you Mrs. Brown?"

"I am." She looked at him warily. "Is Mrs. Turner expecting you?"

"No, but I am her doctor. I was in the area and decided to look in on her."

Mrs. Brown peered at him under wrinkled, hooded eyelids. She seemed to take him at his word and stepped back to let him inside, and he stomped his feet outside before entering her home. Walking ahead of him up the stairs, she knocked and announced his presence before the door opened wider, the creak from its hinges rending the air and causing Rebecca to cringe as she stepped forward.

A smile formed of its own accord on his lips. Jared hadn't realized how much he'd looked forward to seeing Rebecca until she appeared before him.

"Good day, Miss Turner. I came to check on your mother." It was a flimsy excuse, but he hoped that wasn't apparent. He wanted to ask about Alicia too, of course, and find out why he had not seen the Turners out since that morning nearly a week before.

"Please, come in," she said, moving to allow him room to enter. She smiled at her landlady, and Mrs. Brown left, retreating back downstairs. Once the door had closed behind them, Rebecca lowered her voice. "You'll have to excuse Mrs. Brown. She doesn't appreciate male callers. You must have told her of your occupation."

"I did."

"Yes, I assumed as much. I'm certain she would not have allowed you entrance otherwise." Gesturing toward the open doorway, she said, "If you'll give me a moment, I will fetch Mama."

Jared excused her and walked to the window. He gazed outside at the partially sunny sky. Well, sunny was a bit of a stretch. It lacked rain, but the cover of clouds remained. Still, it felt like a reprieve from the dreary weather, the gray-cast world brighter than it had been in days.

"What a lovely surprise," Mrs. Turner said, coming from the door on the far end of the room. She smiled sleepily at him, and he was disappointed to see that a greenish tint yet remained on her skin. He'd hoped that the medication would have made more of a difference for her already.

"I wanted to take advantage of the reprieve in the rain and ask if you would be available to ride with me out into the country. Though we can certainly remain close by if that is preferable to you."

Rebecca's face brightened, and she looked to her mother, but then quickly shuttered her expression. She gave him a tight smile. "I'm afraid it is not an option, Mr. Cooper. We have no horses, as I believe I mentioned before."

"I have borrowed two mares from a friend of mine at no charge." Had she changed her mind? He thought she'd already agreed to the scheme. Jared had urged her to take him at his word, to trust his honesty that it was in no way putting him out. He'd seen to Thomas's men more than once when injuries had arisen from the stables, and Thomas owed him the favor. But more than that, Thomas was always willing to supply horses when Jared wished for a ride, especially when Thomas was included in the invitation. Their friendship was borne of their shared appreciation of horses and had strengthened through the equines with each of Jared's visits to Bath over the years.

But Jared could see that he'd yet to convince Rebecca. Her heart-shaped face tipped down, her eyes appraising him. He laid a hand over his chest. "I promise he was more than happy to lend them, as he would like the excuse to join us as well. You might remember Mr. Hawkins?"

"Yes, I do. That is very kind of him."

"He is a lover of horses and has quite a few at his disposal. I assure you, this bears him no hardship."

Rebecca smiled, and Jared's chest burned with accomplishment. She turned to her mother. "What do you say, Mama? Are you feeling up to it?"

Mrs. Turner agreed, and Jared left the women to change into their riding habits, promising to return with the horses in a half-hour. He was slightly disappointed to have missed the opportunity to speak to Rebecca alone, but surely he could contrive a way to do so on the ride.

He climbed into his saddle and rode toward Thomas's livery. It mattered not that clouds still gathered in front of the sun and it was so cold Jared could hardly feel his toes. His day was looking bright, and he was excited for the ride to come.

———— ∽ ————

Rebecca hurried to the shared writing desk in her and Mama's bedchamber and pulled out a sheet of paper. She had determined not to write a single solitary deceitful word to Mr. Cooper, even going so far as to avoid the places she believed he would be in the last week so she wouldn't have to disappoint him. She hadn't been looking forward to telling him that Alicia had failed to reply to his note. Especially after reading his letter and realizing that it held no lovelorn poems or confessions of his heart.

It had merely been a question: did she approve of William Blake's interpretation of tigers?

But Rebecca saw that as the wrong question to ask in regard

to the poem, for it wasn't about the tiger itself, but it was about the beauty that God could create. She didn't know if Jared meant his question to be a trick or not, but she decided that she could not allow the hope that had shone in his eyes to be in vain. She liked him excessively, and Alicia's lazy attitude regarding their correspondence did not mean that he had to stop receiving letters. Not when Rebecca could supply them.

Alicia mentioned herself that she would be glad to continue a relationship with the man. Rebecca was only helping them, really.

But it was more than that. It was her mother. Rebecca couldn't accept charity, regardless of how expertly Mr. Cooper had wrapped it in flowery explanations. The horses were an expense to *someone*, even if Mr. Hawkins provided them as a favor to a friend, and Rebecca would rather forgo the outing altogether than accept charity. But her mother needed this, so she would pay in the currency that was available to her: she would write one letter.

Dipping her pen in the ink, she hurriedly wrote.

Mr. Cooper—

I approve of Mr. Blake's attempt at capturing the beauty of the ferocious cat through his words. I have never seen a tiger myself, so I must defer to his expertise on this matter. Whether or not I approve of his interpretation of tigers, however, is moot. I believe his intention was to compare the tiger to the lamb and marvel at God's ability to create. In that regard, I find it fascinating.

Yours.

. . .

Her pen hovered above the last word, and she found she could not bring herself to sign either Alicia's full name or her initials. Blowing on the ink, she left the paper on the desk and went to change into her habit while the ink dried.

Mullens brought the plum-colored wool costume to her and assisted Rebecca into it before fastening it at the back. Mama was dressed and eating a quick meal of mackerel and bread in the dining room, and Rebecca couldn't seem to tear her gaze away from the paper resting on the writing desk.

Her actions were deceitful, but she had to make concessions in order to continue receiving help for her mama. Was it so horrible of her when she had been given Alicia's permission —nay, her *persuasion*—to write to Mr. Cooper on her behalf? She would not sign a false name, and if Mr. Cooper asked Rebecca directly who the author of the letter was, she would answer truthfully. The words belonged to Rebecca, and she would claim them if she needed to.

She just hoped he wouldn't ask.

———————— ⟡ ————————

Mr. Hawkins waited atop a steed in the street, fingering the sleeve of his blue coat, the brim of his hat bent enough to cover most of his face as he looked down. Mr. Cooper assisted Mama and Rebecca into their borrowed saddles and took his own seat as the proper introductions were made between Mama and Mr. Hawkins. The party turned in the direction of Prior Park, which would lead them out of Bath and into the countryside for some much-needed clean air and beautiful views of the city.

"It is so cold outside for May," Mama said, a shiver gently shaking her shoulders.

"Shall I turn back and fetch you another wrap?"

Mama smiled at her kindly. "No, Rebecca. I am warm enough. I only meant to remark on the unseasonable weather."

"Indeed, ma'am," Mr. Hawkins said. "This weather is quite the topic of conversation these days. No one can seem to make sense of the lasting chill." He cleared his throat. "Mr. Cooper tells me your husband is in France?"

Mama nodded, bringing her horse up beside Mr. Hawkins. "He is in the business of selling wine."

"French wine?"

"Indeed."

Mr. Hawkins grinned. "I might need to have a conversation with him upon his return."

Mama laughed before launching into a lengthy explanation of the wines Father offered.

Mr. Cooper brought his horse up beside Rebecca's. "Does your father intend to return to England soon?"

"I'm not certain what his plan is, exactly. He had a very loose idea of his schedule when he left us, but it was his hope to return before the end of the summer."

"That is not too much longer."

"No, but it is hard to know if he intends to keep to the original plan. We haven't heard from him in a few months, and it was tentative to begin with."

Mr. Cooper's eyebrows lifted. "Is that reason for concern?"

"I'm not sure." Rebecca lowered her voice a little to avoid worrying Mama, though she felt safer from that possibility with Mr. Hawkins fully engaging her mother in conversation. They weaved slowly through the sparse traffic on the road and began the ascent away from the city. Rebecca's lungs expanded, the exercise doing both her mind and body good.

She looked to Mr. Cooper, surprised to find him watching her closely. "You were saying?" he prompted.

But she wasn't. That was the extent of what she had to say

about her father. Her worries and concerns were unfounded, and she felt discomfited by Mr. Cooper's ability to see through her, to recognize she had anxieties left unspoken. "It is nothing more than conjecture, really. I cannot know if anything is wrong."

"What do you believe to be wrong?"

She held his pale blue gaze, her chest inflated with pent-up breath, and doubt trickled down her spine. She had not voiced these worries aloud to anyone, fearing she was merely borrowing concern. But Mr. Cooper had thus far proven himself to be a trustworthy man, and he had a level-headed countenance that she admired. If nothing else, perhaps he would be the voice of reason to bring her inflated worries back down to a reasonable size.

"My father is sometimes absent-minded, and his failure to write to us in some months is not very shocking, but this feels different."

"In what way?"

Warmth bled up her neck, spilling up into her ears. "Money," she said simply. "He was meant to send us some and he hasn't yet. It isn't like him to fail to hold to his word in that way. If he were unable to send funds, surely he would write to us and explain why."

Mr. Cooper nodded. "Have you written to inquire with him?"

"I wrote to inform him that we were leaving for Bath to seek treatment for my mother about four months ago, and he replied then that he had arrived in France safely and was beginning his work. But I've written to him again a handful of times since, and none of my missives have received a reply."

"Strange," Mr. Cooper said, rubbing his chin. "Do you have another contact in France?"

"No. My father has a cousin in Paris he planned to work with, but that is where I've sent his letters."

"What does your mother think of all this?"

"If she's worried, she has yet to show it. I briefly mentioned some of my concerns a few weeks ago, and she didn't pay them any heed. She is attributing the lack of letters to his general forgetfulness, and I do admit I am more prone to worry than she is."

"All the same, I will give it some thought." Mr. Cooper looked up toward the cloud-covered sky as though he were thinking that very minute. "My father has a good friend in Paris. Perhaps I can send him a letter and ask him to check in with your father."

"Oh, would you?" Rebecca's body tightened with hope. "I wouldn't wish to embarrass my father, but I would deeply like to know that all is well."

"It won't be any trouble at all. My father's friend is a physician he knew from university many years ago, but they have kept up well over the years. I'm certain he would be happy to drop in if it is not too out of his way." He reached across the space between their horses and tugged on the reins to pull her a little closer as a carriage passed close beside them. She shook herself. She hadn't even been paying attention to the traffic on the road. "If you can write your father's name and direction for me, I will be sure to send a note in the morning."

"I'm not sure how I can sufficiently thank you, Mr. Cooper. It seems that every time I feel my debts are paid, you only perform another kindness for me."

His head bent slightly, and he looked at her from under his lashes, a smile hitching half of his mouth up and that blessed dimple appearing. "I do not see my assistance as something that needs to be repaid, if that is worth anything."

"I'm beginning to believe everything you have to say holds a magnitude of worth. But no, *that* is utterly worthless."

Mr. Cooper barked a loud laugh, garnering the attention of Mama and Mr. Hawkins ahead of them and bringing a soft blush to Rebecca's cheeks.

"You shall see, Miss Turner," he said, loud enough for all to hear. "I will find a way to prove my meaning."

Unable to dampen her smile, Rebecca turned away, but not before catching a satisfied smirk on her mother's lips.

CHAPTER TWELVE

They stopped at the gates of Prior Park and Mr. Hawkins left them to inquire with the owner if they would be permitted to ride through his vast parkland.

"The views from here are said to be the very best of Bath," Mr. Cooper said. "Or so my mother tells me."

"It is true," Mama said. "My sister has expressed the same opinion to me."

Mr. Cooper cleared his throat. "How is Mrs. Langley?"

Rebecca looked from the doctor to her mother. Surely his strain was obvious to her as well, proving further the need Rebecca felt to distance herself from the man. Her heart hadn't seemed to understand, however, for it failed to temper its increased pace whenever he spoke to her.

"She is well. Though, time will only help."

Indeed. For with time, Alicia would be able to return to Society, and everyone in her household would find that a blessed relief. The poor girl was going mad with the extension of her mourning.

Mr. Hawkins appeared on the other side of the gate wearing a broad grin. "We've been granted access."

The rest of their party filed onto the lush, well-maintained lawn and up the slope, following Mr. Hawkins toward the top of the rise. A long, yellow stone house sat ahead of them, regal and stately with its columns lining the front portico in perfect symmetry. When they turned their horses around, the view stole Rebecca's breath, robbing her of air. Green rolling hills spread out below them, trees lining the edges of the manicured gardens and stretching either direction away from Prior Park's lands.

Bath spread out in the distance in tidy rows and sloping streets, the curved rooftops of the Circus obvious even from this distance. The hills on the other side of the city were covered in trees as though Bath itself was nestled into a small bowl. Lines of houses stacked beside each other, smoke billowing from their many chimneys. Rebecca could have remained there all day if her mare had not stamped impatiently and drawn her attention down. She caught sight of a covered bridge at the bottom of the hill crossing the small river, its perfectly spaced columns and light stone lovely even from this distance. The bridge was a miniature representation of the house.

"What is that?"

"The Palladian bridge?" Mr. Cooper asked. "Shall we go down and cross it?"

The group agreed and made their way toward the bridge, leaving their horses secured to a tree on the side of the bank before moving on foot up the shallow steps of the stone structure. Water ran beneath them as they stood in the center, looking down at the dam and the reflection of the bridge against the still, glassy water.

The air smelled damp, but whether it was due to the recent rain or the impending storm was anyone's guess. Looking out over the gray sky, Rebecca wondered if they would be caught in a downpour on their return to Bath. She found these sights far worth the trouble were that to occur.

"I must confess," Mama said, looking out over the water, "that I do agree with the general consensus. I do not believe there could be a more beautiful image of Bath than the one we have here."

"Perhaps standing just over there"—Rebecca pointed to the hill in the distance rising from the far side of Bath—"is lovelier, because Prior Park is included in the view."

"Perhaps." The group was silent for a minute until Mama drew in a long breath, releasing it in a shudder. "I'm afraid my stamina is not what it used to be. I must rest for a short time."

Mr. Hawkins immediately offered his elbow. "Allow me, ma'am. Let us return to the horses and find a place to rest."

"Thank you, sir." Mama took him by the arm and walked away, lifting a staying hand when Rebecca moved to follow her. "Do not leave until you are ready, dear." Her gaze flicked to Mr. Cooper. "You will not be out of my sight."

Her mother's logic was sound, but even if the men could not see through her ruse, Rebecca saw it as clear as the water below her feet. Mama had told her that she understood Rebecca's qualms, that Mr. Cooper's attraction to Alicia was enough for her to never consider him a suitor. So why was she trying to push them together now?

Rebecca stepped to the edge of the bridge and rested her hands on top of the cold stone.

"I hate to be so bold," Mr. Cooper said, approaching her, his hands behind his back. "But I wanted to ask if Miss Langley received my letter."

The poor man must have been in a state of despair after a week without a response from the object of his affection, and it was bittersweet that Rebecca could now put his mind to rest. In a way, Alicia *had* received the letter, she just had not accepted it. "She did."

Mr. Cooper looked at her, but her gaze was pasted to the water below, outlining the edges of the trees with her eyes as they tripped over the banks of the pond and crawled over the blue-gray water.

"Do you have another letter for me?"

She sucked in a silent breath. He'd not asked if *Alicia* wrote a letter, merely if Rebecca had one. Her hand sought the reticule hanging from her wrist. "I do."

Mr. Cooper stepped closer to her, facing the water, his shoulder pressing lightly against hers. "May I have it?"

She dug into her reticule, her fingers closing around the rough paper rectangle. Glancing over her shoulder, she confirmed that her mother was speaking to Mr. Hawkins, holding the man's attention.

"Of course," she said quietly.

Mr. Cooper dropped his hand to his side, and Rebecca discreetly placed the letter in his palm, her cold glove-encased fingers brushing his. His hand curled around hers for a brief moment, and she quietly gasped.

He released her hand, stepping away, but not before the damage was done. His warmth permeated the layers of leather between their skin, and she wanted to draw closer to him, to feel again the glow that heated her from within.

He was silent, no doubt eager to be removed from their outing so he could read the words he believed came from Alicia, and the truth of Rebecca's situation reared its ugly head. She shook herself from her childish, romantic feelings and set her focus on maintaining an appropriate distance from this man —both physically and within her heart. She'd set this into motion through her choices alone, and she could blame none other than herself for the difficulty.

"Tell me more about your home, Mr. Cooper," she said, hoping to steer her mind back to neutral territory. "You hail from Wiltshire?"

His mouth tightened, and it was his turn to look away, seemingly avoiding her gaze. "I do. A small country parish called Derham. It always was so idyllic, and I was quite happy there until recently."

"You must have missed your parents deeply after they left."

He smiled. "I did, indeed. But I have a sister in Derham. She is married to the vicar and about to have their first child, and I am rather close to her."

"Then it must have been difficult to leave her behind."

"It was, but she and her husband are happy. My mother intends to go to them and support my sister until the babe is born, so it is good that I will be here with my father. His gout is inflamed and makes it difficult for him to walk without assistance."

A heron swooped down from between the trees and skimmed the top of the water before landing on the shallow shore. Its blue-tipped wings tucked into its sides, and it pecked the water as though searching for food.

"Some poor fish is about to be made into a meal," Rebecca said, watching the bird seek its prey.

"People can be predators, too." Mr. Cooper's voice was quiet, his brow troubled. "Sometimes they wear a deceitful cloak of friendship, and it can be difficult to determine who is friend and who is foe. I understand the plight of the fish."

She faced him. "What happened to you, Mr. Cooper?"

He seemed unable to tear his focus away from the heron. "I was the object of prejudice, and it . . . ." He looked up at her, smiling ruefully. "Suffice it to say that I do not intend to return to Derham."

"So you mean to stay in Bath?"

He shrugged, his blue eyes clear and deep. "I haven't yet decided if I want to remain. I am not used to the bustling of Bath."

She laughed, and Mr. Cooper chuckled. "Have you been to London, sir? I do not think Bath bustles when compared to that great metropolis."

"No, but when compared to Derham, Bath is positively lively."

She nodded in understanding. "My home is very much the same as Derham, it seems." She turned toward her mother and Mr. Hawkins, afraid of what either of them would think if she remained on the bridge alone with Mr. Cooper for much longer. He fell into step beside her, but their pace was reluctant, as if they had equal awareness that once they reached the end of the bridge, their conversation would cease. "It is a very small parish on the southern edge of Somerset. I am eager to return to our cottage there, and the fresh air and horses, but we cannot go until Mama is much better."

"Oh, dear, Miss Turner, you've put me into something of a predicament."

She paused just before the shallow steps that led down to the walking path and faced him. "What is that?"

Mischief played over his lips. "I have never before wished for a patient to both be healed, and to not quite feel well enough to leave my care."

Her heart hammered against her breastbone. "Oh?"

"It is naturally my desire to see your mother well, but I would equally prefer that you remain in Bath."

Rebecca couldn't dim her smile. She forced herself to remember that Mr. Cooper valued her presence for the services she provided in delivering his letters to Alicia, but she would be lying if she said that he did not care for her at all. It was clear in Mr. Cooper's regard that he valued her friendship.

But friendship wasn't enough for her, and it was too bad he did not want more.

--- ∽ ---

Jared pulled in a deep breath of fresh air and sighed happily, directing his horse back onto the road into Bath and out of Prior Park's land. He was far more comfortable outside of the cramped city roads, and the break in dreary weather was a blessed relief.

Thomas had patiently spoken to Mrs. Turner for the duration of the ride thus far, and while it was only fair to switch partners for the return journey into Bath, Jared was hesitant to give up his place beside Rebecca. He wasn't finished speaking to her yet, and there was so much more he wanted to ask her opinions on. Opening up about his troubles in Derham had felt healing, and there was much more he could have said.

Thunder rumbled in the far distance, and the clouds above Bath looked to be pregnant with rain. Thomas lifted his eyebrows. "We should make haste."

"I concur," Mrs. Turner said. Her skin looked bright and flushed from either the cold or the exercise—most likely both—and she appeared healthier than she had when Jared first met her. Whether it was due to the medicine or the exercise was anyone's guess, but Jared was glad something was working for her benefit. Green sickness was a nuisance of an ailment that hindered one's life greatly, despite the fact that it was not terminal. What sort of life was a physically miserable one? It was vastly uncomfortable, in the least.

Regardless of what he had said to Rebecca in a joking manner, he did want Mrs. Turner to heal fully and swiftly. But he also wasn't prepared to say goodbye to the Turners just yet.

Shoving down his desire to pull back and ride beside

Rebecca again, Jared took the lead, drawing alongside Mrs. Turner as Rebecca and Thomas fell in line behind them. Guilt nipped at him for desiring her company so acutely. A twinge of disloyalty to Miss Langley struck him, and he shoved the feeling away, turning his smile on Mrs. Turner. "I'm glad to see you looking so well, Mrs. Turner."

"I must be glowing. It does my heart happy to see Rebecca so joyous," she confided. "It has been a long while since I've heard her laugh."

Jared glanced at Rebecca over his shoulder just as she threw her head back and laughed again, as though she performed for her mother's benefit. Her eyes sparkled in amusement and she continued to chuckle at something Thomas had said, and Jared knew a moment of envy that the laugh had not been credited to him. He shook his head, facing forward again. It mattered not who made Rebecca laugh. She was not the object of his desire anyway. She could laugh with any man she pleased, and Jared needed to reconcile himself to it.

"How have you been obtaining your daily exercise?" he asked. He knew it wasn't from promenading in the Pump Room, for he'd gone there every morning and hadn't seen the Turner women present in nearly a week.

"Usually walking to my sister's house and home again. It hasn't amounted to the recommended two hours every day, but when the rain isn't as strong, we've lengthened our rambles a little here and there."

"Is that more exercise than you were receiving before?"

Mrs. Turner nodded.

"And how is your level of energy? Are you sleeping better?"

She faced him, the smile spreading over her mouth, wrinkles fanning from the edges of her lips. "You make a good, caring doctor, Mr. Cooper. I am quite glad my daughter met you at the cricket match."

His neck warmed, and he dipped his head against the praise. Would the woman believe these things to be the case were she to learn of his past? Of his failures in treating Lucas Hollingsford in Derham, and how it cost the young boy his life?

Jared did his best at doctoring, but he was not a good *man*. A good man would have set aside his insecurities and frustrations and gone to the Hollingsfords' estate despite the new physician in town and the Hollingsfords' prejudice. It had pained Jared, body and mind, to sit and wait after news reached him of young Lucas's fever, but he'd been assured that Dr. Gould had been sent for by the family.

One horrible misunderstanding had ended the life of a young boy and forever changed Jared's reputation in the town that raised him. He would never again hesitate to treat a person in need, but he would carry the shame of that day with him always.

"Mr. Cooper?"

He pulled himself from his musings and gave Mrs. Turner his full attention again. "Pardon me, ma'am. I was woolgathering."

"That is quite all right. I only asked when I should expect the regimen you designed for me to work in earnest."

"I'm afraid it is different for everyone, but I do believe you should begin to feel more the thing within a fortnight of beginning the medication. If nothing has changed, I will alter the dosage more drastically than I originally intended." He paused, looking over his patient. "Excuse my noticing, ma'am, but you do appear better already."

"Well, as I mentioned, it does my heart good to see my Rebecca so happy."

Jared nodded, turning his attention to steering his horse around a small, covered landau idling in the street.

"Above all things in life, it is a mother's wish for her child to be happy," she said.

Jared looked down at the reins lying limp in his hands. Did all mothers feel this way? Surely if that were true, it would not matter that he'd done things he regretted and that Derham had all but ceased speaking to him after the wrath of the Hollingsfords had been placed at his doorstep. Surely if a mother's wish was for her child to be happy, then Jared's mother would understand the awful position he'd been in and love him despite his faults. If only it were as easy to speak his mind to her in truth as it was in theory. He had just under three weeks to inform his mother before she left to stay with Julia, and time was quickly running out.

"I do believe Bath has been good for Rebecca," Mrs. Turner continued, unaware of the personal turmoil roiling within him, and he glanced at her to find a troubled expression on her furrowed brow. "But I do not think we will remain much longer. Has she told you of my husband's business dealings in France?"

"Yes. Though I'm unfamiliar with the wine trade."

"It is like all business," she said, waving her hand through the air. "It comes down to who one knows, and we are fortunate that my husband's cousin lives in Paris, owns vineyards, and knows quite a few people in London as well. But my husband will not remain in France much longer, and I think when he does come back to us, we will return to Welton."

Jared had to agree with Rebecca in that it did not sound as though Mrs. Turner was concerned about the well-being of her husband. Perhaps she had not given the matter much thought, or perhaps she was an optimist by nature. Either way, it was likely better for her health if she did not worry unnecessarily over her husband.

Jared would ask his father to write to his friend in Paris; surely the old doctor would be willing to meet Mr. Turner and assure them of his general health and well-being. If nothing else, it would give Rebecca peace of mind. Perhaps then she could enjoy Bath before quitting the city for her rural oasis.

The idea of Rebecca leaving made Jared's stomach clench, and he glanced back to find her watching him. She ducked her head, a rosy blush spreading over her cheeks, and he turned away so as not to be caught staring.

There was nothing for it. He simply must enjoy her company while he had it.

CHAPTER THIRTEEN

Rebecca pulled her horse to a halt just before the door to Mrs. Brown's townhouse. A cool breeze slipped over her skin, bringing the smell of impending rain. It was a scent she enjoyed, but its relentless presence had begun to wear on her lately. It was summer, for heaven's sake. When was the sky going to catch up to the calendar?

Rebecca had enjoyed the ride—far more than she ought to have done. Spending time with Mr. Cooper was growing into one of her most favorite things. She had to repeatedly remind herself that he'd noticed Alicia first. Who wouldn't? With her radiant, ethereal beauty, Alicia was hard not to notice.

Gray clouds rolled overhead like a slow creek moving over a rocky bed. Their heaviness threatened rain, and Rebecca was eager to get her mother indoors. Mr. Hawkins and Mr. Cooper slid down from their horses and approached the women.

Rebecca's heart galloped when Mr. Cooper stood before her, his hands rising. "May I assist you, Miss Turner?"

"Certainly," she said, tempering her smile. He'd been so vulnerable sharing pieces of himself on the bridge earlier, and it had made her wish to know more, to share more with him. His little confidences were breadcrumbs of what she assumed was a large loaf of bread, his trials so much bigger than the minuscule offering he gave. It made her eager for another letter, as much as she knew she shouldn't want it. They were not truly for *her*.

Rebecca was a good Christian woman, but she couldn't help but feel as though her actions were careless, even if born of desperation. She rejoiced in the opportunity to pay Mr. Cooper for his services—indeed, after Mama's debt-ridden childhood, she would not abide debt of any kind—but Rebecca's payment methods did not sit well with her soul, and the guilt of writing the letter ate at her. She'd never been so eager to do something she knew wasn't exactly right. She vowed to someday tell Mr. Cooper the whole of it. *After* Father finally sent money and she was able to pay Mr. Cooper for his services outright.

Lifting her leg from the curved pommel, Rebecca attempted to turn in the seat when something pulled at her hip, keeping her in place. She tugged again, but the tightness grew, and she looked down to find a string from her riding habit knotted and caught on the leather of the saddle.

"Are you having trouble?" Mr. Cooper asked. Mr. Hawkins had helped Mama down and they were walking toward the front door.

"My skirt is caught." Rebecca tugged at it again, but it would not release its hold on the saddle. Her dratted gloves kept slipping, unable to find purchase on the string. She pulled her right glove off one finger at a time and held it out toward Mr. Cooper. "Would you hold this, please?"

He took the glove, and she proceeded to work the string loose with stiff, bare fingers. It had caused a small hole in her skirt from the unraveled thread, and she would need to mend it later, but if she held the skirt just right then surely no one would notice.

Mr. Cooper shoved the glove in his pocket and raised his arms again to assist her down. Rebecca rested her hands on his broad shoulders, doing her best not to notice the firmness of his shoulders beneath his thick coat, or how they bunched when he took her by the waist and helped her down from the horse.

Once her feet touched the ground, Rebecca took a quick step back, willing her heart to calm, and Mr. Cooper's hands dropped from her waist. Her cheeks infused with warmth, and she avoided his gaze, skirting the horses to approach her mother. She should not feel so excited by the touch of a man who did not regard her with any special affection. It would do no good.

"Thank you, Mr. Hawkins, Mr. Cooper," she said, taking her mother's arm and opening the front door. She hoped to avoid Mr. Cooper's gaze, to hide her blush. "That was an excellent way to spend the afternoon."

"I would be very gratified if we can do so again," Mr. Hawkins said, his smile widening beneath freckled cheeks.

Rebecca took a moment to give him a genuine smile. "As would I."

Mama thanked the gentlemen, and Rebecca snuck a quick look at Mr. Cooper before slipping inside and closing the door behind her. He'd been watching her closely, a small line creasing his eyebrows. Oh, dear heavens. She could only hope he'd not noticed her particular attention or the way her heart pulsed around him.

It would not do to fall in love with a man who wanted to marry her cousin.

—⁓—

Jared clutched the tan kid glove in his hand, running the smooth leather through his fingers as he made his way toward the Turners' townhouse. He'd stuffed it into his pocket the day before in order to help Rebecca down from the horse and had forgotten to return it. Though, he likely would have remembered to give it back to her if she hadn't run from him like a frightened rabbit.

That had been odd, and for the life of him, he could not discern what had made Rebecca run, quite literally, out of his hands. Jared would be lying if he tried to pretend that he hadn't reacted to the feel of Rebecca in his arms, and it had taken him by surprise. It had been purely physical—the increase of his pulse, the feel of a hot brick laying on his chest—and a complete betrayal to Miss Langley.

He could not write to one woman while harboring feelings for another. He needed to squash the feelings that had kept him up late into the night. Rebecca was lovely, her friendship important to him, and she did not deserve to be cut from his life simply because he could not manage his own base reactions.

It was with this in mind that he chose to return her glove forthwith. He would not gain control over himself if he did not practice.

Rapping on the weather-beaten door to the Turners' townhouse, Jared stepped away, rocking back on his heels. He had a letter for Miss Langley in his pocket as well and hoped to be given the opportunity to pass it to Rebecca.

Mrs. Brown opened the door, rosy-cheeked, and he smiled down at her. "Good day, madam. Is Miss Turner at home for visitors?"

She sent him a harassed expression. "They're not in at present."

"Oh." His shoulders fell, deflated like the sudden loss of wind from a sail. "I came to return a glove Miss Turner left behind on our ride yesterday." He fished the evidence from his pocket, but Mrs. Brown didn't look the least inclined to allow him entrance. Frustration seeped into his limbs, his hands fisting around the small, worn glove. The Turners could do much better than a landlady who treated their callers so ill.

A loud creak split the air, and Jared looked past the landlady and up the staircase. The squeak *had* to have been from their sitting room door. The sound was jarring. He kept the irritation from his face, but thought very little of the short, unpleasant woman before him. She could not even take it upon herself to repair a squeaky hinge—the work of a minute, if that.

She began to close the door. "I'll tell Mrs. Turner—"

"Wait," he said, lifting his hand. Someone just went through the Turners' sitting room door. "Is the Turners' maid within?"

"Miss Mullens?"

He did not know the woman's name, but he was fairly positive the Turners only had one servant. "Yes."

Mrs. Brown hesitated only briefly before nodding. "She's upstairs."

Of course she was. Anyone standing within the general vicinity likely heard the squeaky hinge that had given away Miss Mullens's location. "May I speak to her?"

Mrs. Brown stepped to the side, allowing him to enter. "Wait here."

"Of course." Jared removed his hat and gloves, tucking them between his elbow and his side. Mrs. Brown disappeared slowly up the stairs, the old wooden steps creaking beneath her feet. It took a few minutes before the maid appeared at the top of the staircase.

Miss Mullens. He recognized her immediately. Her graying hair was pulled back in a tight knot, and apprehension was splashed over her thin face.

"I've come to return Miss Turner's glove," he said, holding up the article as she came down the stairs toward him.

"Thank you, sir. I will see to it that Miss Turner receives this." She accepted the glove and held it in both of her hands.

He cleared his throat. "I also wondered if I might take care of something while I am here."

"What did you have in mind?"

Jared glanced up, hoping not to offend the maid by his request. "I wanted to repair that wretched door," he said softly, so as not to be overheard by Mrs. Brown.

Miss Mullens's lips twitched, her eyebrows lifting. "You'll be speaking of the squeak, if I understand you correctly. I've been meaning to—"

"I am certain you have enough to keep you busy, Miss Mullens," Jared said at once, hoping to put her mind at rest. Yes, she likely could have fixed it herself, but it was not her responsibility. When the landlady had been asked repeatedly with no action taken, that was a fault of hers, and hers alone. "Perhaps you will allow me to do this for the Turners."

Miss Mullens hesitated. "She doesn't like charity, Mrs. Turner. She's a proud woman, you'll understand. And you wouldn't want to ruin your nice clothes, sir."

"Surely even the proud can decipher the difference between charity and an act of service from a friend," he said gently. Lightening his tone, he gave the maid his warmest smile. "And while I am not entirely certain I can handle a little oil without spilling it on my waistcoat, I do promise to give it my best effort."

She nodded. "Oh, very well. It'll be her wrath you'll have to face if you're wrong."

Jared couldn't help but grin. "Will you be able to obtain a feather or a small square of flannel and some sweet oil? Or perhaps tell me where I can locate those items?"

"I'm not certain we have a feather, but I will look. You go on upstairs and wait for me there, and I will fetch those items straight away." Miss Mullens had a no-nonsense way about her that Jared liked immediately, and he promptly did as he was bid, watching the maid disappear around the corner as he mounted the stairs.

The light wasn't great in the dim corridor, but there was enough to see by. Miss Mullens returned shortly with the oil and rag, apologizing for not having a feather on hand, and Jared set to work applying a bit of oil to the flannel before rubbing it along the hinges. They were stiff, and Jared felt internally chastised when it was far longer than the work of a mere minute, as he'd thought earlier. He worked the oil into the brass creases, opening and closing the door until the hinges made nary a sound.

The front door opened downstairs, and quiet, feminine voices filtered up to him. His heart raced as he rose from his knees, and he caught Miss Mullens's gaze from where she stood in the bedchamber doorway, a handful of laundry in her arms.

She approached him and held her hand out. "I'll take that oil and flannel, sir. You best be devising your explanation." She closed the door to the sitting room and disappeared in a flash, escaping no doubt to the servants' stairs hidden somewhere behind him.

"Mr. Cooper," Rebecca said, stalling in the center of the stairs, her hand resting on the banister, her mother behind her.

"Well, go on," Mrs. Turner said. "Do not keep the man waiting."

Jared wished he'd escaped down the servants' stairs behind Miss Mullens. He swallowed, bowing to the women as they stood before him. "I came to return your glove, Miss Turner."

"Oh, I thank you. You needn't have gone to the trouble." She quickly clasped her bare hands behind her back and Jared was glad he *had* gone to the trouble. That was likely her only pair.

"It was no trouble at all," he promised. Mrs. Turner looked worn, as though she needed to rest, and Jared would not stand in the way of her health. "I will leave you now. I wouldn't want to impose on your time."

He bowed to the women and moved aside so they could enter their sitting room.

"Mr. Cooper?" Rebecca called to him, and he paused at the top of the stairs. "My glove?"

"I gave it to your maid."

She nodded, her hands still behind her back, and gave him a smile. An invisible length of thread spun from her smile to his heart, and his chest constricted. The temptation to remain as they opened their door, to see the looks on their faces when they discovered its smoothness and silence, was great, but Jared turned swiftly and went down the stairs. He had only been acting as a friend.

Retrieving his hat and gloves from the table beside the door where he'd left them, he tugged on his black gloves before setting the hat on top of his head. He hadn't heard the women enter their room, and that alone sent a flood of achievement coursing through him. When he hazarded a glance up the stairs, he stilled, his body losing the ability to so much as breathe.

Rebecca stood at the top of the staircase, looking down at him with curiosity and admiration. She descended slowly, her bare hand sliding down the polished railing as she lifted her hem slightly to keep from tripping, her gaze fastened on him.

Jared's throat grew thick, and he wanted to bolt, to fight the steadily increasing pulsing in his veins.

"You did that, didn't you?" she asked quietly when she came to stand on the floor in front of him.

Was she angry? Her voice was so low and smooth, he could not decipher which emotion brimmed behind it.

"Indeed."

Rebecca pushed her spectacles up her nose, drawing a ragged breath. "I cannot . . . that is, I do not know what to say. Thank you, Mr. Cooper."

"The pleasure is mine," he said, and he meant it. He'd enjoyed serving these women. "It was a simple fix."

Rebecca laughed, and the sound pressed a smile to his lips. "Indeed. I wonder if Mrs. Brown understands how simple." She paused. "How do *you* know how to fix a squeaky hinge?"

"I have oiled quite a few hinges in my lifetime, Miss Turner." Indeed, he'd seldom had more than one servant in his home growing up, and Jared was accustomed to taking care of small things like this himself. "Will your mother be upset? I would like to plead the case that this was not charity, but an act of service from a friend."

"My mama is quite as impressed and grateful as I am, I assure you."

Jared reached for Rebecca's hand before he could think better of it, her gracious acceptance of his kindness at odds with the prideful woman he'd painted her to be. Bringing her fingers up to his lips, he placed a kiss on the back of her knuckles. Her skin was cool, the smell of soap wafting to his nose.

He heard her sharp intake of breath and released her fingers, remorse and guilt washing over him in waves. He needed to take a step back, both literally and internally.

Securing his hat on his head, he smiled briefly. "Good day, Miss Turner." Escaping through the door, Jared was already more than a block away when he realized that he hadn't even given Rebecca the letter.

CHAPTER FOURTEEN

Throughout the previous week, Rebecca had either written or received letters nearly every day, finding ways to hand them off to Mr. Cooper discreetly at the Pump Room or the various events at the assembly halls. She had never before been so social in her life and found that while it was nice to get Mama out of their rooms for fresh air every day as Mr. Cooper had originally prescribed, the consistent gatherings were wearing on her a little.

She sat at a table in the Gastrells' parlor holding cards in her hand and waiting for her mother to take her turn. They partnered against Georgiana Gastrell and her mother at whist, and the game was nearing its end, the Gastrells clearly in the lead.

Mama had known Mrs. Gastrell for quite a few years— they'd made their connection through Aunt Langley—and the Turners often found time to pass in the Gastrells' drawing room when they visited Bath. This was the first time they'd been completely trounced at Whist.

"How is your husband enjoying Paris?" Mrs. Gastrell

asked, eyeing her remaining cards in her hand as she absently petted the small, white dog on her lap.

"He's never been fond of the city, actually, but he loves his cousin quite a lot. I'm certain their time spent together balances his distaste for being away from us."

"Surely it must. He does not intend to stay in Paris long, then?"

"We hope not," Mama said, pulling a card from her hand and laying it on the table.

Rebecca analyzed her remaining cards, swallowing the concern that crept into the tightness of her body when she thought of her father. Mama did not sound in the least concerned that they hadn't heard from him in nearly two months now. "We miss him heartily."

A shadow hovered over Rebecca's shoulder, and she glanced back to find Henry Gastrell there, looking down at her. His dark hair was styled in the Brutus, disheveled and pushed forward, giving him a rakish charm. She didn't yet know what to make of his character. Henry had seldom been in residence the times they'd visited in her youth, for he'd been away at school himself. But he seemed to have a good relationship with his sister and a ready smile.

None of which explained why his presence made her uneasy.

She tipped her cards away to hide them. "Have you been sent by Miss Gastrell to ascertain my hand?"

Henry scoffed. "Of course not. If I was to assist anyone at this table with cheating, it would not be my sister."

"Thank you," Georgiana said wryly. She laid a card on top of Mama's and wrinkled her nose at Henry.

"I suppose I should have to prove myself in the next game," Henry said with an air of nonchalance. "Will you partner me, Miss Turner?"

Rebecca resisted the urge to slide her spectacles higher on her nose and nodded. "I should love to."

"Perhaps I will ask Mr. Cooper to partner me," Georgiana said, leaning over to peer around Rebecca.

Was he here? Rebecca hadn't seen him come in, but she had told him of her intent to attend the card party, and she knew he likely had a letter for Alicia. He had made the Gastrells' acquaintance at the assemblies and had quickly made his way into their good graces. It was no wonder Mrs. Gastrell had extended an invitation to Mr. Cooper.

Rebecca found herself holding her breath and turned her head slightly, catching sight of Mr. Cooper near the door, speaking to another gentleman, his sandy-brown hair brushed away from his face and his dark gray jacket pulling taut across his broad shoulders.

"It is your turn, Rebecca," Mama said, snapping her attention back to the table. Rebecca laid her final card, and Georgiana did so after her, taking the trick and winning the game.

Georgiana rose, slipping her hand around her brother's arm. "We will fetch a fourth for our game and return promptly."

"I suppose that means we are dismissed," Mrs. Gastrell said with a chuckle.

Mama gathered the cards on the table and stacked them. "My old brain needs a break anyway."

"Shall we find ourselves some tea? My cook made a splendid poundcake for tonight."

"That sounds lovely." Mama looked to Rebecca, her eyebrows slightly raised as if to ask if she would be all right, and Rebecca nodded her head, smiling in confirmation. She fingered the emerald brooch attached to her fichu, watching her mother walk away on the arm of her friend, the little dog trailing their feet.

"Good evening, Miss Turner," Mr. Cooper said, resting his smile on her across the table.

She gathered the rest of the cards where the Gastrell women had discarded them and stacked them into a pile. She tipped her head back to see him, for when standing, he was enormously tall. "Good evening, Mr. Cooper. Have you come prepared to lose?"

His grin widened. "I see that you don't take lightly to friendly games of whist."

"I've done nothing but lose all night, and I'm eager to prove that I'm not fully inept." She looked to Henry standing on his other side. "Though you may rest safely, Mr. Gastrell. If we are to lose, the blame shall clearly rest on my shoulders."

"Nonsense," Henry replied gallantly, pulling the chair out opposite her and seating himself. "I would never admit such an ungentlemanly thing aloud."

"Better to keep it in your mind, of course," Rebecca agreed, laughing. Perhaps she'd misjudged the man. She bent her head and pushed her spectacles higher on her nose, hoping they would quit slipping during the game. Georgiana took her seat, and Rebecca gave the cards to Henry to distribute.

Georgiana's raven hair was styled high on her head, with tight ringlets framing her eyes. She thanked Mr. Cooper for helping her sit before he took his chair across from her, and Rebecca focused on putting her cards in order.

"I adore your brooch, Miss Turner," Georgiana said. "It matches your eyes so prettily."

"I'm certain my eyes are not as green as this," Rebecca said, chuckling to dispel her discomfort. She was not used to receiving compliments, though she certainly appreciated Georgiana's kind words.

"Miss Gastrell is correct," Mr. Cooper said thoughtfully. "It is nearly the same color as your eyes. The brooch really is beautiful."

Rebecca's cheeks flushed, and she forced her gaze to his, fighting the temptation to dip her neck and hide away. "Thank you. It has been in my family for four generations and holds a very special place in my heart."

"How is it that some family heirlooms are so lovely, and I am stuck with a hideous, gaudy necklace I shall never wear?" Georgiana asked. "It is so heavy and thick, it would surely weigh me in place."

"You will don it one day," Henry said, playing his card. "Perhaps when you are Mother's age, it will look more appropriate."

Georgiana scoffed, tossing her card on top of her brother's. "You've only made my point more, Henry. Of course I would prefer an heirloom I can wear now."

"Perhaps your husband will have one," Mr. Cooper said cordially.

Georgiana grew silent, assessing him. "I had not thought of that, but you make a very good point. Do you have any family heirlooms, Mr. Cooper?"

He shook his head. "Nothing worth mentioning. I do have a pocket watch that carries special meaning, but . . . ." His cheeks grew ruddy, and Rebecca found herself watching him, despite it being her turn to play.

"What is the significance?" she asked, unable to contain her curiosity.

Mr. Cooper shrugged. "It is nothing to anyone but me, of course. I saved my wages from my first few months of work and bought myself the pocket watch."

"That is very admirable, Mr. Cooper," Rebecca said. "Surely you must be reminded of your dedication to your occupation whenever you check the time."

"It is a good reminder," he agreed. "But more than that, it helps me to recall my own humble upbringing. I do not have expensive things passed down to me from my father's father. Indeed, my parents came into some money a few years ago after the passing of my aunt, but growing up, we had a very simple but happy home."

The Gastrells remained quiet, but Rebecca nodded in understanding. Her cottage in Welton could be described as simple, but she had found immense happiness within its modest walls, and she admired Mr. Cooper for the importance his humble home still held for him.

"What of your brooch, Miss Turner?" Henry asked. "Is there a significance to it, or was it merely passed down from generation to generation?"

"My mother's grandfather gave it to his wife when they married. It has been given to each oldest daughter on her eighteenth birthday in my family, and I hope to do the same one day with my own daughter."

"What shall you do if you only have sons?" Georgiana asked, her brown eyes wide.

Rebecca shrugged, laying down her card on the center of the table. She was more concerned with what she would do if she never married, but she suppressed that thought. "I suppose I will pass it to my son in that case."

"I'm sure it will look dashing on him, too," Henry said, grinning.

"Or his wife," Georgiana added.

Mr. Cooper nodded in approval, selecting a card and adding to the stack. "Whatever happens, I'm certain you will make the right choice."

Rebecca hoped that would be the case. "What faith you have in me, Mr. Cooper."

He looked up, spearing her with his steady blue gaze. "Of course. Did you doubt me?"

She certainly hadn't known that he carried such faith in her, and it buoyed her. Pushing her spectacles higher on her nose, she shook her head. "No, Mr. Cooper. How could anyone doubt you?"

He laughed heartily, his eyes sparkling. "Perhaps they should."

"Oh, nonsense," Georgiana said, fluttering her dark lashes. "I cannot imagine any doctor more deserving of our trust than you."

Mr. Cooper's attention shifted to Georgiana, and then down to his cards. "You truly are too kind."

Rebecca caught discomfort in the undertone of his words, but he seemed to shake it off, and inquired of Henry about whether he believed the races would still be held in Newmarket in July with all this rain. They broke into their own conversation, and Rebecca looked at her cards, doing her best not to analyze how warm and complete she felt when Mr. Cooper praised her.

CHAPTER FIFTEEN

The moment Rebecca and her mother stepped into the Langleys' townhouse the next afternoon, they were set upon by Alicia and Aunt Langley. Alicia took both of Rebecca's hands in her own and squeezed fiercely, dragging her further down the corridor and away from the drawing room.

"If I do not escape this house for an hour I will expire immediately."

"Has your mother approved an outing?"

She nodded with enthusiasm, taking Rebecca's bonnet from the entryway table and placing it back on Rebecca's head. "Only a short walk, but I hardly need more than that. I long to feel the sun on my face and the earth beneath my feet."

"You will feel neither of those things due to the cloudy sky and your shoes, Alicia, but I understand your meaning. Come, let us go while the rain has taken a small break."

Alicia's grin widened, and she reached up to tie Rebecca's limp bonnet strings to the left side of her chin. They readied swiftly in cloaks and gloves and let themselves outside, turning toward the street that would lead them to Queen's Square.

"If I have to listen to another monologue on the merits of Margaret's Lord Buxton or my uncle's gracious charity, I might very well go mad."

"Then let us speak of neither of those things," Rebecca said. A cold wind whipped past her, and she pulled her cloak tight at the neck. They crossed the street and continued down the walking path.

"Agreed. I would prefer to hear about the good doctor," Alicia said, grinning.

Rebecca floundered, unsure what to say. Her pride prevented her from admitting that she was developing a fondness for Mr. Cooper, but she didn't think that was what Alicia wanted to hear anyway. His friendship was growing increasingly important to her, and the contents of the letters growing in familiarity. They were steadily coming to know one another, and to her dismay, Rebecca very much liked the man she discovered Mr. Cooper to be.

Guilt crept over her body slowly, filling her chest. Mr. Cooper believed he was coming to know Alicia, and that was the ever-present truth gnawing at the back of her mind.

"The doctor, Rebecca?" Alicia prompted.

"He has been diligent in seeing to Mama's health," Rebecca said. She cleared her throat, hoping her voice sounded as it usually did. "And writing you letters."

"More of them? Are they very romantic?"

"Not at all, actually." Not unless asking her favorite season, her favorite color, or her favorite poet were meant to lead to romance. Oh goodness, she hoped they weren't. She'd been answering his queries with her own opinions.

Alicia frowned. "But you do write back to him, yes? You are sharing *your own* thoughts?"

Rebecca hurried to explain. "Yes, and he is philosophical, actually. Thus far, he's analyzed the meaning—"

"That is quite enough," Alicia said, yawning. "You've bored me already. Oh, look. There is Mrs. Gastrell with Henry and Georgiana. Let us go and greet them."

Rebecca snapped her mouth closed. If Alicia was uninterested in learning of the letters which were supposedly from her, could she really hold much interest for Mr. Cooper? Surely if she cared for the man, she would at least wish to know what he had said. The undercurrent of scheming that Rebecca had detected in Alicia was brought to mind, and Rebecca pulled on her arm, bringing them to a stop in the center of the walking path.

"What is it?" Alicia asked, her blue eyes rounding.

"What is your objective here? If you do not wish to court Mr. Cooper once you're out of mourning, why am I writing him letters?"

Aside from the need Rebecca felt to pay him in this way for Mama's care, but that was irrelevant. She needed to understand her cousin's motivation, for surely she had some.

Alicia's mouth fell open. She glanced to the Gastrells, who were quickly approaching, and something akin to panic shone in her eyes. "Of course I wish to form a relationship with the man. But courting? Heavens, Rebecca. I hardly know him."

Surprise robbed Rebecca of words as Alicia tugged her along toward their friends. Had she labeled Alicia as more interested in Mr. Cooper than she truly was, or had she been misled? If the letters were not to benefit Alicia, then what could she possibly have schemed for?

The Gastrell family approached. Georgiana was resplendent in a blue pelisse, her raven hair swept up beneath a stylish bonnet with a matching ribbon, while her brother looked every bit the gentleman from his well-cut coat to his stiff cravat and sharp shirt points.

"Good day," Henry said, sketching a handsome bow, his

dark hair maintaining its Brutus style despite the flopping of his head. He must have used an entire vat of pomade in order to accomplish such a feat.

Pleasantries were exchanged, and the health of Aunt Langley remarked upon before Mrs. Gastrell lowered her voice conspiratorially. "Have you heard the news of your uncle, Miss Langley?"

Alicia perked up, her eyes snapping to attention. "What news?"

"It is being said that Mr. Arthur Langley arrived in Bath last evening without any warning to his servants and with no notice of how long he intends to remain."

Alicia frowned. "But my uncle has been in Brighton."

"Perhaps he wished to take the waters," Georgiana offered, shrugging her delicate shoulder.

"Without warning?" Mrs. Gastrell *tsked*. "I've known your uncle for a long time, and in my experience, he does not do anything without great design. Something urgent must have occurred to bring him to Bath with such haste. Is the rest of his family not in Brighton?"

"Indeed, they are. My sister Margaret is with them."

Rebecca slid her arm around her cousin's, hoping that by tugging on her elbow, she would remind Alicia to avoid gossiping about her family member. "I am certain your mother knows the situation, Alicia. Perhaps it is of a delicate nature." The mild rebuke halted all further conversation on the matter.

Henry stepped forward, a wide smile on his congenial lips. "Have you come to take the air, or do you have somewhere you need to be? I would love to offer you use of my arm for a stroll about the square."

"That would be most welcome, Mr. Gastrell," Alicia said, batting her eyelashes perfectly. She was so talented at artful flirtation without saying a word, and Rebecca felt a modicum of jealousy sprout in her gut. Though she could hardly see through her spectacles due to the misty air, so slowly sweeping her eyelashes would undoubtedly be fruitless. If she couldn't see through the glass, it stood to reason that others wouldn't see her attempts at flirtation anyway.

Henry offered his arm to Alicia and lifted his other elbow toward Rebecca, surprising her. She paused, unsure whether to take it and leave Georgiana and Mrs. Gastrell to walk alone. But he stood there expectantly, and Rebecca had no reason to refuse the man aside from her own insecurity. Surely he was only being kind to her, and his preference lay with the blonde, blue-eyed woman on his other arm. Rebecca wouldn't fault him for it. That was typically how it went.

"Did you hear that Frederick Monson is engaged to Fanny Gould?" Henry asked after they began to walk the length of Queen's Square, his mother and sister following close behind them.

"No," Alicia said, gasping. "I was unaware that Fanny had any affection for Frederick at all."

Henry smirked. "I'm not sure she did, but she was found alone with him in the library at the Simpson's ball Friday last, and her father forced him to offer marriage. Or that is what I've heard."

"Some women value their reputations so little that they're willing to risk everything. I could never," Alicia said, shaking her head. "My name is far more important than a quick . . ." She failed to finish the sentence, but Rebecca imagined Henry had no trouble filling in the remainder of her thought easily enough. She was nearly positive Alicia meant a quick *kiss*, and Rebecca had to agree. What kiss was worth forever ruining one's name and reputation for? None, she believed.

Mr. Cooper's pleasant face came unbidden to her mind, the soft curve of his smile, the faint dimple that appeared to the side of his mouth. If he kissed her . . . well, that didn't bear thinking about. Rebecca was his friend. He only had eyes for Alicia.

Though their reputations—and Alicia's—were very much in danger were they to be discovered passing letters. It left the question hovering on the edge of Rebecca's mind: if she did not write them for the benefit of Alicia, and her mother had begun the process of healing, why was she continuing to write so frequently?

Because she wanted to. Because she adored the letters, the conversation, the connection. Because she wanted Mr. Cooper to continue seeking her out in ballrooms and visits. The weight of admitting the truth to herself was startling and frightening. She began the deceit mostly for the benefit of her mother, the excuse of helping Alicia an additional motivator, but she had certainly *continued* to write for herself. Yet Mr. Cooper had no idea it was her.

"We've missed seeing you, Miss Langley," Georgiana called from where she walked behind them, holding tight to her mother's arm. Her voice pulled Rebecca from her musings, and she glanced up to find Henry regarding her thoughtfully. She gave him a tight smile.

"I am eager for your return to Society," Georgiana said.

"As am I," Alicia said with feeling. Despite her black clothing, she did not appear grief-stricken. Indeed, it was odd to continue one's mourning like this, and the Gastrell family was likely wondering why Alicia was not in attendance at the assemblies already. If they weren't careful, Alicia would reveal her uncle's admonishments and her mother's acquiescence, and Rebecca was quite certain that was a rumor her aunt would never wish to be spread about Bath.

"Rebecca," Mrs. Gastrell called. "How does your mother

fare? I have been seeing quite a bit of her this week, and it does my heart well."

Rebecca removed her hand from Henry's elbow and slowed her steps to walk alongside Mrs. Gastrell and Georgiana. Henry dipped his head in acknowledgment and turned to say something quietly to Alicia, which she responded to by tipping her head back in a musical laugh.

"Mr. Cooper's help has done wonders for Mama's health," Rebecca said. "His advice to go on daily walks has persuaded her to leave the house more, and I think that has been a huge motivator in helping her attend more social functions."

"Your aunt's mourning has undoubtedly helped as well, I presume? Of course your mama does not wish to keep *you* from balls or parties."

Rebecca hadn't considered that, but Mrs. Gastrell made a valid point.

"It will be such a relief when Alicia is able to join us at the assemblies. Henry has become so distracted lately, he is no fun at all to be around," Georgiana said, huffing.

Mrs. Gastrell made a humming sound in her throat. "I would not be surprised if he has taken a liking to a young woman. He is acting so odd, gone so many hours and never home until late. It is a rare occasion that we can persuade him to walk out with us like this."

"Well," Georgiana added, lowering her voice, "I also over-heard him telling his valet not to cut his hair too short, for his friend liked it precisely the way it was. He clearly has a woman in mind."

"Do you have any inclination as to who the woman is?" Rebecca asked, looking at Henry swagger ahead of them. Alicia laughed again, drawing closer to his side, and unease fell over Rebecca in a soft haze.

She took comfort in the fact that Alicia was relegated to her own drawing room, for the most part, so she could not possibly be the woman holding Henry's affections. Not if he was seeing her at social functions as his mother and sister believed.

"It could be a number of women," Mrs. Gastrell said. "I haven't the slightest who, though I've been trying to pay special attention to him in order to figure that out."

Alicia slowed her steps, her hand still tightly gripping Henry's arm, and gave Rebecca a pointed look. "Look, Rebecca, it is the doctor."

Rebecca's neck prickled with apprehension. It was precisely her luck that soon after she determined she harbored affection for the man, he would appear before her. So long as she didn't permit Mr. Cooper to speak to Alicia and her without the Gastrells present, he would not be able to mention the letters.

It would only take one wrong comment for their ruse to be revealed and for Mr. Cooper to learn of Rebecca's duplicity.

She glanced up to find Mr. Cooper walking toward them on the path, a tall, black-encased blur through her wet spectacles. He wore the same black greatcoat and black hat, carrying the same black umbrella at his side. Rebecca removed her glasses and wiped them on her skirt, managing to clear most of the misty smudges away. Hooking them back over her ears, she looked up to find Mr. Cooper nearer still, and finally a little less fuzzy. He was still covered in black from his leather-encased hands to his boots, but she could now see the details of his apparel. The gold watch chain hanging from his pocket in a half-circle through the opening in his unbuttoned coat, the white of his cravat peeking up from his light blue waistcoat. She wished to see him without the greatcoat to determine if the blue of his waistcoat made his eyes brighter.

"Good day, Mr. Cooper," Alicia said as their walking party

formed a soft semi-circle around the doctor. "Do you know the Gastrells?"

"I do," he replied, offering a courteous bow. His gaze was pasted on Alicia, cutting a slice of hurt through Rebecca's abdomen. She pushed her glasses up her nose but briefly considered removing them so she wouldn't be forced to see the lovesick look in Mr. Cooper's eyes.

"It is good to see you looking so well, Miss Langley," he said.

She bowed her head meekly. "Thank you, Mr. Cooper."

He seemed to remember himself and looked up to Mrs. Gastrell. "Will I have the pleasure of seeing you all at the concert this evening in the Upper Rooms?"

"I'm afraid not," Alicia said, pouting prettily.

Georgiana stepped forward the slightest bit. "You shall see us there, Mr. Cooper." She looked eager, her brown eyes bright, and it occurred to Rebecca that perhaps Georgiana had aims at obtaining Mr. Cooper's affection.

The doctor seemed genuinely pleased by this news. "I am glad to hear it."

Mrs. Gastrell nodded. "I have heard lovely things about the soprano's voice. I do look forward to hearing her sing."

Mr. Cooper's gaze swung toward Rebecca then, just when she'd begun to wonder if he'd even noticed her presence, and a glint of amusement sparkled in his eyes. Was he thinking of her neighbor in Welton as she was?

His pleasant smile moved back to Alicia. "We all look forward to the day when you can once again join us for a concert."

"Perhaps soon," Mrs. Gastrell agreed. "Certainly attending a concert is above reproach."

In any normal situation, surely. But Aunt Langley was concerned with her brother-in-law's opinion, and it was important to her to keep him happy. Rebecca imagined it would be even more the case if Arthur Langley truly was in Bath like Mrs. Gastrell had predicted.

"You shall soon." Alicia's words sounded very much like a promise. She turned her suggestive smile on Henry. "Though it is not concerts but balls which I long for. I am eager for the night when I can dance again."

Rebecca swallowed nervously. What would Mr. Cooper think of this blatant flirting? "I believe we ought to be going, Alicia."

"But we only just came—"

"We need to return home," Rebecca pressed, and her cousin acquiesced. They bade their friends farewell and turned to go when Mr. Cooper lifted his hat.

"Will you allow me to walk you home?"

No. No, no, no. This was not good, not if Rebecca wished to keep her authoring of the letters a secret. Surely Mr. Cooper would say something and expect Alicia to know what he meant, but Alicia didn't have the faintest idea of what had been discussed in the letters, nor the opinions she allegedly shared. Rebecca wished she had pressed forward and told Alicia all earlier during their walk. But it was now too late.

She hurried to dissuade him. "We are not walking very far, Mr. Cooper. I think—"

"That would be lovely," Alicia said without allowing Rebecca to complete her sentence. "I thank you, sir."

Mr. Cooper dipped his head. "It is my pleasure."

Of course it was.

Jared offered Miss Langley his arm, gratified when she placed her hand on the crook of his elbow. He hadn't realized when he cut across Queen's Square that he would be so fortunate as to see Miss Langley and Rebecca, and his heart had picked up speed when he'd caught sight of the light glinting off Rebecca's spectacles, confirming her identity. He lifted his other arm toward Rebecca, and she seemed to hesitate before taking it, surprising him.

"Are you well, Miss Turner?"

"I am," she said. He heard no dishonesty in her tone, but it gave him pause, nonetheless.

Turning his attention to Miss Langley, he considered the woman he knew from her letters, the serious, thoughtful one, and had trouble reconciling the woman in the letters to this lively, flirtatious creature. But she must be the same, for he had the missives piling in his drawer with her opinions on poetry and ethical dilemmas to prove her thoughtful side existed.

"I could wait to read it later, of course, but I am interested to know what your preference is—"

Rebecca coughed loudly, barking like an unkempt mutt.

"Preference?" Alicia asked, screwing up her eyebrows. "What do you mean?"

"Between the seasons. My best guess would be spring or autumn?"

"Oh, I suppose they aren't so very different. But no, my favorite is summer, I should think." She scrunched up her nose. "Which is why I am so vexed. It is supposed to be bright and beautiful, but we've seen nothing but rain and cold."

Rebecca's hand tightened on his arm, and she delivered another set of great chest-wracking coughs. Jared looked at her, and her cheeks were flushed, her eyes wide. "Are you certain you are well, Miss Turner?" He'd heard many coughs in his time, but hers sounded very odd. Almost . . . well, he hated to so much as think it, but her coughing almost sounded *fake*.

"Yes," she said, her voice raspy. "I'm quite well. Alicia, were you not recently mentioning to me that you adored the cooler weather in the autumn?"

Alicia screwed up her mouth in thought. "I do not believe—"

"Good heavens, look at the clouds over there," Rebecca exclaimed. "It looks like rain."

"It has not ceased to look like dratted rain for months. Summer has forgotten that it's meant to be warmer and sunny." Alicia stopped, pulling Rebecca toward her and pressing her palms to either side of her face. Looking deep into her eyes, she stared hard. "Are you well?"

Jared stepped back to give them space as Rebecca whispered something frantically to her cousin.

The women both turned to him in unison with a uniform smile, and he felt, in that moment, that he must be the object of a joke.

"Of course, I do love autumn, with the golden trees and . . ." Miss Langley trailed off, evidently unable to think of another reason for her love of the season. Something was most certainly bubbling beneath the surface of Rebecca and Miss Langley's conversation at present, and Jared was uncertain he wanted to learn what it was.

They reached the Langleys' street, and Miss Langley pulled to a stop, her lips parting in surprise. "Oh, dear."

"What is it?" Rebecca asked, looking from Miss Langley to the black carriage parked on the road outside her door.

"My uncle is here." She left before she could say another word, all but running down the walking path and up the steps to her house.

Rebecca remained by Jared's side, seemingly as stunned as he was. "I did not think she cared for her uncle's opinion."

"I beg your pardon?" Jared asked.

Rebecca faced him, her eyes widening. "I'd forgotten . . . it is only that she mentioned earlier that she cared not for her uncle's . . . well, I suppose that is private." Her cheeks blushed a very becoming shade of pink, and she ducked her head.

Jared wanted to reach forward and tip her chin up so he could better see her eyes, but he imagined such an intimate gesture would not be welcome.

She obliged him anyway, smiling briefly. "I must go after her. Good day, Mr. Cooper."

Rebecca bobbed a quick curtsy before hurrying after her cousin, albeit at a slower pace, and he watched her go.

CHAPTER SIXTEEN

J ared wrapped his freshly pressed cravat around his neck and tied it into a semblance of a knot. He'd left a very anxious Miss Langley with a calming Rebecca at the front door of the Langleys' townhouse earlier that day, but oddly enough, that was not what had plagued his mind for the last few hours. No, what had bothered Jared was the odd behavior exhibited by Rebecca. He'd known the woman for less than a month now, so he was the first to admit that their relationship had not been long enough for him to know her well, but he felt the opposite to be the case. He'd spent a great deal of time with her over the previous few weeks, and it might be presumptuous of him, but he'd come to count her as a friend.

Her behavior during the walk was that of a distressed woman, and while he'd been glad to see Miss Langley, he was more concerned with Rebecca's apparent discomfort. The coughing fits, for one. The harried, whispered conversation. Stopping her cousin from speaking her thoughts. It was all very odd. *Very* unlike the Rebecca he'd come to know.

To say nothing of the fact that Alicia had brazenly flirted

with Henry Gastrell in front of Jared. What exactly did *that* mean?

Mother stepped into his room, her hair done up tastefully, simple pearls hanging from her earlobes. "I must admit I'm looking forward to the concert."

"As am I," Jared said.

"You have become rather social in the last few weeks." She hesitated before continuing. "Is there a particular woman you have your eye on?"

"Perhaps," he said, focusing on his cravat through the tall looking glass.

Mother seated herself on the edge of his bed. "Do I know her?"

He kept silent. While he'd been bettering his relationship with Miss Langley and coming to know her through her letters, it was certainly too soon to claim an attachment.

"Will you not say?" Mother pressed. "I suppose that is only fair."

"I would not wish to give you any false sense of hope, Mother. When I have something to report, then I will most certainly share it with you."

"Are not your aspirations something to report?"

"My aspirations," he said, chuckling, "mean nothing if the young lady does not wish her name to be linked with mine."

Which, when he boiled it down to the dregs of his concerns, was where his truest worry lay. Miss Langley had made a connection with him privately, but he'd seen the way she openly flirted with Mr. Gastrell at Queen's Square, and the way she clung to the man, giggling as they bent their heads together before Jared had reached their walking party. While shocking, it'd also proven that Alicia was not as focused in her affections for him as he was for her. It had been eye-opening and a blow to his pride.

After professing his love to Evelyn Trainor two years before and subsequently being rejected, opening himself and his heart again hadn't been easy. What if it was all for naught, if he was preparing himself for another rejection, for more hurt? Was it worth continuing down this path?

A folded sheet of paper lay on the table containing his response to her most recent letter. He planned to give it to Rebecca at the concert that evening, and in it was the question he'd intended to ask earlier that day when Miss Langley had been overcome by her uncle's presence and fled inside so quickly.

"You will find love and happiness one day, my son," his mother said, drawing his attention away from the letter. He had become careless, leaving it out for anyone to find, and he needed to hide it before Mother noticed it and inquired about its purpose.

He yanked at his cravat, pulling it from his neck and smoothing it out before attempting to tie it once more. He carefully avoided his mother's face in the reflection. Love and happiness, she had said. He couldn't help the wry smile twisting his lips. "Are the two synonymous?"

"In my experience, they have been. I believe that to be the case for your sister as well. You do not *need* love to be happy, Jared, but it will enhance your life. Of that, I do heartily believe."

"Then why is love so blasted hard to find?" He cringed at the use of his language, but his mother ignored it.

"Perhaps it seems so difficult to find because you have struggled with rejection. Miss Trainor was a lovely girl, but her refusal, as difficult as it was to endure, should not keep you from enjoying your future."

He smiled at his mother, for he knew she meant well, but the truth of her words hurt all the same. Evelyn's rejection *had* hurt, and he was afraid of hurting again. Miss Langley was easy to talk to—well, to *write* to—though, and he was comfortable building their relationship slowly. He would never wish to rush a woman out of mourning, especially for her father.

Mother crossed toward him and squeezed his forearm. "Keep your secrets, Jared. I don't wish to pry. But know that when you are ready, if you need someone to speak to, I am here to listen."

She left the room, and he had the oddest feeling that she meant to include more than his romantic leanings in her offer. But surely she did not already know what had occurred with the Hollingsfords in Derham. His sister, Julia, had promised not to say anything to their parents until he'd told them what occurred, and she would never break a promise.

Picking up the letter for Alicia, he tucked it into his coat pocket and patted it flat. He could tell Mother of his failings with the Hollingsfords and how his town subsequently dropped him, but first, he would tell Rebecca. He trusted her, and perhaps her reaction would prepare him for what lay ahead.

When Jared arrived at the Upper Rooms with his mother on his arm, he was pleased and relieved to spot Rebecca right away on the other side of the entrance hall.

"Look, there is Mrs. Turner," Mother said, leaning in. "Shall we go greet them?"

He could have kissed her. Affecting nonchalance, he shrugged softly. "Yes, I suppose we should."

Mother gave him a funny look, which he ignored. He led her through the groups of people toward the only woman in the room he had an interest in speaking to.

Jared analyzed Mrs. Turner's skin, satisfied to find the greenish tint replaced with a healthier glow. Her eyes were worn and tired, rimmed in purple shadow and evidence of fitful sleep, but she was improving.

"Mrs. Cooper, I have been meaning to ask your opinions on the menu we spoke of at the assemblies Tuesday."

"Oh, yes," Mother said, releasing Jared's arm and giving Mrs. Turner her full attention. The women had become fast friends and now bent their heads to the discussion of which soup was better paired with braised lamb, white or pea soup.

Rebecca stepped around the mothers, amusement curling her lips. "We must pay close attention, or we're bound to miss the beginning of the concert."

Jared nodded, his voice serious. "Agreed. Our mothers have become a couple of gabbing girls."

"I, for one, am gratified by the connection."

He stepped closer, lowering his voice as though he were imparting a secret. "As am I."

Rebecca tipped her chin back, grinning, and he smiled, looking down at her. Her green irises were magnified behind her spectacles, and he was struck by the beauty in them. Try as he might, he couldn't remove his gaze from her. The smile slid from her lips, and she swallowed noticeably.

His heart drummed a steady beat, increasing in rhythm as he considered Rebecca's countenance. He couldn't mistake the reaction he felt to her wit and companionship, and guilt weaved through him like the curling smoke from a snuffed candle. He shouldn't be feeling any of these things for a woman who was not Alicia, not when he'd pledged himself to her by continuing to write.

He suppressed the warmth in his chest and put it aside to examine later. Something about Rebecca gnawed at him. Something was different, and he couldn't tell exactly what it was. Her hair had not changed, and she wore the same gown he'd seen her in at least twice before. The same thin, wire-rimmed spectacles framed her long-lashed eyes, and she wore no rouge on her pink lips.

"You are staring, sir," she said, though he noticed that she had not made an effort to step back, either.

He tried to shake himself out of the odd trance he was in, but it was no use. Rebecca had enchanted him, and it was bothersome that he did not know why. The troubling thing was that he had a letter for the woman he felt honor-bound to in his pocket, but the only woman he cared to think about at present was standing before him right now.

———— ∞ ————

Rebecca felt stricken. Mr. Cooper regarded her like a confusing puzzle, and his proximity was intoxicating, his familiar scent embracing her in warmth. She'd been worried that he would have accusations to lay at her feet after the debacle at the park earlier with Alicia misremembering her supposed favorite season, but that seemed far from his mind now.

"Have you brought a letter?" she asked, steering her thoughts back to the woman who held his affection.

He nodded, slipping his hand in his pocket. His gaze swept over her. "You brought no reticule this evening?"

Rebecca could have kicked herself. She hadn't even worn a gown with pockets. "Drat."

"It is no matter." He flashed a smile and drew his hand from his pocket, patting the square where the letter remained. "I actually wanted to ask your opinion on something."

"Mine?" She couldn't help the surprise in her tone. Mr. Cooper didn't seem the least bothered that he would be unable to pass her a letter this evening.

His eyebrows knit. "You needn't sound surprised. I've often begged for your opinion."

That was true. Far more than he realized, in fact, if one was to count the letters.

"Do you think it is wiser to find a good seat near the front of the music hall or choose a safe seat in the back in the event that the soprano is not quite as trained as they've advertised?"

"The back."

Mr. Cooper nodded slowly. "Why is that?"

Rebecca did her utmost to keep a straight face. "In the event that the soprano sounds more like my neighbor from Welton, it will be easier to hide our shock and discomfort from the back. But of course, there will be no escaping the sound, no matter how far away one sits."

"Very astute observation, Miss Turner. I shall take your advice into consideration when choosing my seat."

Mama came to stand beside Rebecca. "Did I hear you mention that we ought to choose our seats?"

Rebecca nodded, taking Mama's arm, and followed Mr. Cooper and his mother into the concert room. The Coopers chose seats and indicated the two empty chairs beside them, and Mama ushered Rebecca into the chair beside Mr. Cooper.

"Right in the middle," Rebecca said, nodding. "I approve."

He grinned. "I did think it was the safest choice. Would you like to know what I have been wondering?"

"I'm not sure, but I suppose you intend to tell me."

His smile widened, revealing his delicious dimple. "Do the smudges on your spectacles bother you, or are you so accustomed to them that you hardly notice them?"

Heat crawled up her neck and warmed her cheeks. The din in the room grew as the crowd filed in and took their seats, and Rebecca removed her glasses and tried to wipe the glass lenses on her skirt.

Mr. Cooper lifted his hand, hovering it over the spectacles she clutched in her fist before he flexed it and placed it back onto his lap. It was better that he hadn't touched her, but that didn't make her want it any less.

"I didn't mean to embarrass you," he whispered, pulling a handkerchief from his pocket and offering it to her.

"You didn't," she lied. She took the handkerchief and wiped her lenses clean. "But I suppose that answers your question, does it not?"

A smile broke out on his lips. "I suppose it does."

The evening progressed smoothly, the concert beginning with the lilting strains of the violins. Rebecca closed her eyes and listened to the music, letting the powerful sound of harmonizing instruments filter through her body and soothe her mind. Though her mother tolerated concerts, Rebecca had inherited her appreciation for music from her father. Their shared interest had extended to their shared discomfort over their neighbor's loud braying, and the transcendent voice now filling the room made Rebecca miss her father acutely. If only he would write back to her.

When the soprano's passionate voice ascended through the room, Mr. Cooper pressed his shoulder lightly against Rebecca's, and she smiled softly but kept her eyes closed.

He leaned over and whispered, "Is she much better than your neighbor from Welton?"

"Indeed," Rebecca said. "She sounds nothing like a dying pig."

Mr. Cooper snorted, and Rebecca's eyes flashed open to find some of the nearby women casting surreptitious glances their way. His softly shaking shoulders still pressed lightly against her arm, but she didn't want him to move away.

"Cease your mirth, Mr. Cooper. You are bound to have us thrown out."

"Trust me," he said, his low voice tickling her ear. A shiver swept down her arm. "I am doing my best."

As was she. Rebecca was struggling to remain unaffected by the handsome man who set her heart to racing. But try as she might, it was futile. He had a grip on her that was powerful, and despite the way she would never measure up to Alicia in beauty or the art of flirtation, and despite the fact that this man believed he was building a relationship with Alicia, Rebecca couldn't help it.

She was falling in love.

CHAPTER SEVENTEEN

When the concert had ended and the groups were gathered in the hall to discuss the beauty they had been witness to during the last two hours, Rebecca found herself waiting patiently beside a column against the wall for her mother to finish speaking to an old acquaintance of her father's.

She heard bits of the conversation, enough to confirm that Mama was explaining Father's purpose in France, and pressed her lips together in tight frustration.

Ought they continue to tell their friends that Father was selling wine and sending it back to English patrons when he had not sent so much as a letter in two months?

Mr. Cooper sidled up beside her, concern etching lines onto his brow. "You cannot cease thinking of your neighbor in Welton, I assume?"

That pulled a smile from the depths of Rebecca's worries, curving her lips softly. She clasped her hands lightly behind her back and leaned against the cool, marble wall. "The singer did a splendid job of removing my old neighbor and all sounds of dying pigs from my mind completely."

"I applaud her."

"What do you applaud?" Georgiana asked, appearing just before them and startling Rebecca. Her eyebrows lifted, and Rebecca thought for a brief moment that the girl had yet to learn all of her manners.

"Miss Turner was merely relaying her appreciation for the music."

"Oh yes, it was magnificent," Georgiana said. A small smile fell over her petite lips. "Though a little too long."

Rebecca nodded but didn't agree. She felt it could have gone on twice as long.

Mrs. Gastrell approached them and took her daughter by the hand after relaying her greetings. "Come, dear. I have someone I'd like to introduce you to." She gave Rebecca an excited smile and lowered her voice. "He is a *viscount*."

"Where is Henry?"

Mrs. Gastrell pointed to the far side of the room. "Fetching Miss Morgan a drink." She leaned forward and whispered. "She is an *heiress*."

Rebecca located Henry as the Gastrell women took their leave for more elevated conversation and watched him deliver a cup into a young woman's hand. His roguish smile got under her skin, but she didn't know why it bothered her so greatly. Perhaps it was that he had flirted so obviously with Alicia earlier that day and seemed to have no loyalty. The man was a cad, and for Alicia's sake, Rebecca certainly hoped he wasn't on his way to becoming a rake. Her cousin's affections were evidently not settled on any one man, but regardless, she did not want Alicia to be hurt.

"Care to explain the look of utter contempt you are wearing?" Mr. Cooper asked, obviously amused.

Rebecca tore her gaze from the rake-in-training and tried to push him from her mind. "Just worrying about things that I should leave alone. It is a fault of mine." She straightened. "Speaking of things that worry me, I don't suppose you've heard from your father's cousin in Paris yet?"

Mr. Cooper's amusement fled. He leaned against the wall beside her, shaking his head. "I wouldn't expect to hear back from him for a few more days at least. More likely another week, perhaps longer."

Rebecca's shoulders slumped. "I do know that, but I was hoping you'd gotten a letter earlier than usual."

"Forgive the indelicacy of my question, but you are not having trouble obtaining the medicine I've prescribed for your mother, are you?"

"No," she said quickly. She watched her mother bid the man farewell and move over to speak to Mrs. Cooper once again. "You needn't fear on that score. We have sufficient funds for our needs."

He lifted an eyebrow, and shame flooded her belly. If she truly had sufficient funds, she would not need to pay Mr. Cooper for his services by acting as a post carrier. In truth, she could likely scrape enough together to pay him properly, but then she would not be able to eat. It really was such a bother, paying for food, but it was equally a necessity.

"I vow to bring you word the moment I hear anything," he said, his voice low and promising. He held her gaze, and despite the minor smudge in the edge of her left eyeglass, she believed his rapt attention to be the most handsome sight she'd ever beheld.

"I know you will," she said softly. "I trust you."

He straightened, clearing his throat. "Perhaps more than you ought."

"What do you mean?"

His lips twisted into a rueful smile, void of warmth. "I have done something I'm not proud of, and I'm certain I don't deserve your explicit trust, Rebecca."

She stilled. Had he realized he'd used her Christian name? He didn't appear affected in the least, though she felt as though she'd been wrapped in a warm blanket and set before a roaring fire. Her cheeks bloomed with heat, and she swallowed past a suddenly dry throat. It was all so much to absorb, his heady scent, his proximity, his low voice saying her name.

"I can see that I've distressed you—"

"No, I was only considering the suitability of asking you to explain yourself."

He tilted his face toward her. "I . . . I have made mistakes, that is all."

She nodded. If he wanted to speak no further on the subject, that was his prerogative. "I'm sorry I cannot take the letter from you now. I've nowhere to hide it."

She could slip it into her bodice or tuck it into her stays, but not without someone in the room noticing her attempt to conceal it, certainly.

"Perhaps I shall have to walk you home then, Miss Turner."

Blast. He'd gone back to using her surname. She'd really hoped that wouldn't be the case. Though the fact that this man had just declared his need to walk her home so that she could better transport a letter to Alicia was glaringly present in her mind. She would do better to be called Miss Turner by a man who didn't care for her in equal measure.

"That would be lovely, Mr. Cooper."

They collected their mothers and their coats and found themselves outside in the rain a short while later.

Mr. Cooper opened his umbrella. "Perhaps I ought to hire a bath chair for you, Mother."

Mrs. Cooper shook her head, drawing her arm through

Mama's to better fit under her umbrella. They shared a conspiratorial smile, and Mrs. Cooper looked back to her son. "Offer Miss Turner use of your umbrella, Jared. Do not leave her standing out in the rain."

Spots of color bloomed on his cheeks, and he set to holding his umbrella over Rebecca's head. The mothers walked ahead of them, sharing the coverage of the Turners' bent umbrella, and Rebecca swallowed her pride, stepping closer to Mr. Cooper to be protected from the rain. He offered her use of his arm, and she took it, allowing him to draw her close against his side.

Rain fell harder around them, wetting Rebecca's skirt and misting her spectacles. She wiped at them, blurring her vision but making it easier to see where she was walking. Water soaked through her thin shoes, squelching between her toes.

"I think our mothers have become good friends," Mr. Cooper said, amused.

"It is good for my mama. She has not been used to coming out with me at all since arriving in Bath, but lately, it seems as though I cannot keep her home."

"Ah, yes. Your Aunt Langley has been acting as your chaperone?"

"More often than not, yes. Generally, Mama was too tired by the evening to fathom a night out at a ball or card party." She tried to look up at him, but the darkness made it difficult to see, and the black umbrella cast shadows on his handsome face. "We have you to thank for her improvements."

"She has a fair distance to go yet before she will feel herself once again," he cautioned. "But I'm optimistic. Her progress thus far has been incredible. Did you know she credits some of her healing to your improved happiness?"

"No, but I wonder at the validity of that." She sobered.

"How many more recipes for medicine do you think she will need?"

"She might very well need to consume some sort of medication containing iron for the rest of her life. This green sickness is manageable when cared for closely, but the trick is keeping up a healthy regimen as I've outlined for her."

The rest of her life? The words sliced through the rainy, dreary evening and stopped Rebecca in her tracks. She yanked her hand free of Mr. Cooper's arm.

He hurried back to her, stunned.

"She will need regular visits from the doctor *forever?*" Rebecca asked. She couldn't fathom how much that would cost them. Surely Mr. Cooper would not need Rebecca to pass letters to Alicia forever. After learning of Alicia's disinterest in the man, Rebecca wasn't sure she could even stomach writing another letter.

"Yes, it would be good to maintain medical care. Your mother will need the recipe for her medication managed, though I imagine it will reach a point where we will not change the ingredients or amounts any longer. Then she will be able to go a long while between visits."

That was somewhat comforting. Mr. Cooper offered his arm again, and Rebecca took it, allowing him to lead her home. She would have to hope that Father's business would be sorted, and he would be returned by the time Alicia was finished with her mourning. Alicia's uncle had been in the drawing room when they'd returned from their walk earlier that day, and his stiff, clipped behaviors were not promising of an early end to Alicia's social isolation. Which was only good for Rebecca, of course.

Mr. Cooper stopped on the walking path and held Rebecca's arm until she was stalled beneath his umbrella beside him. His eyebrows pulled together, and a stormy expression glittered in his eyes, but she could hardly make out the rest of his features. The night was dark, and the lack of streetlamps paired with the rain made her feel as though they were completely alone. Their mothers had undoubtedly hurried home, for they were nowhere to be seen.

"Your mother and her health are important to me, Rebecca. I would never forgo offering the help she needs, regardless of payment." He seemed to hesitate, his chest rising and falling rapidly, brushing against her coat with every inhale. "Of course it is important to be paid for my services—I would not be able to afford to live otherwise—but you must know that payment is the least of my concerns. I made the mistake once of letting unimportant things get in the way of offering medical care, and it cost a young boy his life. I'm not certain if I could have saved him had I rushed to his house instead of allowing the family to depend on another physician, but I ought to have tried. I ought to have put aside my pride and healed in the way that God has blessed me to."

"Surely if they had another physician—"

"They did not. He never arrived." Mr. Cooper ran an agitated hand over his face. It was as if the dam had broken, his words spilling from his mouth like a rush of water. "He had been poaching people from my care for months, and when someone knocked at my door to inform me of a young boy's fever, they also told me that this other man, Dr. Gould, had been sent for by the family. I knew the family preferred him for a number of reasons, the least of which was their connection to him and the way they'd sung his praises around Derham, telling all who would listen that Dr. Gould was the superior choice, and I was better left to *assist* the man."

"How awful." Rebecca's heart reached out to him, to the pain he must have felt being so rejected and humiliated.

"It felt awful. I didn't wish to help them. But I should have gone, at least to ensure that Dr. Gould had seen to the boy." He paused, drawing in a ragged breath. "I didn't know Dr. Gould had gone to London that morning, and by the time I was sent for again, it was too late."

He sighed, his shoulders bending forward, and Rebecca wondered if he had unloaded a long-held burden. The way he had hidden his secret could not have been easy for him, nor the guilt he must have felt. She did not want to belittle his trial, but he needed to remove the shame and guilt from his heart if he wanted to heal.

Rebecca swallowed, praying she would say the right thing to put his mind and heart at rest. "We all make mistakes."

"But mine cost a boy his life."

"You cannot know that," she said gently. She couldn't understand the intricacies of medicine or healing, but she knew Mr. Cooper well enough to understand that he would never intentionally hurt a soul. The pain in his eyes reached out and touched her heart, and sorrow filled her for the boy and his family, and for Mr. Cooper's grief. "None of us can change the past, but we can use our faults to grow from and to better ourselves. You needn't pay penance for the rest of your life, either. You mentioned that God has blessed you to be a healer. Do you not think He wants you to use your talents and skills to help others? He doesn't wish for you to destroy yourself with guilt."

"How can you know that so unconditionally?"

"Because I know He is a loving God. Of course He wants you to forgive yourself, and likely to apologize to the family for your mistakes, but He loves you, Mr. Cooper. He doesn't wish for you to suffer."

He smiled down at her. "And my mother? What will she think of my grievous behavior?"

Rebecca sucked in a quick breath. "She does not know?"

He shook his head. "She goes to Derham in under a fort-night to see to my sister and her new babe, as I've told you." He ran his free hand through his hair. "It wasn't just the family. The people in town blamed me as much as I blamed myself. They stopped calling on me to tend to illnesses and injuries, and I'm certain my mother won't be able to step more than five feet into Derham before hearing of my faults."

"She needs to hear this from you, first."

He was silent, and the rain roared around them, hitting the umbrella like a thousand tiny pellets. "I know, but it is hard."

Nodding, Rebecca placed both of her hands on his forearm and squeezed. "It will be very hard, but it is important. You will feel better for having relieved yourself of the burden of this secret, and your mother will be glad to hear this from you instead of the first gossiping old woman who crosses her path. Your mother loves you, and she knows your heart, Mr. Cooper. You needn't be afraid."

"You are correct, of course." He spoke so quietly she almost didn't hear him, but she could easily see the soft smile curving his mouth. "As always, you have said the perfect thing to put me at ease."

His praise buoyed her, but just as quickly as her spirits lifted, she crashed to the earth again. It was all right and good for her to preach to him the merits of being a good Christian, of the endless love of God, but what worth did her advice hold when she was herself making a wrong choice every day that she pretended to be Alicia in her letters, pretended to deliver his words to someone else but instead read them herself? She had been dishonest over and over again, and now lectured him on the importance of honesty? Rebecca stepped away from him, disgusted with herself.

She needed this to end tonight. She would have to find another way to pay him. If he would, indeed, choose to continue seeing to her mother's health after learning of Rebecca's deceit. She would sell the brooch, or swim to France and collect her father herself if she must.

"Come back under the umbrella."

Rebecca shook her head, sending droplets through the pouring rain. "I must confess something to you first."

"Can you do so while we walk? Our mothers are likely growing concerned by now."

She couldn't be near him again or she would lose her nerve. Stepping back, she shook her head again. "I need to say this now. I cannot take your letters any longer."

He looked up, his eyebrows raised. "Has Alicia said something?"

"No, Alicia has said nothing. That is the problem, Mr. Cooper. It has been me the entire time. You've been corresponding with me."

Shock hung his mouth open. "I do not understand . . ."

"You do, but you likely don't wish to. My cousin despises correspondence. She didn't wish to write. She did write that first letter, but when you continued to correspond . . . well, I was so worried about being able to afford care for my mother that when Alicia suggested I write to you instead . . ." She shook her head. She was making an utter mash of things. "The reasons matter little now. Please know that I am sorry."

CHAPTER EIGHTEEN

Jared stood in the rain, heedless of the water soaking through his clothing and running down the back of his neck. His umbrella had fallen limp at his side, forgotten, and he could not seem to tear his gaze away from the drenched, lying minx staring at him through wide, blurry eyes. How could she even see him through her water-spotted spectacles?

He shook the thought. He should be less concerned with her ability to see and more wary of the shocking explosion she had just hit him with.

"When did you plan to tell me?" he pressed.

Determination seemed to set her brow. "I planned to tell you, but I hadn't gone so far as to choose when to do so. I'd hoped that when Alicia put off her mourning again we could tell you together, and it would all be a good joke." The power in her words trailed off as though she was not convinced of what she said. She closed her eyes, shaking her head. "Though in reality, a small part of me had hoped you would never learn of my duplicity."

"I am such a fool," he said to himself. "Come, we must get you home."

He was tempted to leave her in the street and storm away, to show her how angry and hurt he was, but he couldn't bring himself to abandon her, not in the evening and certainly not in this weather.

"You are not a fool," she argued. "Alicia and I have very similar handwriting. It was that feature which gave her the idea."

He couldn't believe she was continuing to speak to him, attempting to explain herself. He had to be a gentleman and make sure she arrived home safely, but he needn't socialize with her as he did so. He was so utterly mortified that he had been an object of some game. He'd spent all that time imagining he'd been writing to Alicia, but it had been a ploy.

"I *am* a fool," he said bitterly, unable to help himself. "I believed we had something of an alliance, that we had an equal partnership, each of us with something to help the other. I thought . . ." He stopped and threw his hands out to the side, the swinging umbrella sending water toward the street. "I thought you were my friend. Now I'm humiliated, without a friend, and without a romantic liaison."

"But when it began, Alicia expressed—"

"Please, no more explanations." He couldn't listen to another word. It hardly mattered now. His vision was clouded in anger, and he only wanted to be alone.

Rebecca remained blessedly silent, and Jared was grateful when they turned onto her street and would soon be parted. The front door was cracked open and warm light spilled onto the wet paving stones at their feet. Jared clenched and unclenched his jaw, completely furious with himself for falling victim to such deceit.

Rebecca pushed the door open to reveal their mothers,

huddled together in the entryway beside a flickering lamp on the table near the door, their smiles wide. They glanced between Jared and Rebecca expectantly, and he flushed, angry and embarrassed to arrive in this manner. He was certain his anger was rolling off him in hot, flammable waves.

"If you two are finished with your scheming, we should be going," he said to his mother, trying to maintain an even tone. The mood immediately shifted between the women from anticipation to apprehension, and Jared knew a small moment of guilt for being the cause. But, no. Surely they should know that a match between himself and Rebecca was impossible. She was not interested in him as a suitor, which had been made painfully obvious to him by her willing participation in the ruse to press him toward Alicia.

"Goodnight," Jared said, bowing to Mrs. Turner. He wasn't sure how he was going to continue to see to her health when he did not wish to ever see Rebecca again, but he would find a way to manage it. As he'd said earlier, he would never again allow his pride to come in the way of seeing to his patients' needs.

Mother slipped her arm around his and took shelter beneath his umbrella as they started toward home. She waited until they'd crossed the street to speak. "I will not pretend I didn't notice the discomfort between you and Miss Turner. You did not set out from the concert in that state."

"Are you planning to ask me a question, Mother, or are you merely relaying the facts of the evening?"

She nudged him softly with her elbow. "I was giving you the opportunity to talk, Jared. I do not wish to pry into your affairs, but I must admit that I am saddened by this."

"By this? You know not what occurred."

They made it to their home, and Jared helped his mother inside, removing her sodden coat and giving it to their manservant. Jared shed his wet things with jerky, irritated motions, completely aware of Mother's watchful eye on him.

When the servant left, taking with him their wet coats, gloves, and hats, Mother cleared her throat. "I've enjoyed my conversations with the Turner women, and while it is clear that something grievous has occurred between you and Miss Turner, you must allow me to tell you that I extended them an invitation to dinner in a couple of days."

Jared scoffed. "You did not."

"Was I meant to predict that you would become angry with Miss Turner in the time it took you to walk her home from the concert? You both seemed positively chummy all evening."

"It was an illusion," he said bitterly. An illusion even to him.

"But my invitation to dine was not, and I refuse to redact it."

"Then you must excuse my absence to your guests, for I refuse to be there."

He could tell he'd shocked her. Closing his eyes, Jared pressed his fingers to them and rubbed along his brow. He'd been shocked himself this evening and needed time to soak in the full meaning of the events which had transpired. Drawing in a sustaining breath, he did his best to smile, though he was certain it looked more like a grimace. "I will see you at breakfast tomorrow. Goodnight, Mother."

She said nothing, surprise lifting her eyebrows and parting her lips. Jared leaned forward to kiss her cheek before beating a tired retreat.

The same fatiguing, deflating feelings of rejection and remorse flooded him that he'd experienced when he'd been denied by Evelyn Trainor two years before, and he trudged to his bedchamber as though he'd been filled with stone. Why could he not find a woman to love who would return his feelings in full? Evelyn Trainor's response to his proposal had been that she simply did not love him, and now this? Dejection bent his shoulders, and he could only conjure Miss Langley's image in his mind with disdain.

When he'd seen Miss Langley at the park earlier, her open flirtatious banter with Mr. Gastrell only seemed to give Jared pause. That burst of attraction he felt whenever he saw her was missing, and he hadn't understood why. Hurt at her disloyalty, perhaps? But even that hadn't rung true in his soul, and he'd done his best to explain both of those things away. Something had failed to spark within him, and now he questioned everything.

As far as pursuing Miss Langley, he was through. She was party to the deception. If Rebecca was to be believed—which was debatable at present—then the whole scheme had not only had Alicia's blessing, it had been her idea.

What an utter sham.

The odd thing was that though Miss Langley was the woman to whom he'd given his affection—or so he thought—when he considered his loss, it was not the blonde angel's image who surged pain through his heart, it was Rebecca's.

CHAPTER NINETEEN

Rebecca had ruined everything, but she had simultaneously removed the burden of deception, and she would be lying if she pretended to be sorry for that. It was a blessed relief to know that she no longer had to lie to a man she had developed feelings for, even if it meant pushing him away.

Adjusting her bonnet over her plainly arranged hair, Rebecca clutched the fabric-wrapped emerald brooch her mother had given her on her eighteenth birthday and opened the shop door. She should have done this weeks ago to pay outright for her mother's care and ease some of her own worries but hadn't been able to bear the thought of parting with the only family heirloom she had—the one her mother had specifically asked her not to sell.

Now, she had no choice.

"Can I help you?" the man asked from behind the counter, a set of narrow, half-moon spectacles resting on the bridge of his nose.

"I would like to sell this brooch," Rebecca said, placing the heavy golden-inlaid piece on the glass counter with a thunk.

She unwrapped the linen covering it and slid it toward the jeweler, and he picked it up, holding it by the fabric.

"It's lovely," he said quietly, retrieving a magnifying glass from a nearby shelf and holding the jewelry up to the light. "How did you come by it?"

Rebecca swallowed against a dry throat. "It was given to my grandmother's mother by her husband."

He nodded as though he'd expected its origin to be decades in the past. "I can give you a fair price."

That was all she'd wanted. They discussed the parameters of the sale and arranged the paperwork to Rebecca's satisfaction, but when it came time for money to change hands, she balked.

Holding the brooch in both of her hands, she pressed it to her heart and shut her eyes. She was certain she looked a fool, but she cared very little for the jeweler's opinion, be it poor or otherwise. Sending up an apology to her angel grandmother, she placed the brooch back on the counter and stepped away from it. Watching him count her pound notes was a slight balm on her bruised feelings, and she felt comfort in the fact that she would now be able to pay Mr. Cooper in full.

"What do you plan to do with it?" she asked, indicating the brooch with a flick of her head. "If I were to return in a few weeks with the exact amount you've paid, would you be willing to sell it back to me?"

His chin jutted forward in thought, his finger stroking the largest emerald. "I could be persuaded to hold on to it for a fortnight or so before displaying it on my shelves, if you were able to present the full amount plus an additional thirty-five percent."

Thirty-five percent? That was an outrageous sum. She gave him a tight nod. "Very well. I thank you."

Rebecca folded the thick stack of pound notes and stuffed

them into her reticule. If she was to save as much of this money as she could, and father miraculously sent what he'd promised, she just *might* be able to come up with the money to pay the jeweler the amount he'd given her. But the extra thirty-five percent? That was simply impossible.

It was a problem of her own making, however, and she accepted that. Pushing open her broken, bent umbrella, Rebecca lifted it above her head and let herself into the rain. She would only make one stop at the bookstore to retrieve a new novel for Mama, and then she would go home. She should have brought her mother's maid with her on these errands, but Mullens was needed at home, and truly, what were the chances she'd see anyone she knew? With the current downpour, she was certain everyone of her acquaintance was at home, waiting out the storm.

A bell rang overhead to indicate her entrance into the bookstore, and Rebecca went straight for the gothic novels, her mother's favorite. She turned the corner sharply to find Henry standing beside a petite brunette who looked familiar, his hand subtly playing with the fabric of her skirt. Miss Morgan, the heiress from the concert, if Rebecca was not mistaken.

Henry caught her gaze and dropped his hand to his side, smoothly resting his other fist against his waist. "Good day, Miss Turner. Are we obstructing your search?"

They were standing before the exact section of novels she hoped to look through. "You are, but I am perfectly content to wait my turn."

"I think I'm finished," Miss Morgan said to Henry, flashing him a coy smile. She held *The Mysteries of Udolpho* in her hands, and Rebecca wondered if this sweet young woman knew exactly what she was getting herself into with that book. Hopefully she had a healthy tolerance for frightening stories.

"My mama is waiting for me," Miss Morgan said sweetly.

Henry offered her his elbow. "Please, allow me."

The women exchanged swift curtsies before Henry led Miss Morgan to the counter to purchase the book, after which they met an older woman near the door. The bell rang to signal their exit, and Rebecca moved toward the bookshelves, doing her best to shake the odd sense of discomfort flitting through her. Surely Mrs. Morgan approved of the book her daughter had purchased. Though if she approved of her daughter hiding in the back of a bookshop with a man who was doing his best to earn the title of cad, then perhaps she was not paying close enough attention.

The bell rang again, and a man approached the counter, asking the clerk for a specific text in his quiet, deep voice. Rebecca searched the shelves for a volume her mother had not yet read as the man's voice grew in volume, and she froze. She would know Mr. Cooper's steady tone anywhere, and the sound of it now, when she hadn't expected it, was like a knife to the gut.

Looking over her shoulder, she caught sight of Mr. Cooper speaking to the bookshop owner, his hands casually slung behind him as he spoke. "I would not be opposed to any recent medical texts, of course, but I'm particularly interested in the *Edinburgh Medical and Surgical Journal*."

"I will write to my man and see what I can do."

"Thank you, sir."

Mr. Cooper looked directly behind him as though he could feel the weight of her gaze, and Rebecca ducked behind the bookcase of gothic novels, pressing her back flush against the wall. She could see her chest rising and falling rapidly and hoped the motion would not give her hiding place away. Though the term was used loosely, for there was nowhere to truly hide in this tiny shop. She wished she could slide between the floorboards and disappear.

"Miss Turner," Mr. Cooper said, his voice resigned.

She straightened. "Good day," she croaked.

His smile was anything but good. It looked pained. "I trust you are well, that your mother is in good health."

"She is, yes."

He nodded. She could see he was about to leave, and she did not blame him. It had been within his rights as a wronged man to give her the cut direct. That he had approached her at all was proof of his good character.

She spoke quickly, lowering her voice so as not to be overheard. "I intend to pay you for the services you've rendered my mother."

He waved a hand through the air but would not look at her face.

"I plan to, Mr. Cooper, and I will."

He faced her, lowering his voice. "Do you not think it is best to leave our dealings in the past?"

"I shall endeavor to remain away from you, but I will pay you what I owe."

His blue eyes flashed. "Did you not do that already when you acted as a courier?"

His words stung, but she kept her chin up. "I believe my deceit voided those transactions."

A muscle jumped in his jaw, his eyes glittering in anger. "I did those visits for your mother, and I would have done so whether or not you could afford to pay me. As you well know, I could not let things go without seeing to her health, and I do not regret the care I rendered her. Keep your shillings, Rebecca. I do not want them."

He may as well have struck her, for his words did the same damage as a fist. She swallowed, nodding in acceptance. "Be that as it may," she said, proud of the strength in her voice. "I intend to pay you, and I shall."

Mr. Cooper scoffed lightly, shaking his head. "You do not give up, do you?"

"I wasn't raised to quit when things grew difficult, no."

"But were you raised to graciously accept defeat?"

"I was raised to have integrity."

Mr. Cooper opened his mouth but seemed to think better of it, and he turned away from her, fleeing the building into the rain without another word. It had been his intention, she assumed, to make a comment on her lack of integrity the past month, and she could not fault him for such anger.

But she still planned to pay him.

Rebecca had one last letter to write.

CHAPTER TWENTY

Rebecca took her mother's hand and led her up the stairs of the Langleys' fashionable townhouse in the early afternoon. A strong male voice came from the drawing room, warning them of the presence of Mr. Langley, Aunt Langley's brother-in-law, before the Turner women entered the room.

"Perhaps he does not intend to stay long," Rebecca whispered, hovering in the corridor.

Mama shot her a mildly rebuking expression. "He is perfectly amiable, if a bit stuffy."

Rebecca tried to suppress her snort, and the sound sounded more like a cough. "Perfectly amiable to control your sister-in-law and nieces? I do not understand why he has come to Bath at all."

Mama lowered her voice. "He came to Bath for the waters, did I not tell you this? He's been suffering with headaches for some weeks now with very little reprieve."

Rebecca hadn't been told this at all. "I knew he had a headache yesterday, but I was unaware that it was so recurring."

Mama placed a hand on Rebecca's arm. "I understand it can be difficult but show a little Christian charity and put up with the man politely." She lowered her voice and leaned closer. "And all the while thank the Lord that He saw fit to make certain Arthur is not *your* uncle."

Mama pushed the door open, and Rebecca followed her inside, suppressing her grin. Aunt Langley rose from the sofa to greet them. Mr. Langley reclined on a wingback chair near the fire, opposite the sofa, and Alicia was perched on the piano bench.

"Good afternoon, Sister." Aunt Langley wore a harried expression, her eyes too wide and her smile too forced. Taking Mama's hands, she pulled her toward the sofa to sit beside her.

Rebecca dipped a curtsy to Aunt Langley and Mr. Langley before she crossed the room to sit beside Alicia at the pianoforte.

"You wouldn't believe the crush at the Pump Room this morning," Mr. Langley said. "One would think that all this dreary weather would force people to remain at home and protect themselves from the cold."

"The weather has done little to slow Bath's social calendar, from what I have seen," Mama said.

"Hmm." Mr. Langley pulled an eyeglass from his pocket and brought it up to his eye, sweeping his gaze over Mama. "I did not think you were well enough to partake heavily of Bath's social calendar. Indeed, are you recovering well? You do not appear very different from the time I saw you last. When was that? Just six months ago or so, I believe."

Mama's cheeks suffused with color, and irritation swooped upon Rebecca like a diving dove. Perhaps Mama was heeding her own advice and praying right now, grateful Mr. Langley was not *her* brother-in-law.

Alicia snatched Rebecca's forearm, squeezing softly. "Do not say anything to anger him," she whispered.

She hadn't planned on it, but Alicia's plea rankled, nonetheless. "Whyever not? He certainly is not acting the part of a gentleman."

Alicia spoke through her teeth. "But he only just threatened to extend our mourning again, and I simply *cannot* allow that to happen."

"So I must remain quiet while he insults my mother?"

Alicia squeezed harder. "Please bite your tongue. For me."

"What earthly reason could he possibly have for lengthening your mourning again?"

"He claims that his brother deserves better than for us to cast off our black and return to life as though nothing has happened. I do not know what his aim is beyond flexing his control, but I refuse to lose the comforts I've grown accustomed to. Until I can marry, we must abide by his strictures."

"That is vastly unfair."

"It is not unfair," Alicia said with feeling. "It is *barbaric*. That does not make it any less real."

"Your mother is putting up with this?"

"She must. She does not wish to lose our benefactor, either."

Disgust rolled through Rebecca. She did not know if she was more disturbed by Mr. Langley's need to control his nieces and sister-in-law or perturbed that her family members were submitting to the schemes of a madman.

"Tell me something interesting," Alicia begged. "I must be diverted before I fall into a total fit of despair."

Rebecca swallowed the inclination to reveal what had occurred with Mr. Cooper. She was certain it would be an interesting tidbit to her cousin, but it hurt to think about, and she wanted to guard it close to her heart.

"Alicia," Aunt Langley called, saving Rebecca from being persuaded to reveal too much about herself. "Do play us something nice. Perhaps a duet?"

"Of course, Mother."

Alicia retrieved her music from a nearby bureau and thumbed through the pages until she found something that interested her. She spread it out on the pianoforte's music stand and Rebecca rested her reticule on the back of the instrument, then warmed up her fingers on the cool keys.

"Has Mr. Cooper written anything romantic yet?" Alicia asked softly, placing her fingers on the starting position.

They dove into the song together. It wasn't one Rebecca knew well, but she could hold her own. She cleared her throat. "No."

Alicia frowned. "Have you tried to steer him in a romantic direction?"

"No."

Alicia huffed a frustrated breath. "Some men must be helped along, Rebecca. If you do not steer him, he may not understand where you would like him to go."

Rebecca found her fingers hitting the keys harder than she meant to. "Mr. Cooper is a ship now?"

"Yes. He is a ship in the ocean, and if left to his own devices, he may travel clear to . . . to Antigua. There is nothing wrong with Antigua if that is your destination, but let us pretend that love is found in India. You must steer Mr. Cooper toward India, or he shall find himself floating in the Caribbean."

"In this analogy, what is the Caribbean meant to represent?"

"Well, friendship, of course," Alicia said, as though it were obvious. "Friends are all fine and good, but not when one wants the man in question to become a husband instead."

"You forget one important thing, Alicia," Rebecca said, leaning closer to the sheet music to decipher a particularly difficult portion of the song.

"What is that?"

"I do not wish for Mr. Cooper to be my India. I am perfectly fine with him being my Antigua." If he was willing to even be so much as a friend, now that he'd learned of her deceit.

Alicia grumbled a frustrated sound, and Rebecca immediately felt silly. Of course Alicia knew that she didn't want Mr. Cooper to write romantic letters to *her*, the letters had always been meant for Alicia. Even if Alicia did not appear to want them.

"Of course, if you are implying that he should write letters of an Indian nature to *you*—"

"Good grief, Rebecca, enough talk about countries. I do not want Mr. Cooper for myself. I never have."

Rebecca ceased playing the music, shock sliding down her arms and freezing her fingers where they hovered above the keys. "What do you mean you *never* have?"

A loud thud sounded in the room, shaking the floor with a vibration, followed by a long, high-pitched scream. Mr. Langley lay on the center of the rug, his face pressed into the carpet, his body still and unmoving.

Aunt Langley continued to scream, standing over him, her hands flapping wildly as she seemed to struggle with words.

"Uncle!" Alicia yelled, running toward him and falling to her knees. She attempted to rouse him to no avail.

Rebecca scurried to the door, swinging it open. "Someone help us!" she shouted. A maid appeared in the corridor, her eyes wide. "Run and fetch Mr. Cooper at 42 Hart Street with great, *great* haste. Mr. Langley has fallen on the floor and will not be awakened."

The maid turned and fled down the corridor, and Rebecca crossed back to the man and knelt at Alicia's side. Mr. Langley's form lay unmoving except for the subtle rise and fall of his back.

"Look," Rebecca said, trying to calm her hysterical aunt. "He is breathing."

Aunt Langley fell to the sofa, dropping her forehead on her bent arm.

"Should we move him to the sofa?" Mama asked, perched on the edge of her seat and reaching for her sister.

Aunt Langley popped up, fanning reddened cheeks, and the harried look returned to her eyes. "We cannot lift him! He is enormous."

Mama remained calm, her voice soothing. "Perhaps I can fetch some footmen to do it for us?"

"Oh, yes. That would be good. You always know just what to do, dear sister," Aunt Langley said with feeling.

Mama left to fetch some servants, and Rebecca remained on the floor beside Alicia, hoping to offer her support in whatever way she could.

Alicia glanced up. "You must move to another chair, Mama. That is the only piece of furniture large enough for Uncle to lie on."

"You are quite right," Aunt Langley said feebly. "Though I'm finding it difficult to stand. The shock of this is quite a burden on my poor nerves."

"Allow me to help you," Rebecca said. She helped her aunt rise and steered her toward the wingback chair but met with resistance.

"I cannot sit *there*. That is where it happened."

"No, of course not." Rebecca directed her toward the other chair further from the fire. "I should have thought better."

"It is all well, dear," Aunt Langley said, her voice faint. "It is difficult to think logically when men are dying in one's drawing room."

"No one is dying, Mama," Alicia said, though the worried gaze she swung toward her uncle spoke to her concern on that very matter.

"What will we do, Alicia?" Aunt Langley asked, her chest heaving as her breathing grew more labored. "I cannot . . . if he is not to make it . . . oh, what will we *do*?"

"You always will have a home with us," Rebecca reminded her, hoping to put her at ease.

Aunt Langley's eyes widened, but she had the grace to nod appreciatively. It would be a step down for certain.

"At least we will not go to the poorhouse," she whispered, as though consoling herself.

Rebecca made a very great effort not to sigh. It was all well and good for her and her mother to live within meager means, but heaven forbid Aunt Langley was forced to give up her grand house and subscriptions to the assemblies.

Well, that was unfair. She had paid for Rebecca and Mama's subscriptions this year as a gift, and Rebecca had enjoyed them thus far, even if accepting them had rankled.

"We needn't worry yet, Mama. Besides," Alicia added hesitantly, "I could very well receive an offer of marriage soon."

Rebecca looked at her cousin sharply. Surely Alicia meant that it would not be hard for her to obtain a husband, and not that she already had a beau. She'd been mostly housebound for the last few months.

The door swung open to reveal Mama followed by two tall footmen. Alicia and Rebecca stepped back and watched them make quick work of picking Mr. Langley up and laying him on the sofa. His feet hung off the end, and his head lolled to the side, his ruddy cheeks pressing into the pillow.

The footmen left, and Mama posted herself to the side of

her sister's chair. Aunt Langley stared at her brother-in-law in mild panic, her mouth drooping down at the ends. "I do believe this is much worse than his position on the rug. At least there, we could not see his face."

A quick knock preceded the door opening once again, and Rebecca's heart felt as though it jumped a hedge when Mr. Cooper strode into the room. He immediately set toward the prone Mr. Langley, his gaze subtly passing over Rebecca and Alicia before landing upon Aunt Langley.

"Oh, Doctor! I am so glad you've come," Aunt Langley said. "And with such haste. You do us a great service."

"I was intercepted on my way out the door, as it was. What happened to the gentleman?"

"We do not know. One moment he was sitting right there"—she pointed to the empty wingback chair near the fire, wariness in her eyes as though she worried it was cursed—"and the next, he ceased talking and crumpled to the floor. It was all so sudden."

Mr. Cooper hummed a thinking sound and knelt before the sofa, feeling Mr. Langley's neck as the women watched on in anticipation.

Rebecca swallowed, her throat dry and sandy. She watched Mr. Cooper methodically check Mr. Langley with the care and precision of a man used to doing his job well. He continued to make small thinking sounds, and Rebecca appreciated the opportunity to watch him work, admiring the concentration in his blue eyes and the firm set of his handsome jaw. His hair was damp, made darker by the rain, and looked to be slightly mussed, as though he'd run his fingers through it more than once.

Mr. Cooper rose, the serious lines crossing his brow speaking to the severity of what he was about to explain. Alicia stepped toward her mother and took her hand, squeezing it in both of her own.

"This is Mr. Langley?" he asked.

"Yes, he is my brother-in-law."

Mr. Cooper nodded. "Mr. Langley appears to have suffered an apoplexy. Does he have a room in this house?"

Aunt Langley's eyes widened. "No, he has his own house, but I daresay he would prefer to remain here where he can be watched over." She turned to Alicia. "Fetch Abbot and direct her to have a room made up for your uncle."

"Any room cooler in temperature or with a window we might open near the bed would be best."

Alicia left straight away to see to her task. Mr. Cooper's gaze followed her out, then flicked to Rebecca. He looked as though he wanted to say something, but his eyes hardened, and he cleared his throat, directing his attention back to Aunt Langley.

Shame for her behavior and hurt over his dismissal—as deserved as it had been—enveloped Rebecca in a thick cloud, and she wanted nothing more than to flee the house. Rebecca had not allowed herself to think of Mr. Cooper again except to pen him a letter that thanked him for his assistance; she had folded it around a sum that she believed to be fair for the services he had rendered her mother.

She'd yet to give him the letter. It sat heavily at the bottom of her reticule, which was now resting on the hood of the pianoforte like a pudgy, squat bird.

"You will not leave us, will you?" Aunt Langley asked, panic lacing her tone.

Rebecca ripped her gaze from the reticule and found, to her dismay, that Mr. Cooper stood near the door.

Apologetic wrinkles lined his eyes. "Do forgive me. I do not believe there is anything else that can be done beyond the instructions I have just described. He could awaken in as little as eight hours, or as many as twenty-four, and I do hope you will send for me the moment he does so."

Rebecca had not been listening to his detailed instructions, and she was certain her aunt hardly retained a word, but Mama would have listened. They could count on her.

"Will you not remain?" Aunt Langley pleaded. "I do not believe we can do this alone. Oh, dear. I must send word to Christine. His wife will certainly wish to be here."

Mr. Cooper hesitated. His gaze swept to Rebecca, melting her body from her toes to her forehead with his pure displeasure. He was certainly wishing she had not been present. Would he have stayed if she had not been there?

"I will leave," Rebecca said, the words out of her mouth before she could think better of them or what they would imply.

Mr. Cooper dragged a hand over his face, expelling a long, patient breath. "No, that is unnecessary. I do believe you are capable of managing your brother-in-law at this point, Mrs. Langley. And yes, do send word to his family quickly. But if it will relieve your burden to retain my presence, I would be happy to stay."

Palpable relief lowered the shoulders on both Aunt Langley and Rebecca. The door opened and Mr. Cooper stepped aside when the two footmen of before reentered the room and went to Mr. Langley's side, Alicia shortly behind them. They began the arrangements of how to best carry the man up the stairs in his unconscious state, with Mr. Cooper adding his opinion that they ought to maintain elevation in the man's head. Rebecca stood back, watching them.

She caught Mr. Cooper's eye, hoping he could feel her gratitude, but he looked away again.

He was hurt and likely embarrassed. It was not lost on her

that he must be thinking of Alicia and her unwillingness to write to him, and it could not have been easy to enter her home. But Rebecca had been correct in her estimation of his character. He would not leave a man in need without medical care, and furthermore, she had not known any other doctor to call upon.

Mr. Cooper was a good man. It was only too bad that he could never be hers.

CHAPTER TWENTY-ONE

J ared wanted to leave the Langleys' townhouse, to crawl into his own bed and fall asleep, but he couldn't make himself go. He stood in the doorway of Mr. Langley's dark bedchamber, watching Rebecca curled up in the chair she'd dragged over by the fire, her head nodding off only to snap back to attention. She had come to sit at Alicia's side, but her cousin had long since fallen asleep in the other chair nearer the bed.

It had taken a long while to move Mr. Langley upstairs, properly set up and elevated in his bed with the window open just so and the warmers at his feet. Jared knew it was important to coax the man's blood away from his head, but it had not seemed to help thus far.

Rebecca's mother had been escorted home by a footman, but Rebecca had chosen to remain and offer her much-needed assistance.

She had removed her spectacles, and they sat folded in her lap. Her long lashes fanned over her cheeks, and her neck drooped again. Jared couldn't very well leave them like this, not when the two women who had offered to sit at the sickbed were sleeping. Who would alert Jared when the invalid awakened if they were both asleep? No, he needed to stay. He could remain another hour or so, and that would allow these women to sleep.

Resigned to his fate, Jared left the doorway and helped himself to the short footstool that accompanied one of the large armchairs the dainty women had inhabited. He moved it quietly toward the fire and sat upon the tufted seat, watching the flames flicker, casting dancing shadows over the stone hearth.

It had been a shock to arrive at the Langleys' townhouse and find Rebecca present. He'd yet to forgive her for her deception, but that did not stop his traitorous heart from leaping in excitement at the sight of her. He'd grown to like and appreciate Rebecca's company and friendship. It had been quite a blow to lose her.

He frowned. He supposed he had not lost her, not exactly. She was sitting a stone's throw from him right now. But how could he ever think of her as a friend again after what she had done to break his trust? He found himself grieving not only for the loss of Rebecca's physical company, but also her witty correspondence and thoughtful prose. He had reconciled the woman in the letters to be Rebecca since learning the truth. How had he ever believed those thoughts and words would come from someone the likes of Miss Langley? She was sweet, but he did not imagine her analyzing poetry or sharing profound observations about Bath Society.

But the letters carried Rebecca's essence, and he missed them. He missed *her*.

A motion caught his attention to his side, and he turned to find Rebecca stirring in her chair, lifting her head and blinking slowly in the direction of the invalid's bed. She slid her glasses on her wrinkled nose and ceased squinting. She seemed to sense Jared watching her and looked his direction, startling slightly when her gaze met his.

"I did not know you remained, Mr. Cooper." Her voice was raspy and low, laden with remnants of sleep.

He spoke quietly so as not to disturb Miss Langley. "I thought to watch over Mr. Langley while you got some rest or until the maid returned."

"I sent her to bed," Rebecca said, smiling guiltily. "I hadn't realized I would be so weak in my resolve to stay awake, and I thought she could use the sleep before rising early to see to her duties."

Of course she had been that thoughtful and selfless. It was precisely the sort of thing he expected from her, and it rankled, because a kind, selfless soul did not perform the deceit she had.

"My aunt has long since retired for the night," she said quietly, careful to allow her cousin to sleep. "You may leave, and I will have you sent for the moment Mr. Langley awakens."

"It is not your responsibility to remain by this man's bedside." He found the words leaving his mouth before he thought better of them. He should be stronger in his resolve to keep his distance from her, to only speak to her when forced, but he couldn't help himself. It was easy to break with his resolve in the dead of night, in the time between days when most souls were sleeping, with no one nearby to catch him breaking his objective. He could slough off his pride and his willpower briefly and start afresh tomorrow.

Holding her gaze, he whispered, "You are not his family."

"No, but members of my family have suffered a great ordeal this afternoon. To say nothing for the fact that his wife and children are in Brighton, so the burden of his care is resting solely on my aunt's shoulders until they can be notified."

Jared wanted to argue further, to vent his frustrations on

her in one way or another, but they were bound to wake Miss Langley if he persisted.

Rebecca must have had a similar thought. She stood, stretching her arms above her head before picking up her footstool and placing it before the fire near Jared's. She remained far enough away to grant him space, but close enough to absorb warmth from the dancing flames. Smudges on her spectacles clouded the view of her green eyes. How did she see through such dirty lenses?

"My aunt has always had her husband nearby to manage things for her. This was the first time, I believe, that a great thing has happened since losing her husband, and I could easily see the strain and toll this fright took on her."

"I believe the neighbors to either side of the house also heard the strain and toll this took on your aunt," he offered. She had endured fits on and off all evening, varying in volume and intensity.

A whisper of a smile passed over Rebecca's lips. "Indeed, that is possible. If I can ease the burden for my aunt or my cousin, then I am willing to help, even if that means sacrificing one night of sleep."

"Most people would not do as you are. Most people would likely not think that way." Indeed, Jared had not even thought of Mrs. Langley's distress in this light—his thoughts had been for his patient. All he had felt for Mrs. Langley throughout her outbursts had been irritation. "Your own mother went home."

"My mother is ill herself," Rebecca gently reminded him. "It took a great deal of convincing to persuade her to leave me here."

"Of course. I wasn't thinking." The smudges on her glasses distracted him. Was it not defeating the purpose of her spectacles when she wore them with such awful smears across the glass? Certainly the world was still blurry through her eyes.

Reaching for her, he tipped his chin down. "May I?"

Rebecca looked stunned, her eyes widening like a gentle, cautious doe. She nodded, and Jared removed her glasses. He pulled a clean handkerchief from his pocket and wiped the glass clean, running the cloth over each side in a circular motion. He held them up to the light of the fire and the clear lenses sparkled.

"You do not need to do that," she whispered.

Jared didn't respond. Perhaps he shouldn't have removed her glasses. She looked vulnerable and exposed without her wire-rimmed spectacles, but he could better see the gentle slope of her nose and the height of her cheekbones. She was beautiful, with or without the glasses, and he certainly did not need more appealing images of this woman to store in his mind.

He moved to return them to her face, and she leaned closer so he could slip the ear pieces in the correct place. His fingertips brushed her cheekbones, and she shivered. "Do you need to move closer to the fire?"

"No, I am close enough. I fear I am always cold."

Jared leaned his elbows on his knees and directed his attention to the dancing flames, anxious to lead the conversation onto safe, neutral ground. "Your mother is looking well."

"Her energy is growing by bits every day, or so she says." Rebecca's voice was raspy, and she cleared her throat. "I have seen that she is far more tired in the evenings, but growth is something to celebrate, even if it is not as fast as I would like."

"I've done a little further research on green sickness to ensure that I was providing your mother with the best advice I could, and from what I have read, her progress is typical, if not faster than average. Most physicians warn that restoring full health can take upwards of a year. The body responds well to iron and sunlight, but it does so at a snail's pace."

"I must rejoice that my mama is the enigma then." She hesitated, drawing his attention back to her. "I thank you for taking such care. You needn't go to further effort than you already have."

"I will never do less than I am able, and I believe you well know that."

"Yes, but to steal your words from a moment ago, *most* people would not do as you are. Most doctors would offer the knowledge they have and be done with it."

Jared's chest burned with satisfaction, warming from her praise. Her soft lips were fighting a smile, as though she'd won. He chuckled, then paused. He didn't know whether or not her lips were soft, but they looked as though they were, and he wondered if he was correct in his assumption. Though now he had spent far too long staring at this woman's lips, and her smile had slipped away.

Rebecca watched him closely. "Have you spoken with your mother?"

He swallowed hard and shook his head. "No. I would like to say that I have not found the right moment to tell her, but that wouldn't be true. I have simply been putting it off because it is an uncomfortable task, and I hate uncomfortable tasks."

"None of us enjoy being uncomfortable, but it will be worth the brief unpleasantness for how much better you shall feel afterward."

"Can you promise that?" he asked.

"No. But I can share from a recent experience I had. You see, I was dishonest with a friend of mine. Once I told him the truth, I ceased to feel as though I was carrying a heavy bag full of stones with me everywhere I went. My heart is sad for the pain I caused, but my shoulders are lighter."

"You forget one thing," he said coolly, his heart tugging at her admission despite his best effort to remain unattached. "I was not dishonest with my mother."

Her lips flattened. "The concept is applicable all the same."

"I do agree with that. I should not . . . forgive my candor, Rebecca. I am finding great difficulty in forgiving you."

She nodded but said no more, and silence fell between them. Temptation badgered him like a relentless pecking bird, and he wanted nothing more than to drop the discomfort between them and carry on as they had before. He wanted her letters again, her conversation, her arm wrapped around his at the assemblies and when promenading the Pump Room.

She stood, wiping her hands quietly down her gown. "I should go. Or you may leave . . . whichever you prefer."

Jared stood as well, bringing them much closer than he anticipated. He looked down at her shadowed face, the orange glow from the fire reflecting on her skin. She tipped her head back to look into his eyes, and he gazed down at her, yearning to forgive her, but afraid. How could he know that she would not do something dishonest again?

"I am sorry, Mr. Cooper," she whispered, as though she knew his mind and what he longed to say. "I wish I could return to that day we rode out to Prior Park and never have written the letter. I wish I had been honest with you—"

He stepped back, and the tenuous thread which bound them snapped. "It is done. It cannot be changed. I will take my leave, Miss Turner. Send for me when Mr. Langley awakens, and I will return with haste."

She nodded, and Jared turned and strode from the room. He didn't inhale a deep breath until he had cleared the doorway and was in the corridor, his heart pounding hard in his chest. He was a fool, and he would do better to leave Rebecca behind. But he couldn't seem to cease thinking about her.

It was not Miss Langley he was angry with, or hurt by, or always on his mind. It was Rebecca. His feelings for her had begun to run deeper than friendship, or he would not be missing her so keenly. The truth of the situation hit him like a cricket ball to the face. He felt blinded by the shock and leaned his shoulder against the wall as he gathered his wits again.

"Wait," Rebecca called softly from down the corridor. The wall sconces burned low, giving them very little light to see by, but he could clearly discern the hesitation in her worried eyes.

She held out a white rectangle. "I promise this is the last one."

His breath caught as he actively worked to temper his elation. As badly as he wanted it, though, he could never accept another missive from her. "A letter? You cannot—"

"Please," she said quietly, continuing to hold it out before her.

Her meager plea beat at his resolve. Swallowing, he accepted it, his hand brushing hers. He would take the letter, but he didn't promise to read it. Rebecca turned away and left him, and he hated watching her go.

Whatever his feelings for Rebecca, he would need to squash them until they dissipated into nothing. He could never love a woman who'd lied to him. Fisting the letter, he shoved it into his coat pocket and left.

CHAPTER TWENTY-TWO

J ared hadn't slept much at all the previous night, and he found himself at the door to Thomas's stables the next morning, having left strict instructions with his parents' servants to retrieve him immediately if he was sent for by anyone from the Langley household. He'd left the letter from Rebecca in his room, hidden away in a drawer of his shaving table.

He would open it later, maybe. Now, he was too afraid of what it would make him feel.

Jared picked his way through the stables, past rows of fine horses and men mucking stalls and laying down fresh straw. He knocked on the door to the small office at the back and let himself inside. Thomas sat behind a squat desk, a quill in his hand and a sheet of paper spread before him. He wore his riding clothes, but his cravat had been removed, his shirt left unfastened at the neck.

"Good morning, Jared," Thomas said, running a hand through his shock of red hair. "Did you fancy another ride with your lady friend and her ailing mother?"

Jared stilled. "You do know that the ride was for a patient of mine. I explained how it would help her green sickness."

Thomas slapped the desk playfully. "Oh, forgive me. I mixed up the order of my words. I meant: did you want to schedule another ride for your patient and her daughter that you fancy?"

Jared closed the door behind himself, ignoring his friend's facetious barbs and overbearing grin. "Actually, that is partially why I'm here. I'm not certain I will ever need your services for that particular patient again." He pulled out the wooden ladder-back chair and sat across from the desk. The room smelled of leather and polish, and it made him itch to go riding.

Thomas set his pen down and leaned back in his chair, crossing his arms over his chest. "Something must have happened. You look as though someone just told you that they were ceasing to publish your blessed *London Medical and Physical Journal*."

"Surely I do not look as troubled as *that*," Jared defended. But he felt that way, indeed. It was disconcerting how easy it was for Thomas to discern his displeasure.

"Did something occur between Miss Turner and yourself?"

"I tell you that I will likely no longer borrow your horses for Mrs. Turner's care, and you assume that the trouble is with the daughter?" He rubbed a hand over his forehead. "How did you know?"

Thomas was quiet for a moment, watching Jared with amusement. "I was on the ride with you both that day, do you recall? It was no secret how easily you got on, nor how often you found opportunities for quiet conversations."

"Well, I shan't do so anymore. She has broken my trust." Jared shook his head. "Which is all beside the point. I never had any romantic feelings for Miss Turner. I had aims on her cousin, Miss Alicia Langley."

Thomas's copper eyebrows rose, and he snapped his mouth shut.

"What is it?" Jared pressed. "You cannot give such an expression without offering some explanation."

"It is not my place to tell you who to admire."

"No, but you have an opinion, and I would like to hear it."

Thomas hesitated. "Miss Alicia Langley does not seem the sort of woman who would make you happy, that is all."

"And you believe Miss Turner does?" he asked bitterly. It was not lost on Jared that he had a similar thought. He'd misjudged Miss Langley in more ways than one, but evidently, he'd misjudged Rebecca as well.

"She has a steadiness of character that complements you, yes. But it is more than that. Like I said, I was on the ride. I have seen the way you interact. She feels like a woman I could see by your side."

"Well, put the thought from your mind. She has lost my trust, and I'm afraid there is no way for her to regain it."

A beat of silence passed between them, and the air felt heavy, the musk of horses and straw overwhelming the pleasant leather scent.

Thomas speared him with a contemplative look. "You are unwilling to show mercy? Or are her sins too grievous to be borne?"

Jared immediately opened his mouth to confirm the latter but stopped. What right had he to rate the foulness of her sins? He could only say how her actions had made him feel, and at present, such was very confusing. Anger, embarrassment, and betrayal were all fighting the yearning to have her near him again. "It is difficult to say."

Clearing his throat, Thomas leaned forward and clasped his hands on his desk. "You may dislike my boldness, but I must ask, was her intent to hurt you?"

Her intent had been sound, but her honesty lacking. Did intent mean anything when the sin had still hurt him?

"She knew what she was doing was wrong."

Thomas nodded, his lips flat as though he was giving this some thought. "It is difficult to give my opinion when I do not know the nature of her offenses against you."

"I do not wish to blight her character," Jared said softly. He did not mean to sound secretive, but he would hate to give others a reason to think less of Rebecca, not when he knew with surety that she had not set out to hurt him. She should have known her actions would accomplish that, but her reputation didn't need to suffer for it.

"Of course." Thomas rocked his clasped hands, tapping his fingers against the desk in thought. "Perhaps this is entirely irrelevant, but hear me out."

Jared nodded, listening. He was desperate to make sense of the turmoil in his mind, and he knew Thomas to be thoughtful and wise. His friend considered things from every angle before making important decisions, which Jared was certain was part of why he had grown so successful in his business before yet reaching thirty years of age.

"You made a mistake in Derham, which you believe cost a young man his life," Thomas said gently. "You did not directly hurt that boy, and by your accounts, I do not believe you could have done anything to save him."

"I could have eased his suffering," Jared said quietly. His body grew still as the truth of his words settled in his mind. Had that been what really bothered him? That he did not do everything he could, he knew, but that he could have eased the final moments in the boy's life?

"Your intent was not to harm him, though you feel you did so indirectly," Thomas said. He let his words settle in the room, and Jared turned them over in his mind, considering them from each angle as his friend likely had done.

He'd been angry at himself for his own faults, but also at the Hollingsfords and the rest of Derham who had lain the blame on Jared's shoulders for not helping the boy.

"Perhaps Miss Turner's intent was not to harm you, but she did so indirectly."

Jared stood, needing to breathe clean air that wasn't scented with leather and horses. Thomas was correct, though he could not know how near on the mark he truly was. The connection between Rebecca's deceit and Jared's own failures was obvious. He'd only wanted forgiveness, too, and was saddened when his people had not afforded him the opportunity to prove himself again after his misstep.

"Have I said too much?" Thomas asked, rising from his seat.

"No. You've said the right thing, but it is difficult to hear."

"The truth usually is," Thomas said apologetically.

Jared opened the door and paused, his hand resting on the knob. "Thank you, friend."

"You are welcome here any time."

Jared closed the door and set his hat back on his head. Thomas had given him a lot to think on. But first, he needed to speak to his mother and father and tell them what had happened in Derham.

———— ⌒ ————

Rebecca let herself into her sitting room and found Mama on the sofa beside Mullens, wrapping the yarn around Mullens's hands into a ball. They paused their activity and Mama looked up swiftly. "How is Mr. Langley?"

"He has awoken," Rebecca reported. Her body ached from the lack of sleep, and she yearned to lay down and close her eyes for an hour or two. She stifled a yawn. "They sent for the doctor, but I did not remain to hear his opinion. I am quite fatigued."

"I imagine so," Mama said, setting her yarn ball on the cushion and crossing the room toward Rebecca. "Did you sleep at all last night?"

"I slept some." She thought back on her late conversation with Mr. Cooper. "But not much."

"Go and rest. We can return to the Langleys' house in a few hours to offer our help again." She squeezed Rebecca's shoulder. "I do hope Mr. Langley recovers."

"For his sake as well as my aunt's, I hope the same."

Rebecca reached the door to the bedchamber and Mama said, "Wait, we have a dinner invitation for this evening."

"Who would invite us to dine besides Aunt Langley?" Rebecca asked, confusion drawing her eyebrows together. Surely not the Gastrells?

"Mrs. Cooper extended the invitation after the concert the other evening, but I forgot to tell you."

The air swept from her lungs. Dinner at Mr. Cooper's house? Surely he would not be present. He'd seemed bent on avoiding her at all costs until their conversation last night, and even then he'd fled with great haste when it was over.

"Do you think we ought to cancel?" she asked, hoping simultaneously that her mother would both agree and disagree. She wanted to go to Mr. Cooper's house, but the idea pained her as well.

"No. Surely my sister will need rest this evening as well. I am certain she would not expect that of us."

Drat. Rebecca nodded. "Do not let me sleep too long."

Mama smiled. "I was hoping you would wear Alicia's

yellow gown again with Grandmother's brooch. It is so fetching on you, darling. It compliments your hair well."

Rebecca's heart pounded, and she shook her head. "I'm not sure that's appropriate for a dinner."

"I do think—"

"I cannot think of gowns quite yet." She spoke hastily, the words slipping from her tongue as though they were greased with guilt.

"Very well," Mama said, though she sounded suspicious. She returned to rolling her yarn, and Rebecca fled the sitting room.

She shut the door to the bedchamber and leaned against it, resting her head back and closing her eyes. How was she to sit in Mr. Cooper's home and partake of his parents' generosity after what she had done? How was she to tell Mama that she no longer had the brooch in her possession? And where, oh, *where* was Father?

CHAPTER TWENTY-THREE

Rebecca stood in front of the dressing table, the mirror tipped up to better see her empty neckline. She'd donned the yellow gown as Mama had asked of her and contemplated covering it with a fichu before Mama could mention the brooch again, but that wouldn't be honest of her. If she'd learned anything over the course of the last few weeks, it was the importance of remaining completely honest.

"Are you ready, dear?" Mama asked, poking her head through the open doorway. "Oh, you look lovely."

Rebecca shot her a smile. "Thank you, Mama. Shall we be off?"

They intended to stop in at Aunt Langley's house on their way to the Coopers' residence and learn of the progress Mr. Langley had hopefully made since awakening that morning. Mama had allowed Rebecca to sleep far too long, and they'd been unable to go earlier.

The walk was short and blessedly dry, though they brought their umbrella in case they would need it later. Aunt Langley's butler let them inside and led them upstairs to the drawing room. Rebecca's steps faltered when she caught sight of Mr. Cooper sitting on the sofa beside Aunt Langley, Alicia on the wingback chair opposite them.

She hadn't expected to see him again, and the way his eyes lingered on her as she entered the room made her heart speed its rhythm. Was he disappointed to see her? It hurt, though it was deserved.

"Oh Sister, you've come," Aunt Langley said, lifting her feeble hand as though it took a great deal of effort.

Mr. Cooper rose from the sofa to allow Mama to sit beside her sister. "How is your brother-in-law?" Mama asked, taking the seat and drawing Aunt Langley's hand between her own.

"He has awoken, but Mr. Cooper needs more time before he can determine the extent of the damage. We are just grateful Arthur is alive."

"As am I," Mama said.

"We have much to thank our dear Rebecca for," Alicia said, eyeing her with particular attention.

Rebecca stepped back, resting her hands on the back of the empty wingback chair. "I do not—"

"Indeed," Alicia continued, looking between Rebecca on her right side and Mr. Cooper on her left. "She was most generous with her time last night and allowed me to sleep. I was quite fatigued and could hardly keep my eyes open."

"That was kind of her, yes," Mr. Cooper agreed.

Alicia nodded, far too enthusiastically for what the situation warranted. She widened her eyes at Rebecca, who did her best to ignore her cousin. Madness had overcome Alicia in her lack of sleep, surely. She was acting strangely.

"I must be off now, but I will return in the morning to assess Mr. Langley's progress," Mr. Cooper said.

"Wait!" Alicia said, rising. She went to Rebecca's side and

took her hand, facing the doctor. "Surely you want to hear what my cousin was about to say before you leave."

Rebecca looked sharply at Alicia. What was she trying to do?

Alicia eyed her again, her blue eyes wild, and squeezed her fingers. The blonde ringlets brushing her temples were nearly vibrating with energy. "You were about to say something?"

"No, I don't believe I was."

"I know it because we only talked of it yesterday. You were about to speak of *India*."

India? Oh, good heavens. Rebecca slipped her hand free and spoke between nearly clenched teeth. "No, I do not think that would be appropriate at this moment."

Alicia shook her head. "It is always appropriate to speak of India." She swung her radiant smile to Mr. Cooper. "Do you not agree, Doctor?"

"I, uh . . . certainly. I think India must be a nice topic of conversation at any time for those who wish to discuss it."

"See?" Alicia said, satisfied. "Mr. Cooper appreciates India too, just like any other man."

Rebecca tried to smile and found herself clenching her hands together tightly. She would be mortified if anyone else understood that by India, Alicia truly meant *love*. Especially with Mama and Aunt Langley listening on.

"Thank you, Mr. Cooper, but you needn't remain any longer." Rebecca took Alicia's arm and squeezed her elbow. "I have completely forgotten everything I meant to say about India."

"Very well," he said. He bade the women farewell and then looked to Rebecca. "Until tonight." He sketched a handsome bow, which she returned with a curtsy, too stunned to speak, and he quit the room.

Once the door closed behind Mr. Cooper, Alicia took her

by the shoulders and squealed quietly, her grin so wide it could stretch from here to India. "I *knew* he had a marked interest in you. I have a sense for these things."

"What do you mean?" Aunt Langley asked. She looked just as confused as Mama, though Rebecca was doing her best to avoid looking at her mother.

"Mr. Cooper must have a fondness for Rebecca. Did you not see the way he bade her farewell with pointed interest? He is certainly looking forward to seeing you tonight. What is tonight?"

Mama spoke. "We are to dine at the Coopers' house."

Alicia looked triumphant. "Even more proof!"

"We were invited by *his mother*," Rebecca said, moving around the wingback chairs and sitting on shaky legs. Alicia sat in the empty chair near hers.

"It hardly means anything," Rebecca said softly.

"Do not say that yet—"

Rebecca speared her cousin with a look, willing her to drop the matter at once. "I do know that of which I speak. Trust me."

Mama asked Aunt Langley about her plans to care for her brother-in-law, stealing her away in conversation.

Alicia leaned in, lowering her voice. "Why are you so adamantly against this? Mr. Cooper is a fine man."

Rebecca leaned closer. "He knows about the letters."

Alicia stilled, surprise widening her eyes. "You mean he knows—"

"That I wrote them? Yes. He also knows that I was pretending to be you, and he has lost all trust in me." She suppressed the urge to cry, maintaining her low tone so her mother would not overhear. "We were becoming friends, but now he wants nothing to do with me. He told me that he cannot find it in himself to forgive me."

"Oh, Rebecca." Concern lined Alicia's forehead in deep grooves. "I did not know."

"I should have told you, but I was embarrassed."

Alicia nodded knowingly. "Of course you were. I am impressed with how amiable Mr. Cooper just was, given that you completely lied to him."

"Yes," Rebecca agreed wryly. "Though I am sorry that I've ruined things for you in that quarter. I'm not certain he will entertain the notion of friendship with either of us."

Alicia's head snapped up. "You do know that I had no intention of ever letting him pursue me, yes? I mentioned that yesterday. I only pushed you to write those letters so you would grow closer to him. I thought you needed a nudge, and the letters presented themselves as the perfect opportunity to force you to continue to interact with the man." She pushed her lower lip out. "I thought you would make a lovely pair."

"Alicia," Rebecca reprimanded. "You did not hold any interest for him *at all*? Not even in the beginning? You wrote to him first. You were adamant about thanking him for his compliment!"

"Only to force you to go to the assemblies to see him. I assumed that if I gave you a note to pass to Mr. Cooper, you would be obligated to speak to him. I couldn't go with you to make certain it happened, so that was the only thing I could think of." She shrugged. "When you returned with a letter from him, I saw the opportunity and set about trying to convince you to write to him. You are too gentle and selfless to think of your own romance, Rebecca, so a little scheming was in order. Mr. Cooper has just the right even-keeled temperament to complement your steadiness of character."

"You clever little minx," Rebecca said, scoffing. So that had been what the woman's blasted scheming had been about. "I do not know whether to laugh or be mad at you."

"Oh laugh, certainly. That would be far more pleasant." She leaned closer, the light of scheming shining in her eyes once more. "Besides, I do believe I will shortly become engaged. The moment I put off this black, of course." She picked at the black lacy overdress of her skirt, wrinkling her nose in disdain.

A cold river of dread threaded through Rebecca. "Who is the lucky gentleman?"

Alicia looked at her mother before leaning closer still. "I fear mentioning his name aloud will curse our union, but suffice it to say, a gentleman has made me a promise, and with Uncle's poor health, I'm certain I will be able to make an announcement sooner rather than later. I'm hopeful Mother will put an end to this elongated mourning now that Uncle can no longer force us to abide by his strictures. The poor man is struggling to speak at all, let alone command us."

Rebecca sent a quick glance at the mothers to ascertain their attention was elsewhere and was gratified that they hadn't seemed to overhear. "When could you have possibly had the time to make promises to *any* gentleman? You've hardly left your house in weeks."

"Oh, most of it was decided long before Papa died. But I've managed a few covert meetings." Her cheeks bloomed pink, and her eyes sparkled.

Clandestine meetings with gentlemen—presumably after dark—were exceedingly dangerous to both Alicia's safety and her reputation. "Please tell me you have not so much as kissed—"

"Of course I've kissed him," Alicia whispered. "It is what one does when one falls in love."

Love? This was bordering on ridiculous. How could Alicia love a man that she had never so much as hinted about before? "Alicia, you are worrying me. Did you not mention just a few days ago that you value your reputation far more than a kiss?"

Alicia laughed. "Oh, yes. Wasn't that such a lark?"

Reaching for her cousin's hand, Rebecca squeezed it softly. "Now that your uncle is unwell, and the prospect of putting off your mourning is close at hand, please promise me you will not participate in any more covert meetings."

Alicia's mouth pinched closed, and she looked at Rebecca with apprehension. "You will not tell my mother, will you?"

"Just promise me." She squeezed Alicia's hand. "I worry for your safety, and if you will soon be returning to Society, you shouldn't need covert meetings at all."

Alicia seemed to ponder this before sighing and slumping in her seat. "Very well. I promise."

Rebecca settled back in her chair but worry tightened her spine and stiffened her shoulders. She could only hope Alicia would hold to her word until Rebecca had time to learn more.

By the time Rebecca and Mama left for the Coopers' house for dinner, Rebecca was able to consider her cousin's antics without the added thread of irritation. Alicia's reasoning for pairing Mr. Cooper with Rebecca continued to batter her. Alicia believed they would make a good match because their temperaments complimented one another, and Rebecca had to agree. Imagining Alicia at Mr. Cooper's side was both silly and incongruent. While they would make a handsome pair, Mr. Cooper would likely have tired of her relentless energy and need for entertainment. Alicia might be the most beautiful lady in all of Bath—which Rebecca truly believed to be the case, bias aside—but that did not mean she was the best pair for Mr. Cooper.

The reality of that stung. Rebecca had found a man that she thought would make a good partner, and she'd ruined the chance of a relationship through her deceit. Perhaps if she'd allowed things to develop naturally, Mr. Cooper would have come to his own decision about Alicia, and he would have been open to the possibility of a future with Rebecca. But now it could never be. She would be lucky if he agreed to be her friend after all that she'd done.

Mama took her elbow outside and they huddled together beneath the umbrella as a light rain fell around them.

"I will be quite happy to arrive at the Coopers' warm house. I believe they do not live too far."

"No, it should be just up here and around the corner." They would be there shortly, and Rebecca needed to remove the melancholy of lost opportunities before it shaded her mood for the evening.

"Thank you for wearing the yellow gown, Rebecca. I love how it makes your skin glow." Mama bunched her eyebrows in thought. "Did you fasten the brooch on the front again? I do not remember seeing it earlier."

Her heart skipped a beat. "I did not."

"Oh, that is too bad. Perhaps next time."

Rebecca swallowed. "I will not be able to do that, either."

Mama's chin jutted out thoughtfully. "I suppose Alicia will be expecting her gown back at some point, that is true."

"Mama," Rebecca said, tugging on her arm to pull her to a halt. "I sold the brooch." Her mother went stiff beneath her hand, and guilt flooded her. "I had to pay Mr. Cooper for his services, and we have nothing else. Our budget is spent on room and board, and Father hasn't sent any money." She lifted a shoulder in dejection. "I did not know what else to do."

"Oh, Rebecca, you didn't."

"We owed the man, Mama. What else could I have done?"

Her mother drew in a deep breath and blew it out between tight lips. "I do not know, either. Your father hasn't sent anything, and I do not understand why, unless he has not been able to sell any wine. He hasn't responded to any of my letters though, and I'm doing my best not to worry, but I do understand how tight our finances are without the money he promised."

"Could he be hurt?" Rebecca asked, her stomach tightening.

"I surely hope not," Mama said. "But other than continuing to write to him and praying heartily, I do not know what else to do."

Rebecca wanted to tell her that she had enlisted Mr. Cooper's help, but she feared allowing Mama to hope when there was the potential of bad news awaiting them.

"Let us go to this dinner, and we can discuss it more later." She squeezed Rebecca's hand. "All will work out. I understand why you did what you had to do, though I'll admit it hurts my heart."

It hurt Rebecca as well.

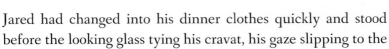

Jared had changed into his dinner clothes quickly and stood before the looking glass tying his cravat, his gaze slipping to the drawer in his shaving table where Rebecca's letter sat. When he'd seen her at the Langleys' house, he'd been overcome with curiosity over what her parting words were. She'd promised it was the last letter, and despite his resolve to put her from his mind, he was now desperate to know what it entailed.

Hastily finishing his knot, Jared retrieved the letter and moved toward the window. He broke the wafer and unfolded the letter, and thin sheets of paper fluttered to the floor. Money? Lifting the pound notes from his carpet, Jared scanned the contents of the missive, disappointment growing into thick sludge in his stomach. It was nothing but a mere entreaty for

Jared to accept payment for the services he'd rendered Mrs. Turner along with Rebecca's deep gratitude.

He scoffed, dropping the note on his shaving table, his hand fisting around the money. He didn't want payment, and he certainly hadn't appreciated a hastily scrawled note detailing what Rebecca believed the money covered. She'd listed the horse rentals, each visit, and his extra time consulting with her.

A knock at the door preceded his parents' manservant, and he swallowed down his frustration. "Yes, Miller?"

"We searched the rooms you visited today and have found nothing yet, sir. But we will keep looking."

"It may not be here at all," Jared said, thinking of the different places he'd gone that day. "But I thank you for looking."

"Of course, sir."

Jared dismissed Miller and sat hard on the chair near the window. He'd returned from the Langleys' home to find his pocket watch missing, its chain dangling empty from his waist. He had immediately set to look for it, but his search had come up empty thus far.

He planned to inquire with the Langleys' butler when he visited Arthur Langley again in the morning. Hopefully, they would find it tucked in a sofa cushion or fallen on a rug somewhere. His mind drifted back to finding Rebecca in the Langleys' drawing room, and Miss Langley's odd talk of India. The whole thing had been strange, though he assumed there was something Alicia was pushing Rebecca to do.

If only Jared could cease his unending curiosity where Rebecca Turner was concerned, that would make it far easier to forget her. As it stood, it was blasted difficult to remove her from his mind.

CHAPTER TWENTY-FOUR

J ared stood beside the mantel, his arms folded over his chest. He tried to ignore the quickening of his thudding heart when Rebecca walked into the room, and he took the opportunity to admire her from a distance while she greeted his mother and was introduced to his father. Her yellow dress was a lovely shade against her skin, hugging her figure just enough and flowing around her in gentle waves as she walked.

Rebecca tilted her face down toward Jared's father where he sat on his armchair, his foot propped up on a stool, and nodded at whatever the man was saying. It likely had something to do with the rain. That seemed to be all anyone could speak of these days, the dreary, unrelenting showers from heaven. It was odd to be so removed from sunlight, particularly during summer, but Jared was just as tired of the rain itself as he was of hearing others speak of it.

Mrs. Turner's voice filtered toward him, breaking through his contemplative cloud as she spoke to Jared's father. "Your son has told us that you were a physician?"

"Indeed," Father said, nodding. "Not any longer, thanks to my gout, but I am still able to discuss medical situations with Jared, and that has brought me a great deal of contentment during my retirement."

"How fortunate that your son has chosen to follow in your footsteps and provide you with this service," Mrs. Turner said.

Father grinned. "I fear I gave him little choice. I took the lad along with me to every visit he could reasonably attend in Derham, and he learned too much not to put it to use."

Jared pushed away from the mantel and crossed to where their guests had grouped around Father's chair near the window. "You claim you tricked me into becoming a doctor?"

"That was my design," Father said.

Mother shook her head. "Jared had an aptitude for healing from a young age. It was not long after his fourteenth birthday that he began diagnosing illnesses."

"Only because Father would quiz me," he muttered.

"You lived for it," Father said, his ruddy cheeks round and jovial.

Jared couldn't help but smile, dipping his head and rubbing the back of his neck. "You are correct on that score."

Rebecca laughed, and the sound was more beautiful than any of the soprano's arias he'd heard at the concert a few evenings before.

Dinner was announced and the families moved slowly into the dining room, Jared falling behind to help his father up from his chair and hand him his cane. When Rebecca stepped through the door into the dining room, she looked back at him over her shoulder, and he had difficulty tearing his gaze away. Her auburn eyebrows were bent into a question, and he longed to put her mind at ease, but he did not think he could. Not yet.

Mother had placed their uneven numbers as best she could around the end of the table. Father took up the head, Mrs.

Turner to his right and Rebecca to his left. Mother took the chair beside Mrs. Turner, leaving the only open seat next to Rebecca.

Jared helped Rebecca into her chair and sat beside her, avoiding his mother's conspiratorial smile across from him as the rest of the party took their seats. When Mother had asked him to reconsider his threat to not attend the meal, he had agreed to be present. But both of them knew that he'd never been serious in his claims to absent himself. He could not bear to be so rude, despite how Rebecca had hurt him. He liked Mrs. Turner and was glad to see her looking so well.

"We've had word from our friends in the country that the rain does not seem to be any better in Wiltshire than it is in Somerset," Mother said, shaking her head. "I had wondered if we should leave Bath in order to enjoy some dry weather, but I'm not sure there is sun or warmth to be had anywhere else in England."

"Traveling in such wet weather is tiresome," Mrs. Turner said.

"Indeed, and I have no choice but to do so soon."

"To visit your daughter?" Mrs. Turner confirmed. "I am certain you will find that journey worth the uncomfortable travel."

Rebecca leaned closer to Jared, lowering her voice. "When did our mothers become such good friends?"

"When we did."

She froze, her eyes flicking up to catch Jared's gaze, and he held it, unwilling to look away. A faint pink bloomed on her cheeks, and her green eyes sparkled behind smudged lenses.

He couldn't help himself. "You do not enjoy seeing clearly, do you?"

She startled. "I do not . . . oh, you mean my dirty spectacles."

He nodded, itching to remove the glasses himself and wipe them clear.

"They are not usually like this, but it is impossible to step outside without getting them wet. I find it more comfortable to leave them be, water spots and all, than to remove them each time I enter a building and draw attention to myself." She took a bite of her roll. "Besides, it is not as though I *cannot* see. It is merely blurry."

She did not want to draw attention to herself? That reason surprised him. "Is it not nicer to see clearly? Surely a little attention cannot be so awful."

"In this, the benefit does not outweigh the cost. I was teased far too often in my youth for these wretched spectacles, and it is better not to concern myself with fiddling with them in public places too often."

"You are speaking clearly, Rebecca, but I cannot understand you one whit."

Rebecca looked to be gauging his sincerity. "I hate my glasses. There, was that any clearer?"

"No." Why was he being intentionally argumentative? He needed to stop, but he didn't want to. "Do you not appreciate how they help you to see better?"

"I appreciate how they allow me to see at all, of course. But I hate how they look and how I must rely on them." She gave an exasperated chuckle. "Are you satisfied? You've made me feel quite vain in forcing me to say that."

He lowered his voice to avoid being overheard by their parents. "I will never be satisfied to hear that you do not like the way you look, Rebecca. Particularly when I think your spectacles are very charming."

Her blush deepened, painting larger red spots of color over her cheeks. "I do think you are trying to flatter me, Mr. Cooper, but I cannot tell why."

"I'm only telling the truth," he said softly. "As I always have."

He did not miss her quick intake of breath, and it only made him feel guilty for his indiscreet barb. He hadn't meant to bring up her dishonesty. Indeed, Jared had decided not to speak of it at all during the dinner.

"Forgive me, Miss Turner," he said, forcing himself to use her surname. "That was not intentional."

"I believe you, but you are not wrong."

He was tired of the discomfort between them and wanted to put an end to it at once. Enough was finally enough.

"Tell me, Miss Turner," Father said, chewing a bite of his lamb. "Have you found Bath to be everything a young lady desires?"

"I have found quite a lot to entertain me," she said.

Mother took a sip of her wine and put her glass back on the table. "Do you believe you will remain in Bath, then?"

The underlying meaning of their inquiry was obvious. Jared's parents wished to know if anyone was keeping the Turners in town. Now that Mrs. Turner had found the root of the illness which was plaguing her, surely she could obtain the medication she needed from any apothecary.

The sudden reality that Rebecca could leave Bath at any moment brought a wave of discomfort and uncertainty over Jared. He did not know if he could trust the woman, but neither did he want her to leave. It was confusing and frightening, but of everything running through his mind and the feelings rushing through his body, one thing was perfectly clear: he cared about Rebecca.

Rebecca was ready to leave the Coopers' townhouse and return to the safety of her quiet, unassuming rented rooms. Mr. Cooper's behavior to her during dinner had been confusing at best, troublesome at worst, and she hated that she could not discern what he meant by it. She sat on the sofa before the fire as the adults reminisced about the way Bath was two decades ago in their prime, and Rebecca's mind drifted once more to Mr. Cooper's words at dinner. *I think your spectacles are very charming.* Charming. The word had such a range of meaning. He could either mean that the glasses were attractive on her or that they made her look like a quaint, sweet old maid.

"Rebecca can play very well," Mama said, snapping Rebecca's attention back to the conversation in the room.

"Oh, how lovely. I haven't been able to play in the last few years with my fingers growing so stiff, and our poor pianoforte has been unjustly neglected." Mrs. Turner directed her attention to Rebecca. "Will you play for us?"

"I'd be happy to." Rebecca crossed to the pianoforte on the far side of the room, and Mr. Cooper followed her.

He rested his hand on the smooth, polished surface. "Will you need help turning the pages?"

"I shall play from memory, but I thank you for the offer."

She lifted the lid on the keys and ran her fingers over them, warming her cold joints and acquainting herself with the Coopers' pianoforte, glad not to stumble on any sticky keys. Mr. Cooper remained at the instrument's side as Rebecca played in earnest, and she focused on her fingers moving with great effort to avoid his distracting presence.

She had made it nearly halfway through the song when Mr. Cooper took a step closer. "You play beautifully. Perhaps I should have opted for those lessons you originally offered."

Rebecca's fingers stumbled, but she continued on, avoiding his gaze. "I'm certain you do not mean that."

"You'd be surprised how deeply I do," he muttered.

Warmth swept through Rebecca's body, starting at her core and filling every bit of her. She focused on remembering the notes to the song so she would not melt into a puddle on the floor, but Mr. Cooper's pointed encouragements were playing tricks on her emotions. It was impossibly devastating to receive such words of affirmation when she knew the man could not find it in his heart to forgive her.

When the song came to an end, light clapping met her ears. The elder Mr. Cooper's warm, deep voice said, "Will you play another?"

She sent a soft smile to her mother and the Coopers. "Certainly."

The parents resumed their conversation, and Rebecca turned her attention to Mr. Cooper. "What do you mean by that?"

He glanced at her through steady eyes and seemed to be weighing his words.

"I cannot . . ." Rebecca took a deep breath. She cared too much for this man to continue playing games which confused her. "If you would like to be my friend, Mr. Cooper, then tell me so. If you are still having trouble forgiving me, then you must cease to . . . to talk so prettily to me. It is unfair to play with my emotions, and you should see that."

Mr. Cooper stepped back from the pianoforte, his hand still resting on the edge of the instrument. "You are asking a lot of me."

"As are you," Rebecca countered. She remained on the seat, her fingers folded on her lap. "I am not asking you to forgive me —though don't mistake me, I would like that very much—I am asking that you do not flirt with me if you cannot forgive me. I would love to be your friend, Mr. Cooper, but right now I do not know what we are, and it's maddening. I cannot think straight."

He stared at her, the silence rolling between them in heavy waves. The room had grown too quiet, and Rebecca noticed that their parents had ceased talking. A warm blush stole over her cheeks and ran up her neck, and she closed the lid to the keys. She could not play another song, not with her heart in such a state. It was disheartening that when she passed Mr. Cooper, he did not try to stop her. She put a bright smile on and stood behind her mother's chair when the door to the drawing room opened and a servant entered carrying a tray.

He crossed to Mr. Cooper, who took the card from the salver and glanced up at his parents. "Thomas is here. I can send him away."

"Do not do so on our account," Mama said, rising from her chair. "I think it is time we are leaving."

Mrs. Cooper looked between Rebecca and her son, worry pinching her lips. "I am glad you were able to join us. I enjoyed our evening very much."

The elder Mr. Cooper remained behind, his injured foot resting on a tufted stool, as Mr. Cooper and his mother escorted the Turner women downstairs.

"Did you hear that the Gastrells left town this morning?" Mrs. Cooper asked as they made their way down the staircase. "It was all over the Pump Room this morning. They've gone to London."

Mama paused. "I wonder if my sister knows. She said nothing to me about this." She frowned and gave Rebecca a light squeeze on the shoulder. "I would have liked to say goodbye."

"Surely we will see them again soon." Though Rebecca agreed that it was odd, particularly when Mrs. Gastrell had requested that Rebecca and her mama be certain to bid her farewell before departing Bath.

Mr. Hawkins stood in the entryway, his hat in his hands, and he bowed to the women as they approached. He had an easy smile and a casual air about him that Rebecca liked.

"Forgive the lateness of the hour. I had hoped to catch Jared alone."

"Is anything wrong?" Mr. Cooper asked.

"No," Mr. Hawkins said, digging into his coat pocket. "One of my men found this in the stables today, and I believe it belongs to you." He opened his palm to reveal a gold pocket watch missing its chain, and Mr. Cooper sucked in a quiet breath.

"You found it," Mr. Cooper said, somewhat awed. "I was convinced I hadn't lost it until this afternoon, so I didn't think to inquire with you. Thank you, Thomas."

Mr. Hawkins nodded. "I will now get out of your way."

"We were just leaving," Rebecca said, hoping to put him at ease.

Mr. Hawkins turned his kind gaze on her. "It is wet outside; will you allow me the pleasure of escorting you home?"

That was not why she'd spoken, and she opened her mouth to refuse him when Mama said, "That would be lovely, Mr. Hawkins."

They thanked the Coopers for a lovely dinner and left. Rebecca had difficulty maintaining conversation with the man on the walk home and settled for listening as he and Mama discussed his horses and how he had begun his business.

"How kind of you to return Mr. Cooper's watch," Mama said when they reached their front door. "You must have known that he would be worried about it."

"Indeed, it is quite special to him. I thought to ease his concerns."

Mama opened the door to walk inside, the warm light from the lamp on the entry table spilling onto the rainy front step. Mr. Hawkins cleared his throat, and Rebecca looked back at him.

"Jared is a very good man who cares a great deal about virtue; just give him time. He will come around."

Rebecca was lost for words, but Mr. Hawkins did not give her the opportunity to reply. He merely nodded and turned away, leaving her with the odd, warm feeling of hope.

Oh, dear hope. What a cursed thing it could be.

CHAPTER TWENTY-FIVE

Jared came down the stairs after helping his father to bed and dropped onto the sofa, leaning his head back and rubbing his hand over his forehead. He closed his eyes and allowed darkness to swoop in, filling each crevice in his mind and pushing out images of Rebecca.

"You appear to have the weight of the world on your shoulders," Mama said, startling him into opening his eyes.

"Just my own stupidity, nothing more," he corrected.

Seating herself on the other end of the sofa, Mother faced him. "If Miss Turner makes you so uncomfortable, you needn't have attended the dinner."

"It is not her, Mother, it is me. I am the one who cannot find it in me to forgive. I am the awful man who is holding her faults against her after I have learned that her character is true, and she has apologized." He shook his head. "Why can I not let this go in my heart when my mind is telling me it is time to forgive?"

"Sometimes the emotions of the heart take time to catch up to the logic of the mind. You can know something is right, but that does not make your contradicting feelings any less real. Sometimes these things just need time."

"I do not want to give it time," he said softly. "I miss her."

"She was here just this evening and has only been gone for a half-hour."

"Exactly," Jared said, holding his mother's gaze. "Rebecca has only been gone a half-hour, and I already miss her dearly. I want her back here, or I want to be there with her. I care not which. I just want to see her, to talk to her, to clean her wretched glasses."

If his mother was put off by the oddness of Jared's desires, she hid it well. "Is this the malady that has plagued you for weeks?"

"Weeks? No. That . . ." Jared found himself unable to continue. How had she known that he'd been so bothered? "That was something which occurred in Derham."

Mother nodded softly, allowing him to continue at his own pace.

It was time to confess his wrongdoings, and despite how much he knew his mother loved him, he was still worried about what she would think. Drawing in a breath to sustain his nerves, he sat up and squared his shoulders. "You recall Dr. Gould?"

"Of course. He has taken over your position in Derham since you left."

"He took over long before I left," Jared said, bitterness edging his words. He told his mother everything, of the way the Hollingsfords brought Dr. Gould in because they felt the town needed a physician and not just a simple surgeon, to how Dr. Gould himself spread around rumors of Jared's ineptness and his ability being better suited to assisting. He told of how a good portion of the town members ceased calling on him for their illnesses and injuries, and how he eventually lost the will to fight for them.

Finally, he told her of the moment when he'd been informed that the young Hollingsford boy was ill, but Dr. Gould had been sent for. How Jared had remained away, not hearing until hours later that Dr. Gould had gone to London and Jared was the only doctor in town.

"When I arrived, it was too late. Little Lucas had not been saved; my pride had prevented me from easing his suffering, from making his death easier to bear."

Mother slipped closer to him on the sofa and took his hand in hers. "That was not your fault, Jared. If you'd known Dr. Gould was gone, you would not have left that boy alone, despite the wrongs the Hollingsfords had done you."

"But I could have—"

"No." Mother was resolute and firm. "You cannot change the past, and you could not have saved him. You said so yourself."

"But what if I could have saved him? I'll never know."

"Precisely," Mother said with compassion. "You will never know. Do not allow this to eat you up. You cannot change the past. You cannot go back and do things differently, despite how badly you may wish it."

"None of that has ceased the slander against my name . . . against *our* name. I've made things difficult for my sister among the parish members, and you will certainly hear of my faulty reputation among your friends."

"Any person in that town who has something ill to say about my son has no business calling themselves my friend." Mother squeezed his fingers again. "You've been hurt by the people of Derham, and I can see how you allowed that to creep into your mind and make you ill, but I am only saddened by the fact that you felt ostracized by your town. I'm certain anyone who knows your true character would understand that you did not know that Dr. Gould had gone away."

He considered his sister and brother-in-law, the vicar, and a handful of others who had stood by his side and continued to call on him when they needed help. But that loyal group was such a small fraction of the town he'd been raised in. "I had hoped so, but you might be surprised by the people who turned on me." He drew in a ragged breath, feeling once again the weight of disappointment in the people of Derham.

"Have you told Miss Turner of these things?"

He sat up, confused. "I have, though I'm not certain how that is pertinent." He gave his mother a bashful smile. "I know I should have told you weeks ago, long before I shared my troubles with Miss Turner. I was gathering courage."

"You can tell me anything, Jared, and I will never love you less. We all make mistakes. Some of them are more costly than others, I'll grant you that. But we do all make mistakes."

Ah, so that was where Mother was trying to lead him. "Even Miss Turner?"

"Yes, even her," Mother confirmed, her lips curving into a smile. "Though that is not what I was trying to tell you. You say you are having trouble forgiving her?"

He nodded, embarrassed.

"Well, I do not know the nature of your disagreement, but I cannot help but wonder if the difficulty lies within you, Jared. Perhaps when you've forgiven yourself, then you'll be able to forgive her."

Jared slumped back on the sofa, the words soaking through his mind and taking root in his heart. "How do I do that?"

Mother chuckled softly. "That is up to you, Son. But I will give you a small warning that you may want to decide what you want quickly. Mrs. Turner mentioned that there is nothing to keep them in Bath any longer, and once she confirms that her sister can bear to part with her, she intends to return to Welton with Miss Turner."

Cold, uncomfortable dread settled like a weight in his gut. "They're leaving?"

"Yes, and soon, I believe. Though even they are unsure of how quickly they can manage their preparations to return home."

But he did not want Rebecca to leave. He wanted her nearby.

Standing, he had the sudden, unaccountable urge to go to her.

"You may not knock on her door this evening, Jared. It is far too late for courting."

How could she possibly know his intentions so easily? "I only want to tell her not to leave."

Mother looked at him shrewdly. "What are you offering her to remain?"

He paused, his mouth hanging open until he closed it again. What *was* he offering? Himself? "I'm not sure."

"Then you mustn't go to her. Do not knock on that poor woman's door until you are certain of yourself. It is unkind to ask her to trail along while you untangle your feelings."

The validity of her point only heightened Jared's need of discernment. He paced to the window, circling around Father's chair and back to the fire, then repeated the motion.

Mother rose, and he stopped before her. "Thank you for listening to me. I am sorry if I disappointed you."

"I am only disappointed that it took you so long to talk to me. I will always love you, Jared, and I know you are a good man. I have never once questioned it."

He kissed his mother on the cheek and watched her leave the room before slumping down on the sofa again and dropping his head in his hands. Drawing in a deep breath, he considered his mother's words: *perhaps when you've forgiven yourself, then you'll be able to forgive her.*

Jared hadn't considered forgiveness in this way. He had been so concerned with the way his mother would respond to the news that he'd done something so awful. But she hadn't reacted poorly, she had been understanding. He knew she loved him, but he'd still expected her to be a little upset.

Rebecca had been correct, though. Telling his mother the truth had lifted an enormous burden from his shoulders, allowing him to feel lighter. She had been able to overlook the mistakes Jared had made in Derham because his character and actions had proven time and again that he was a good man with a good heart.

Had Rebecca not done the same for him? Her character and actions had proven her kindness, selflessness, and goodness. Her poor choices regarding the letters were, at their root, a selfless act. Jared had merely been a casualty of her attempts to help her mother. He felt his pocket for the money she'd given him and frowned.

He wanted to return her money, but more than that, he wanted to see her again. To beg her to forgive his foolishness for taking so long to see what was clearly in front of him.

He wanted *her.*

CHAPTER TWENTY-SIX

Rebecca stood at the window, watching the rain run down the glass panes in rivulets as the morning sun hid behind the clouds, its distant light glowing. She'd made such a mess of things, but she couldn't regret the letters she'd written or the relationship she'd forged with Mr. Cooper, not when it gave her the gift of caring for him, however briefly it had lasted.

She slumped against the window pane, her shoulder pressed into the wall as she rested her forehead against the cold glass.

"Rebecca, come sit by the fire," Mama said. "It is far too chilly near the window like that."

She shook herself out and forced a smile on her lips. "I must continue packing, Mama."

"Leave it for a minute. Mullens will help this afternoon."

"I enjoy packing," Rebecca argued. "It gives me something to do with my hands."

Mama rose from the sofa and came to stand near the window, her arms crossed over her chest. "Why do I have the feeling you are running away?"

"I am not. In order to do that, I would need something to run away from."

She dipped her chin. "You are not fleeing from Mr. Cooper?"

"He was never mine."

Mama's lips pressed together, her shrewd gaze penetrating Rebecca's protective shell. "Are you certain you wish to leave Bath?"

"Father has not responded to us. What other choice do we have?"

Shaking her head, Mama sighed. "I do not know."

"I need to go to the apothecary and collect another dosage of medication for you before we leave." Her gaze fell on the empty pearl-encrusted jewelry box on the dressing table, and she frowned. Coming to Bath had not been useless, for she'd been able to obtain the help Mama needed.

She could not repair her relationship with Mr. Cooper, but perhaps she could retain some of what she came here with. Perhaps the brooch was not lost to her yet. "When does Mullens return?"

"She should be home within the next quarter-hour," Mama said.

Rebecca did not want to wait that long. "I will return shortly. We can finish our packing later this afternoon."

"Is it safe to go alone?"

"I have gone to the apothecary alone a handful of times. Besides, I have tasted independence already, Mama. You will find it very difficult for me to give it up again."

"That does not mean I am comfortable with it. It is one thing to slip down to the apothecary in Welton and an entirely different thing to go alone in Bath."

Rebecca did not reveal how many times she'd gone out alone during their time here while her mother had been sleeping or otherwise engaged with Aunt Langley. She had been referring to Bath when she'd mentioned that she'd already gone to the apothecary alone.

She leaned forward and gave her mother a kiss on the cheek. "I promise to return shortly."

She was glad her mother was too tired to offer to accompany her. It took a few short minutes to tie her bonnet on and slip on her gloves and green cloak. She stood in the entryway, focused on fastening the cloak about her neck when a hurried knock jarred her. It was repeated until she stepped forward and opened the door, revealing a tear-streaked, distraught Alicia.

"Good gracious, what has happened?" Rebecca asked, pulling Alicia inside and closing the door behind her. She rested her hands on her cousin's shoulders. "Is it your uncle?"

"Uncle? No, he is . . . unchanged." Alicia hiccupped, a sob tearing from her chest. "It is . . . it is . . . oh, I am so ashamed."

The air whooshed from Rebecca's lungs when Alicia rammed into her chest, her thin arms going around Rebecca's waist as she buried her face in her shoulder. Rebecca recovered from her shock and rubbed Alicia's back consolingly. "At least confirm that no one is in immediate danger, please."

Alicia sniffed, stepping back and wiping at her eyes, her face forlorn. "That depends on what you define as immediate danger. My heart is surely subject to expire."

That dramatic pronouncement put Rebecca slightly at ease. "What happened?"

"It's Henry," Alicia wailed, another sob bursting from her. "He's gone and left Bath."

"I heard of the Gastrells' departure," Rebecca confirmed. But that did not explain why this was so heartbreaking unless Henry was the man Alicia had believed was going to propose. That ridiculous cad. He should have known better than to string along such a young, inexperienced woman.

Or perhaps that was exactly why he'd strung her along.

"I love him, and he's gone."

Rebecca tempered her irritation, doing her best to offer the man some sort of explanation. "Perhaps he intends to return. London is not so very far away."

Alicia's eyes grew hard. "He will not return. He's followed that *heiress*, Miss Morgan. And his wretched mother has taken Georgiana and gone with him. They are all of them in support of this."

Rebecca's chest constricted in pain for her cousin. "Does my aunt know that you are here?"

"No," Alicia said meekly. "My maid is there to make sure no one interrupts my nap."

Ah, that must have been how she'd snuck out to visit vile Henry as well. "Then come and let us get you home."

Alicia nodded, tears continuing to stream down her face. "I kissed him, Rebecca. I kissed that awful man. And now he has left me behind with little remorse."

"Then clearly you are better off without him in your life."

Alicia seemed to ponder this as Rebecca opened the front door and guided her outside. They walked to the Langley townhouse, and Alicia's tears dried up as they went, her mouth bent into a despondent frown.

"Perhaps you ought to plead a headache and take today to rest," Rebecca suggested when they neared the house.

"It shall not be dishonest, for my head aches something fierce." Alicia pulled Rebecca into a hug. "Oh, how will I ever love again?"

"You shall." Rebecca spoke resolutely. "It may hurt now, but someday you will be grateful you learned Henry's character now instead of long after you married him." *If* the rake had even intended to marry her at all.

Alicia nodded. "Yes, of course. You are so wise. I am going to miss you when you depart."

"We will take our leave of you before we go. I do hope your uncle's family arrives before we do."

"I doubt they will. I'm certain they've received word by now, but Mother does not expect them for a few more days." She tried to smile. "We will simply enjoy the quiet house until their arrival. Uncle will surely be moved to his own house once my aunt has arrived to care for him."

Rebecca considered the indelicate thought her cousin failed to voice aloud, that once her uncle was removed, they would have peace and freedom. Nothing would change in their finances, but he would not be able to control them any longer.

"Goodbye, dear cousin," Alicia said, slipping down to the servants' entrance and disappearing. Rebecca puffed out a heavy breath and turned for the jeweler, considering Alicia's plight. The poor girl had been taken in, swindled by a handsome face and empty promises. All things considered, Henry had not hurt her in a way that she could not come back from. Her reputation remained intact, and her heart would heal.

She only hoped that Alicia had learned from this experience and would be more careful in the future.

Playing with the corded reticule handle on her wrist, Rebecca made her way toward the jeweler who had her emerald brooch. She did not have the funds the jeweler had required, but she had some money. She could make installments and have the brooch paid for within a year, surely. Rebecca was willing to beg. She needed to try to retrieve it at least once before leaving Bath.

The rain was slow and drizzly, fogging her glasses and covering her body with a fine film of water. She let herself into the jewelry store. The bell rang over her head, and she closed her umbrella, leaving it near the door.

"Good day, madam," the man said, coming out from behind the counter to greet her. He seemed to recognize her, his eyebrows raising slightly and his smile faltering.

Gathering her courage, Rebecca straightened her shoulders. "I've returned to discuss my brooch."

The jeweler was already shaking his head and slow dread started in Rebecca's toes and moved up her legs, weighing her down on the wooden planked floor and holding her in place.

"It has sold."

"It hasn't been a fortnight yet, and I believe you told me you would hold it for me."

He shrugged. "I run a business, madam. I could not turn down a sure sale on the basis that you *might* return for the item." He lifted his hands, tipping his head to the side in apology. "I'm sorry, but it is gone. I cannot retrieve it."

Anger ripped through her, leaving a path of hot fire over her chest and bleeding up into her cheeks. She was hurt, but moreover, she was ashamed. Rebecca had made the idiotic choice to sell the brooch, and now it was gone forever. She had no one to blame but herself.

Now it hardly mattered. The reality that she would never again hold the emerald brooch, that she could never hand it down to her own children, cut her deeply.

Rebecca stepped outside and lifted her umbrella, covering her head from the increasing rain falling around her. It took a half-hour to go to the apothecary and fetch another batch of Mama's medication, and then she was on her way home again. The rain had increased steadily, pelting her umbrella in a quick tattoo.

She focused her attention on the uneven, wet paving stones and avoided the larger puddles as she made her way toward home.

A set of boots blocked her path, and Rebecca halted,

cowering beneath her umbrella as she tried to move around the man.

"Rebecca, wait."

She skidded to a complete stop when she recognized Mr. Cooper's familiar voice. She looked up and met his gaze. Rain battered against his umbrella, his face shadowed but securely fastened on her.

"Good day, Mr. Cooper," she said, trying to swallow her disappointment and put on a brave face.

"*Is* it a good day, Rebecca? You look upset."

She shrugged, her heart squeezing at his natural use of her Christian name. "It is nothing important. I am just discouraged."

"I understand that feeling well."

She pressed her lips together, gripping her umbrella handle until her knuckles turned white. "Yes, you do, because I was horrible and lied to you." She scoffed, shaking her head. She had felt awful, but at some point, this man either needed to forgive her or leave her in peace. "How often must I apologize?"

He lifted a hand, his blue eyes widening. "No, you misunderstand me. I wasn't referring to that."

Rebecca had a hard time believing him. She had done nothing but beg this man to forgive her, and while he struggled to do so, she'd remained silently by, waiting with hope that he would. But she was tired of waiting, and she was angry that he would arrive at a vulnerable, difficult time and pour salt over her gaping, wounded heart.

Her father was missing, her brooch was gone, and she'd ruined any semblance of a friendship with the man she had been falling in love with. Rebecca had twisted her own life into this disorder, but she needed a little grace, or she would crumble.

Staring at Mr. Cooper, she clamped her lips shut, refusing to apologize again. She already had, more than necessary.

"I'm sorry for giving you the impression that I was still angry," he said gently. "I ceased being angry with you a few days ago."

"Forgive me if I have difficulty believing that—"

"No, I understand." He scrubbed a hand over his face, dropping his umbrella on the wet ground and stepping toward her. His blue eyes shone with an intensity that stole her breath. "I'm making a mash of things. Rebecca, I can't lose you. I've been foolish, holding on to the anger and hurt that you caused with your letters, but it occurred to me that the reason I was so hurt by what you did was because I wanted the letters to be real, and I feared they weren't. It wasn't anger; it was pain. The pain of losing *you*."

"I cannot . . ." She had no words. Nothing. She couldn't believe him, could she? This man had not been interested in her. "You wanted Alicia."

"I hadn't realized that I was attempting to court the wrong woman, not until I learned of your duplicity with the letters. But when it occurred to me that you were the woman I was falling for, it all made sense. Everything made sense, Rebecca, and I was glad you wrote the letters, because the person I fell in love with was *you*, both through your words and your company."

"But if she'd written—"

He shook his head. "I never loved Alicia. I only loved the idea of her. I worried that I was falling for two women—the woman who wrote to me, and the woman who danced with me. But it was all you. It was always you."

He stepped forward again, rain running down his hat and pooling on the brim before falling over his shoulders and face. He was soaked through but didn't seem to care, his gaze fixed on her as if nothing else mattered. He reached to cup her face and her body moved forward, yearning for the contact and comfort he could provide, but she couldn't believe him. She couldn't reconcile that he felt the same for her that she felt for him.

"Can you forgive me for being such a fool?" His glove-encased hand wrapped around her cheek, his thumb caressing her cheekbone. "I do not wish to lose you, Rebecca. I want you to stay. Stay in Bath. Stay with me."

Rebecca shook her head, her heart squeezing in pain. The umbrella dropped from her hand and rain immediately misted her spectacles. She let them slide down her nose so she could see into his eyes. "I cannot remain. We must go to France—"

"France? I was just at your house, and your mother said you were packing, but I had thought you were going home. You are not returning to Welton?"

"No. We are going to Paris to find my father."

"*Paris?*"

"We must go to him," Rebecca said. "We've not heard from him in far too long, and we cannot wait around for his cousin or your father's friend to write to us. Mama and I must go and ensure that all is well."

Mr. Cooper nodded. "If you'll have me, I'd like to accompany you."

Emotions swirled through Rebecca's body, fighting one another for precedence as she rested her palms on his coat, her hands rising and falling in time with his breathing. Relief, fear, and confusion beat at her in turns. "Mama and I can travel to Paris alone. And we'll have our maid."

"I care about you, Rebecca. I don't wish to merely offer my protection, I wish to offer myself. I love you, and I want to marry you."

Cold shock swept through her body, followed swiftly by a

warmth that filled her chest and made her heart pulse as though it would burst. Never had she imagined that her feelings for this man would be returned. She tipped her head back to better see into his eyes, but her glasses were too wet, the rain too unceasing.

Mr. Cooper removed her wet spectacles, folding the ear pieces and tucking them into his pocket. "They're useless in this rain. Can you see me?"

Rebecca nodded, and Mr. Cooper swiped his thumbs under her eyes and over her forehead, removing the water from her face as best he could. Her hair was plastered to her head and clung to her neck, but all she could focus on was the man before her and his gentle ministrations. His hair darkened from the rain, his blue eyes steadily fastened on her.

"Will you forgive me, Rebecca? Will you be my wife?"

She scoffed quietly, unsure how she'd gone from feeling so lonely to feeling so full of hope and excitement for her future. "Mr. Cooper—"

He growled, the low sound emanating from his throat. "Enough of the blasted mister. If anyone has a right to call me Jared, surely it is you."

She swallowed hard, a tremulous smile flitting over her lips. "I love you, Jared."

A blinding grin spread over his face, and he slipped his hands around her waist, pulling her flush against him. Jared crashed his lips down on hers, taking her in a ferocity that melted her limbs like hot wax. She slid her hands around his neck, returning the kiss, her body warming from the inside and pulsing out as rain fell unhindered on them. She had never felt so whole, so complete, as she enjoyed the comfort of being wrapped in the arms of the man she loved.

Guilt slithered into her abdomen, and she pulled back,

panting in rhythm with him. "I can't . . . I must go help my mother pack. We need to be on our way at once."

Jared nodded, his chest heaving, and he rested his wet forehead against hers. "Allow me to accompany you home. I would like to be of assistance in any way that I am able."

She smiled. "Perhaps you ought to go home and change into something dry first."

He swooped down and kissed her again, and she felt the grin on his lips as they moved over hers. "I will still walk you home."

Jared bent down and lifted their discarded umbrellas, closing hers and raising his above their heads. When they were protected from the rain, Jared tucked the umbrella handle under his arm and removed her spectacles from his pocket. He did his best to wipe them before sliding them back over her ears.

"I'm afraid even my handkerchief is sodden now," he said apologetically.

She glanced at him through wavy, wet lenses and her lips formed a mischievous smile. "It's no bother. It was worth it."

Jared grinned, leaning down to kiss her again, sweet and smooth. He took her hand and led her toward her townhouse. "How soon do you believe we can have the banns posted?"

"I'm certain it won't be possible until I return from Paris."

"You will allow my escort, though?"

"Yes," she said, squeezing his arm. "I would appreciate your escort very much."

CHAPTER TWENTY-SEVEN

J ared stood near the rail as waves lapped against the boat, the steady rocking lulling him with its comfortable rhythm. Rebecca stood beside him, her arms wrapped around herself as she gazed out over the ocean. The sun beat down on them, warming their skin for the first time in weeks, and they soaked in its rays.

"Your mother is resting below deck," Jared said, sidling closer to his future wife. She glanced at him over her shoulder and a smile curved her lips, warming his chest immediately.

"Mullens is with her?"

He nodded, sliding his hands around her waist and resting his head on top of hers. "I want to give you something, but you must promise to accept it without any questions."

Rebecca turned in his arms, leaning back against the ship railing and looking up at him. "What is it?"

"That was a question. I need you to promise you won't ask anymore."

"Very well, I promise."

Jared reached for the small bundle in his pocket and took it out, stepping back to give her space. He placed it securely in her hands.

Rebecca unwrapped the linen covering the object and gasped when the emerald brooch sat in the palm of her hand. She looked up at him, tears gathering in her eyes. "I thought this was lost to me."

"Not any longer."

Shaking her head, she turned the brooch over in her fingers, admiring it from every angle as the sunlight glinted off the deep green emerald. "But how did you come by it? I went to try and convince the jeweler to work out a payment plan with me, but it had been sold."

"It was sold to me, and you weren't supposed to ask any questions."

Rebecca looked up sharply, and Jared sighed and continued. "The clasp broke on my pocket watch, so I took it to a jeweler to have it repaired, and I saw this on the display. When I questioned the man, and he described the young bespectacled woman who brought it in, I knew it was the very same brooch you wore to the Gastrells' card party, and I couldn't leave it so vulnerable." He shrugged. "The jeweler was willing to sell it to me, so I bought it, intending to return it to you."

"I will pay you for it."

He looked at her hard. "You will soon be my wife, Rebecca. The very last thing you need to do is pay for something which is rightfully yours."

"But the money—"

"Gads, woman. At some point, you will have to swallow your pride and allow my profession to provide for us."

Rebecca nodded, chuckling slightly. "It is difficult for me to do so, but I can see I have no choice."

"We may not have an affluent life, but we will have what we need," he said.

"*You* are all I need. Thank you, Jared. You cannot know what this means to me." She reached up on tiptoe and planted a kiss on his lips. Jared's arms went around her, pulling her close, and he lost himself in the warmth of her embrace.

A sailor whistled at them, and they broke apart, Rebecca's cheeks mottling red as her gaze shifted down to the brooch in her hand again. "Thank you, Jared."

"Anything for you, my love. Anything."

———— ⟳ ————

They traveled the cobblestone streets of Paris in a hired carriage, rocking and jolting as it bumped along. Sunlight slanted through the window, highlighting the concern on Mama's face. Rebecca scooted closer to Jared's side and slipped her hand into his on the dark bench, and he squeezed her fingers back. Ever since stepping foot on the boat to cross the channel, Rebecca had been a bundle of nerves about the state in which she would find her father, and Mama fared no better.

They rolled to a stop, and Mr. Cooper opened the door and stepped out before turning to help the women down. They filed from the carriage and up the short steps to knock on the door, and a servant cracked it, eyeing them with apprehension.

Mama stepped forward, speaking to the servant in broken, stilted French. After they went back and forth a little, the servant opened the door wider. "Dr. Bonnet. He is here," she said in heavily accented English. "Come, come."

"Dr. Bonnet?" Jared asked. "That is my father's friend. The one my father wrote to."

Rebecca clutched his arm as Mullens supported Mama up

the stairs and into the house. She was hit with a wave of warmth when she stepped inside and the heavy scent of roasted meat.

A man appeared at the foot of the narrow stairs, his gaze landing on Jared. Light glinted from his balding head from the wall sconces, and his eyes were heavily rimmed in wrinkles. "Young Mr. Cooper," he said, surprised. "It has been years. My, you have grown."

Jared stepped forward and bowed. "You look well, Dr. Bonnet."

"I feel well," he agreed. "Old age has not been terrible to me yet."

Jared smiled. "My father will be happy to hear of your good health."

Dr. Bonnet's gaze slid to Rebecca and her mother, and Jared indicated them. "I've brought the Turners. Allow me to present Mrs. Turner and Miss Turner, and their maid, Miss Mullens."

Dr. Bonnet bowed to them again, dipping his head to Miss Mullens before directing his attention to Mama. "You received my letter, I assume."

"On the contrary," Mama said. "We've received no word at all."

A groove formed between Dr. Bonnet's eyebrows. "It must have missed you by a day, then. You should certainly have received it by now. You may rest at ease, Mrs. Turner, for your husband is on the way to healing. It is safe to visit him now."

Safe to visit him *now*? Rebecca swallowed hard, her hand searching for Jared's. He took her fingers and squeezed them.

Jared asked the question that Rebecca—and her mother, it seemed—could not formulate. "What was the diagnosis?"

"A dreadful case of smallpox," Dr. Bonnet said heavily. "He contracted it a month or so after arriving in Paris. When I came to ascertain Mr. Turner's situation and discovered his condition, I set to seeing to his health right away, and I've returned regularly to ensure that he was properly cared for. It is all in the letter I sent."

"But his cousin," Mama said, looking as confused as I felt.

Dr. Bonnet nodded. "I inquired why no word was sent to Mr. Turner's family, and I was told that his cousin was called away before your father grew ill. He went to see to his vineyard in the south. He's yet to return, so the servants left to care for the house and your father had no way to communicate your direction. Your father was quite incoherent for a time." He stepped forward and lowered his voice. "Though in truth, I am not certain it crossed their minds to write to you."

Rebecca's free hand fluttered over her lips. "But he is well? We may see him now?"

"Yes, please follow me. I will take you to him." Dr. Bonnet turned back up the stairs and they followed him. He paused in the small corridor. "Forgive me, Mrs. Turner. I admit I did not write back immediately, for I had pressing concerns at hand. But I did write to you the moment I had good news, and I'm certain the letter must be waiting in England for you now."

"You cannot know the depth of my gratitude," Mama said, her voice reedy and thin. "Thank you for caring for my husband."

He gave a quick nod and knocked on the door beside him.

A small maid opened the door. "Dr. Bonnet?"

He spoke to her in French, gesturing to the group behind him, and the maid nodded, opening the door wider to allow them entrance; warm light spilled from the room in flickering motion.

Mama went in first, her hand rising to rest against her chest, and Rebecca wrapped her arms around her mother's shoulders, guiding her across the thick, burgundy rug to where her father sat before the fire. He was in an overstuffed armchair, his legs resting on a footstool and his head lolled to the side in sleep. His face was thin, pocked with the marks of his scars, and Rebecca's stomach constricted from the sight.

"We should have come to him weeks ago," she whispered.

"Then you might not be alive," Dr. Bonnet said.

Jared stepped forward, analyzing Rebecca's father. He gave her an apologetic grimace. "As awful as it sounds, Dr. Bonnet is correct. You would not have wanted to be close to him while he was ill with the pox."

"And we cannot change the past," Mama said quietly. She slipped her hand free and crossed the room, kneeling at Father's feet. She took his hand in both of hers and looked up at him as he roused from his sleep. "Philip," she said softly.

He awoke, looking down at her through tired eyes. "Sarah?" Mama nodded.

"You've come," he said, though his voice was raspy and weak. Rebecca could see the physical toll the illness had taken on his body, and she thanked the heavens he was alive and healing.

Turning to Dr. Bonnet, she lowered her voice. "Thank you for all that you've done for us."

He dipped his balding head, a kind smile in his eyes. "I could not do any less."

Rebecca shared a knowing look with Jared. There must be something about men of the healing profession that gave them charitable hearts.

Passing Jared, she took Father's other hand and bent, kneeling beside her mother. "I am so glad to see you well, Father."

He smiled down at her, his green eyes reflecting the fire behind her. "I have missed you so, my little one." He glanced around the room, greeting Dr. Bonnet and Mullens before his gaze settled on Jared.

Rebecca cleared her throat. "We've brought along a friend of ours to meet you. He accompanied us on the journey." Standing, she took Jared by the hand and brought him in front of her father. "This is Mr. Jared Cooper, a surgeon from Bath. He helped Mama learn what has been causing her such fatigue and has been working to ease her burdens."

"I can see that he has helped you, my dear," Papa said, cupping her cheek.

Mama leaned into his touch. "I feel much more the thing."

"Soon, I shall too. What a sorry pair we make."

Light laughter flitted around the room, and Jared bowed. "Pleased to meet you, Mr. Turner."

Mama smiled. "I believe we'll have another announcement to make once Mr. Cooper has had the opportunity to have a private conversation with you, Philip."

Father looked from Jared to Rebecca with an appraising, unsurprised expression. He nodded. "I look forward to it, then."

Rebecca grinned, unable to contain her expression. "We should let you rest, Papa."

He did not argue, and Rebecca kissed him on the forehead before following Jared and Dr. Bonnet into the corridor.

The housekeeper met them when they closed the door behind themselves. Her accented English was thick but easy to discern. "We have bedchambers prepared for you when you are ready. Are you hungry?"

"I am," Rebecca said. "If it is no trouble."

"None at all. Follow me down to the dining room, and I will have Cook send something up."

She turned away and they followed her, Dr. Bonnet trailing

behind them. When they reached the bottom of the stairs, he said, "I will leave you now, but I shall return tomorrow."

"Thank you, Dr. Bonnet," Rebecca said. "We cannot express the fullness of our gratitude."

He took her hand and kissed her knuckles. "Goodnight."

When the table had been set with plates of food and Rebecca and Jared left alone to eat, he reached across the table and took her hand. "Do you feel better now after seeing your father?"

"Much better," she said. The tension of concern that had steadily built over the previous weeks slowly dissipated, and she suddenly grew weary, feeling fully depleted. She was prepared to sleep for the next two days thanks to the comfort of finding her father whole. "My heart is at peace."

Jared ripped a corner from his bread and studied her. "It appears your mother has given her blessing to our union, and your father might readily agree."

"He will trust that the man I love is good and kind," she said with quiet conviction. "And I'm certain he will be amenable after my mother's positive report of your good character."

Jared took another bite as a smile stole over his mouth. "Speaking of the wedding, have you considered where you would like to live after we are married? I wanted to ask what the state of Welton is. Do they have a doctor?"

"We have an apothecary, but not in Welton. It is a good distance to the next town." A grin widened her lips. "Do you wish to fill the need? I might be biased, but I do think Welton is a beautiful place to live."

"I think we must visit it when we return to England." He reached over and removed her spectacles, taking his handkerchief from his pocket and wiping them clean. "Perhaps it would have been easier to see your father had you been able to see clearly."

"I can see well enough," she said. "But thank you for taking care of me."

"It is selfish, really," Jared said. "I would prefer to see your lovely eyes through clearer glass."

Rebecca framed his face with her hands and leaned over to kiss him. "Thank you, all the same."

EPILOGUE

FOUR MONTHS LATER

Rebecca walked to the end of the lane and turned around to appraise the empty, unkempt cottage. It was only a ten-minute walk from the house she grew up in, and the familiar smell of wildflowers and barley fields coupled with the wide, open sky made her feel at home. The cottage was smaller than her house, but the backdrop of red and orange oak trees, their fallen leaves gilding the house and surrounding grass, was idyllic. Once they painted the shutters and trimmed the grass and golden shrubbery, the house could certainly be considered cozy.

Alicia picked her way across the overgrown pathway, her nose wrinkled. "Do you truly wish to live so far away from other people?"

Rebecca nodded, smiling. She was glad Alicia had seemed to come to terms with the deceit she'd experienced at the hands of Henry Gastrell. She was much more herself of late. "As much as I would love to be your neighbor, Alicia, I shall have to settle for periodic visits."

"Visits to Bath, correct?" Alicia said, glancing around again.

She clearly did not approve of Rebecca's quaint home, but that was neither here nor there. Rebecca adored it.

"Yes, of course. How could I ever expect you to visit this far away from civilization?"

Alicia looked at her through a shrewd, narrowed gaze. "I can tell that you are mocking me, but I do not know why. I've gone to visit Margaret and her Lord Buxton since they married *twice* now, and they live a good thirty minutes from Bath in the middle of the country as well."

Margaret and her Lord Buxton lived on a large estate, so Alicia's concession was hardly that. "How magnanimous of you."

"I thought so," Alicia muttered.

Rebecca squinted, blurring the image before her, and she could imagine just how the cottage would look when it was all sorted and repaired, framed by the reds and golds of autumn. It would be her own little oasis.

Jared stepped through the front door and wiped his hands to remove the dust. He rested them on his hips and turned around to take in the view. "Once the place is cleaned, it will not be too bad," he called.

"Your husband is a saint," Alicia said quietly. "You truly are made for one another. Tell me how to find such a perfect match."

Rebecca admired Jared across the distance, considering each of the ways he showed her he loved her. "Find a man who notices the little things. A man who cares about your little comforts. That will be a man for you."

"What little things has Jared done for you?"

"He cleans my spectacles," Rebecca said. Plus, he was willing to move to Welton, to purchase a small cottage in need of repairs, to build a life with her.

Alicia looked unconvinced.

"Jared cares about the little things, about making sure I'm comfortable. My glasses smudge easily, and he wipes them for me when I don't even think about it. Find a man who cleans your glasses without being asked."

"I do not wear spectacles."

Rebecca laughed. "No, but I know you take my meaning."

"I do," Alicia said thoughtfully.

Jared walked toward them, nodding to himself. "It is going to be lovely when we are through with it," he said with conviction.

"I do hope you believe that, and you are not trying to convince yourself of it."

He grinned. "I believe it, my love. This will suit us well."

The three of them turned to walk back to the Turners' house, and Alicia bent to pick a flower, pulling at its petals and scattering them on the ground as they went.

"How is your uncle faring?" Jared asked.

Alicia sighed. "He is not any better. We sent for that physician your father recommended, but he said the same thing. My aunt is taking care of him as best as she can manage, but Uncle will likely never speak again."

"It is not uncommon for victims of an apoplexy to experience a repeat within the year."

"We are doing everything we can to help my aunt make him comfortable, and he is watched over nearly always. But I must admit that things have been much more pleasant since he has lost the ability to tell us what to do."

"He cannot communicate?"

"He can write to us. But with how much Mama has helped to care for him, he has ceased trying to control her. Everyone is much happier in this situation."

"I am glad for you," Rebecca said.

"Do not be too glad. You recall that Mother promised me a London Season next year? Well, now she is saying that we mustn't plan on it for we cannot leave Uncle behind, nor Aunt to manage alone."

"It shall all work out," Rebecca said, taking her cousin's hand and squeezing. She looked at Jared, and he shared a smile with her. "It worked out for me, and it shall for you, too."

Alicia laughed. "Well, you needn't brag."

Jared shook his head. "Enough of this. Have you chosen the color for the drapes, yet?"

"Oh!" Alicia said, grinning. "This is something I can help with. I am quite good at selecting colors. How about a nice butter yellow? Or perhaps a sage green?"

Alicia's color monologue continued until they reached the Turner cottage, and when they got to the door, Jared snagged Rebecca's hand and tugged her back. "The things I put up with for you," he murmured, kissing her soundly.

When Rebecca came up for air, she grinned broadly. "You love Alicia, and you know it. You just won't admit so aloud."

"I do enjoy her company, yes. In *very* small increments."

Rebecca pulled him down for another kiss when they were interrupted by Alicia's voice just inside the corridor. "What about a light blue, Rebecca? Rebecca? Where did you go?"

Jumping away, Rebecca hurried down the corridor. "Yes, Alicia. Blue would be lovely too."

"Anything would be lovely if it put an end to this conversation."

Rebecca grinned. "Says the man who asked about colors to begin with."

Jared smiled, and contentment wrapped around Rebecca like a comfortable blanket. He quirked an eyebrow and reached for her spectacles. She smiled, watching him clean the lenses and replace them on her face before sealing the gesture with a kiss.

Alicia popped around the corner, smirking. "A man who cleans your glasses, indeed."

AUTHOR'S NOTE

Mrs. Turner suffered from anemia, which was then known as green sickness due to the greenish tint often present in the skin. At the time, doctors were aware of the importance of iron in treating anemia, and believed that when medication was paired with sunlight, cold air, and even horseback riding, the patient could heal quicker. The medication Mr. Cooper prescribed to Mrs. Turner was a direct recipe taken from a contemporary source, *Modern Domestic Medicine*, and would have been given to patients at that time.

During the Regency era, there were three avenues for people to receive medical care. *Physicians* were typically gentlemen, were less likely to touch their patients, and went through medical school. They were given the title Dr. before their surname and were more expensive. *Surgeons* were trained on the job in lieu of attending school (as Mr. Cooper was trained by his father and through his own studying), were more likely to physically touch patients or perform surgeries, and were called by "mister." And last, *apothecaries*, who would treat smaller ailments and provide medications.

Though Mr. Cooper was not trained in a university/hospital, he still would've been considered a doctor, he just would not be called Dr. Cooper.

Lastly, you may have noticed that this summertime story was a little wet and cold. 1816 was known as the Year Without a Summer. Due to a massive volcanic eruption in 1815 in what is now known as Indonesia, the world saw severe climate abnormalities and Europe endured the coldest summer temperatures on record at that time. The world experienced great famines and severe weather, and in my story, you see the effects in the lack of sunlight, the cold, and the extra rain. But it led to a rainy kiss, so I'm not complaining, and I doubt Rebecca and Jared are either.

SONS OF SOMERSET

Carving for Miss Coventry by Deborah M. Hathaway

The Stable Master's Son by Mindy Burbidge Strunk

In Pursuit of the Painter by Ashtyn Newbold

An Agreeable Alliance by Kasey Stockton

The Highwayman's Letter by Martha Keyes

ACKNOWLEDGMENTS

Huge thanks must first go to Deborah, Mindy, Ashtyn, and Martha for being so easy to work with and making these series a breeze! Y'all are the best author friends a girl could ask for, and I've loved writing these books together and appreciate how they've brought us closer.

Thanks to my critique group for helping me sort out the beginning and pointing out my weaknesses (and strengths) and being a great support: Jess, Martha, and Deborah.

Thank you to everyone who played a part in getting this book ready: my beta readers: Heidi, Kelsy, Emily, Marlene, Brooke, and Whitney; Ashtyn, who made gorgeous covers for the entire series; Jacquie and Deborah for your professional betas, opinions, and notes—they were inordinately helpful; and Jenny, for all of your edits, your polishing, and your support.

Thanks Jon for being my best friend and my light in the darkness. And thanks to my babies for letting me be both a mom and work this full time author gig: the two things that bring me the most happiness.

ABOUT THE AUTHOR

Kasey Stockton is a staunch lover of all things romantic. She doesn't discriminate between genres and enjoys a wide variety of happily ever afters. Drawn to the Regency period at a young age when gifted a copy of *Sense and Sensibility* by her grandmother, Kasey initially began writing Regency romances. She has since written in a variety of genres, but all of her titles fall under clean romance. A native of northern California, she now resides in Texas with her own prince charming and their three children. When not reading, writing, or binge-watching chick flicks, she enjoys running, cutting hair, and anything chocolate.

Made in United States
North Haven, CT
28 September 2023

42123780R00171